Even You

Even You

Marilyn Oser

mill city press
minneapolis

Mill City Press, Inc.
322 First Avenue N, 5th floor
Minneapolis, MN 55401
612.455.2293
www.millcitypublishing.com

ISBN-13: 978-1-63413-546-7
LCCN: 2015908222

Book Design by Biz Cook

Printed in the United States of America

Author's Note

That my name alone appears on the spine of this book is a publishing convenience. It is also a half-truth. Mary Lou Kallman conceived and began Jessie's story sometime in the 1990s. At the time of her death in 2003, she had written over a hundred draft pages, in which the characters of Jessie, Grandma, Gramp, Uncle Jimmy and others were adroitly developed. Mary Lou felt that Jessie's narrative would not be sufficient to stand on its own, and she experimented with various complementary narratives. It is one of life's hideous ironies that her death provided what was needed by opening the way for Claire's story.

When we wrote together, as often we did, the time would come (after the usual multiple drafts) that we no longer could tell who had written what, and the work had become neither Mary Lou's nor mine, but ours.

This book is ours.

1

Claire

Hutchinson River Parkway, New York
April 1995

It's important to remember that Claire Bramany began her quest without murder in mind. What was in her heart was a different matter—a matter not at all clear to her when she found herself speeding on damp pavement up the Hutchinson River Parkway. A slow drizzle was falling, and she had no notion where she was headed at sixty-five-plus miles an hour. Nor did she care.

Her mind was on the contents of Jessie's desk stashed in a carton in the backseat of her cherry-red Honda. She'd fled from the office with them. A coppery night was coming on under low clouds, and she drove without plan or destination, giving the car its head. It threaded its way through rush-hour traffic north out of Brooklyn, east through Queens, then north again across the Whitestone Bridge and straight up the Hutch. She knew not a living soul up the Hutch.

When the drizzle matured into spattering rain, the car braked, turned and pulled in among a herd of SUVs in the lot at the Mobil Mart. Her Honda, it seemed, was aptly named:

Marilyn Oser

"Goes and stops of its own Accord," she punned—and by long habit listened for an amused groan from the passenger seat. No response came, of course, the seat being vacant as an unfilled grave. But just for an instant—and against all hope—she'd hoped for one.

Compared to today's megaconvenience stores, the parkway's Mobil Mart was small and cramped. A center island with self-serve beverages took up the lion's share of the space, leaving barely enough room along the perimeter for one person to squeeze past another. Burly men were clustered there, and it was there, just hours after finding Jessie's bombshell in the desk, that Claire shoplifted for the first time.

In their stout, weathered barn jackets, the men took up all the space. Their unhurried voices boomed, blustery and good-natured. They chatted weather and sports, waiting to fill up mammoth cups at the caffeinated spigot. With her shoulders hunched and her chin tucked, she sidled past them and fixed a small decaf, adding a spurt of skim milk. Around back, she found the sweeteners and stirrers, the lids and napkins—and stacks of tea bags.

She'd swear what happened next had nothing to do with the little story Jessie had scribbled in the topmost notebook—a short vignette about a whistling kettle for her grandma, who drank sage tea. Claire had never tasted sage tea, though she'd always liked the idea of herbal infusions. Positively witchy, wasn't it?, to come indoors with a handful of blooms from the garden, or better yet a meadow frowsy with wildflowers, and boil up a fresh brew, warm and fragrant and seductive.

Sure, the idea was lovely, though in the end the brew was a complete cheat. One sip, and Claire would be perfumed out, which was the reason she disliked herbal tea. Given her druthers, she'd take strong Colombian hi-test every time. So why her attention was drawn to the packets of tea she couldn't say. Their brightness, maybe. Nothing even faintly unusual or furtive was going on, not then. She was just snapping a lid on her cup and putting it into one of those cardboard sleeves while admiring (arguably) the bright, layered colors.

Yet in the very next moment some switch got thrown inside her, and she shifted her weight onto her right hip, then used her plumpish, middle-aged midriff to obscure the tea display from a dark-bearded fellow in a Yankees cap—an absurd subterfuge, really, since he was intent on loading his cup with sugar and couldn't have cared less what she did.

No onlookers saw her palm the tea bag. No witnesses saw her pocket it. Under the peak of her own cap with its embroidered pink twist, she kept a darting, hawk-like guard. When no accuser stepped forward, she went around to the front and paid for the coffee, all the while telling herself that Jessie had nothing to do with the contraband in her pocket. And neither had the teakettle.

No, nor the letter, either, the one she'd found tucked into the first of Jessie's notebooks. *Fifty years, Claire,* it said. *That's how long it's taken me to face the things that happened in Tulsa. When the words finally came, they gushed out of me onto these pages in a torrent. The words are meant for you, to tell you something I cannot say aloud, something you must know about me. I need you to understand this not from the outside—a set of disagreeable facts—but direct as I can make it from the child who still speaks inside me. Yet so far I haven't been able to bring myself to show you even the littlest bit. I'll do that soon, or I'll destroy everything I've written.*

I hope you will never see this note. I'm only writing it because I don't trust fate, having come so close to dying. If you've found this, and I'm truly gone, I can only hope you'll do away with these notebooks. Shred them or burn them or bury them with me, please. I don't want you reading what I've written without me there. You see, love, it's my story they tell, not ours. So let it be.

My life, joy of my heart, forgive me.

2

From the first of Jessie's notebooks

This is my story, written Spring 1994.
For Claire, joy of my heart.

The place: West Tulsa, Oklahoma
The time: Spring 1944

Grandma's old teakettle is black enamel, that kind with tiny white dots on it, spatterpainted except on the bottom ridge, where the iron stove grates have worn all the paint off, and the rusting shows through like dried-up scabs. You can't see yourself mirrored in it, and it never whistles to let you know it's full of boiling water, waiting for you. You have to come after it, keep checking up on it time and again, which can be a trial. Grandma never has seemed to mind very much, although at night, after she's gone into the living room, if I call her to come through the kitchen into the blackened bedroom she'll like as not holler back, "Land sakes, Jessie, can't you let a body rest sometime? I can't be jumping up and down, running hither and yon. Be a good girl, now. I need my peace."

    If I can find a teapot that will call out when the water is hot for her sage tea, Grandma will have a little peace. I thought this up awhile ago, except I believed it wasn't real, just made up in my mind. Then Aunt Nedra heard me telling John Ellis what I'd buy Grandma for Christmas, a talking pot if only it was invented, and she smiled. Aunt Nedra has a smile so lazy and wide it looks like it began a month ago someplace secret deep inside her and crept up real slow and pried open her mouth until the grin got so big it had to crinkle her eyes. "It's invented," she said. "It's called a whistling tea kettle, and your grandma would love one."

Straight off, Uncle Jimmy said he'd be right happy to take me looking for one, and next Aunt Nedra chimed in how she'd go shopping with me, too. For sure, if I have to depend on Gramp taking me, he'll spill the beans and spoil the surprise. Gramp can't keep a surprise for anything. Like one time he and Uncle Cubby and Uncle Jimmy were up in the hayloft drinking—and it wasn't Dr. Pepper! Uncle Jimmy sells Dr. Pepper, but he also sells whiskey in Dr. Pepper bottles. He brings it down from Kansas in the space between the backseat and the trunk of his 1941 businessman's coupe. Oklahoma is a dry state, which means they don't have any whiskey for sale at all, and maybe that's why my mother doesn't want to be here.

That evening the barn smelled of springtime, of the sweet corn mash that Gramp mixes warm and damp in a bucket and that I help scoop out into small tin bowls for the new-hatched chicks. Men had been coming to visit up in the hayloft and going away with brown paper sacks in their hands, glass clinking inside. I was near the barn door, oiling the tools. Gramp pays me ten cents for the pickax and the scythe, but I have to be careful or the ribbon of red spoiling the shine will be my own blood.

Grandma must have heard the whooping floating down from the hayloft, because there she came whooshing out the back door, letting the screen slap shut right in Aunt Nedra's face, and she planted her feet outside the barn doors below the half-closed hayloft door. "You, Amos Langley," she yelled, and I knew he was in big trouble. When Grandma calls Gramp Amos instead of Doc, which everybody calls him because he runs the Rexall, you know Gramp is in for it. It's like if she calls me Jessica Ann Louise Friedman: I snap to.

Gramp came down all agrumble, like she was his rheumatism acting up. He flat-out told her he'd been drinking, but it was Uncle Jimmy's fault though, because of all that hot Texas chili and corn bread she cooked up for Jimmy, her sweetie pie Jimmy, and Grandpa's poor old tongue was burning so hard that Jimmy took him up to the loft for some Dr. Pepper, but unbeknownst to him it turned out to be some sour mash Jimmy was selling so he could surprise Nedra with those alligator platform shoes she'd seen downtown.

And Aunt Nedra standing there in plain sight all the while!

Grandma clucked a little at Gramp, but mostly she said she'd have to box Uncle Jimmy's ears like when he was just a boy and got into Uncle Cubby's French postcards. French postcards are bad, but I don't know why. They must be very bad if Grandma was moved to box Uncle Jimmy's ears for them. Although maybe it's more like the way mothers in movies spank their kids when they run out in traffic and almost get killed, and the mothers spank them and hug them and cry. My mother says the French are our allies, and they are good, except they can't do much good now, because the Germans have them, and the Germans are bad. The Germans are our enemies.

When I was at boarding school at Monte Cassino in Tulsa, my mother sent me a box of German cookies. I wanted to give them away to the other girls, but I knew they would all make fun of me for getting enemy cookies from my mother. Besides, I didn't want to murder anybody, not even Myra and Myrna, and the cookies, being German, could be poisoned. I didn't know why my mother would want me to be poisoned. But she sent them for me wrapped in a huge bow, and they were a present, so I sat on my bed and I spelled out *J-E-S-S* on my blanket with the cookies, which is as far into my name as they went. Then I started eating beginning with the crossbar of the *J*. I worked the edge of the cookie, nibbling all the way around, chewing with my front teeth and wondering how far into the center I'd have to go to get to the poison, wondering whether I would be able to taste the poison and how long it would take to work once I started swallowing and which cookie in which letter would be the one to finally kill me.

At Monte Cassino I learned a lot about dying and the things that will not kill you. Sister Angeline told us that if we went to bed at night without saying our prayers, we would die and wake up in hell. One night I accidentally fell asleep before I ever got to say my prayers. The lights were still on, and I was in bed reading my book about Cherokee myths and legends for the second time. Uncle Jimmy sent it to me, and it used to be my favorite, and I guess I fell asleep, because when I woke up the sky was blue through the high-up windows in our dormitory and the book was tumbled on the floor next to my bed and I was still alive. Sister was mistaken, because the next night I tried it out again, this time on purpose to see where I would wake up, and the result was the same.

3

Claire

Hutchinson River Parkway, New York
April 1995

"Impulsive" was never a term you would use in the same sentence with "Claire Bramany." "Planner" was. "Bean counter," though not to her face. If given a list of behaviors to sort into Claire and not-Claire, the one you'd instantly pick as not-Claire would be stealing. The last time she'd taken something that wasn't hers, she was not yet ten years old.

On that occasion her dad caught her slinking a small glass creamer out of the roadside restaurant near Baltimore, where their family had stopped for fried chicken in the basket. "The world doesn't owe you a living," he'd instructed, his face filled with disappointment in her. "Blue Suede Shoes" was issuing from the jukebox, and he made her set the little jar, still smeary with cream, on the counter and buy it with an advance on her allowance. "You pay for it if you want something. If you can't pay for it, you don't take it."

But her memory of the shame of it—Dad scolding, Mom staring up at the ceiling as if she didn't know them, the kid in the next booth smirking, while the waitress shrugged and Carl Perkins sang—all of that wasn't, anymore, a recollection of the real event. What she remembered now was the replay she'd told Jessie twenty-some-odd years later, circa 1978 or '9, as the two of them lounged on Claire's old chintz sofa, Jessie's snow-coated shoes and wet socks near the radiator, Jessie's bare feet up on the coffee table, Claire's head in Jessie's lap. Something on the TV must have prompted her memory, and she described the harried waitress, who really would have been happy to leave well enough alone, her mascaraed eyes boring dark holes through Claire's dad for giving her an extra bit of work to do—setting the stupid price of the thing (her slow shrug: two cents), ringing it up on the register, and then the annoyance in her sharp snap of the drawer: was she going to have a problem with the bookkeeper, or the accountant when he came in, over a lousy couple of pennies rung on No Sale, because it wasn't food, and the restaurant didn't offer merchandise? This was what came to mind now while Claire went back to her car flummoxed and ashamed—the memory they'd laughed over one winter night, long ago, too.

What would Jessie think of her now? Granted, swiping a tea bag didn't rank up there with knocking over the First National Bank. Willie Sutton she wasn't; Sadie Sneak was more like it. Still and all, she'd broken the law. Which was why, in a few days' time, when her plunder would come crumpled out of the laundry in its yellow foil wrapper, Claire would be glad not to have used it, glad to have sent it through the wash inside her pants pocket—though not sorry to have taken it. Something about taking it helped her balance out a ledger she carried around in her head, its columns labeled "life's gains" and "life's losses."

And she knew what Jessie would call her if only Jessie could be here. It wouldn't be Sadie Sneak or Shirley Shoplifter or anything mean. It would be her best girl. Thumbing away the worry line between Claire's eyes, she'd croon the first lines of the song in her off-key soprano, the song "My Best Girl" from *Mame*, telling her that nothing she did was wrong. Stolen goods and all, she'd make Claire feel right and good, because that's what Jessie always thought, and what she always made Claire feel, right from the very first.

Back then, at the very first, Jessie's desk was actually Claire's: Claire's calculator on the blotter, her stuff in the drawers, and no nasty surprise stashed in its recesses. One day, Jessie came in and plunked herself cross-legged on the floor, a tall woman a little older than Claire—in her thirties, Claire guessed—with thick, straight eyebrows over steady eyes, a ropy braid down her back, and a stronger handshake than Claire expected from her lanky, freckled arm.

"I need help," she said.

"What can I do for you?" Claire barely knew her, a part-time outreach worker at The Open Door, the social work agency where they both worked.

"I have the stories," Jessie said. "I could tell them so your blood would run cold, the hair would stand up on the back of your neck, your skin would crawl and you'd have nightmares for a week."

Stories about her clients, she must mean—the children of men and women behind bars. But what did that have to do with Claire?

"Problem is, you wouldn't open your wallet."

"I'm working my way through school. What's in my wallet wouldn't do you much good."

"That, too," Jessie said. Her eyes left Claire's face and did a slow transit of the office. "I need a full-time job. A full-time job has to be funded, and nobody will get a grant for me. If I want one, I'll have to rustle it up myself."

What did Claire know about applying for grants? She was only an administrative assistant. She said Jessie would do better trying someone in development or personnel.

Jessie scratched her head. Her blouse was sleeveless, underarm unshaven, a nickel's worth of auburn fuzz floating in bottomless cream. "Oh yeah, I've made the rounds. I'm told money comes from people who don't want to hear clients' stories: anecdotal evidence, not important. They want numbers."

Later they would learn this wasn't entirely true, that a good story well told by a grateful client made a great little fund-raiser. But that was to come later.

"So will you help me? Show me how to tell my stories in numbers?"

Claire said, "Teach you how to lie with statistics?"

Jessie's quick grin was wide, lopsided, astonishingly lovely.

That was 1973, Watergate summer, and Claire had the hearings on all day, the radio played low so nobody would hear. Her boss Ray Hammond said he heard, though. "Your entertainment is not an agency perk," he told her. "You can't use our electricity for your private enjoyment." She bought batteries and kept listening.

Politics as usual, her coworkers scoffed. Not exactly news—was it?—this government's absence of integrity. Not worth bothering about.

She had her heroes, though, and that summer they were the people's representatives doing the people's business. Howard Baker, Daniel Inouye, Sam Ervin: the guys asking the sharp questions about the Watergate break-in.

And Barbara Jordan. Claire idolized Barbara Jordan; so did Jessie. After the statistics briefings ended—one or two sessions, that's all it took, and Jessie was up to snuff—she'd stop by Claire's desk to catch up on the hearings. Before long she was bringing two sandwiches in what she called a "sack" no matter how often Claire told her it was a paper bag. What began haphazardly soon became a habit of eating lunch together early or late, the hour scheduled so as not to overlap the hearing's midday recess. If not for Nixon and Deep Throat and the shoddy pranks of the Committee to Re-elect the President, their friendship would never have blossomed. Talk about a silver lining!

By the time Claire got her degree, sat for the CPA exam and passed two parts, she'd lost interest in public accounting. She liked working at The Open Door, liked social workers and the things they did for people. A job opened up for an assistant controller—glorified bookkeeper would have been a truer job title, but it was the first step toward becoming the agency's CFO someday—and she applied, believing she'd have the inside track. Ray Hammond was CFO then, a bitter man who was counting down the days until his retirement. Literally counting them: he had a two-foot-square orange chart on his office wall that showed 343 on the day Claire heard someone else was to be hired—some guy from the outside. It took her until day 340 to get up the nerve to confront Ray.

"I was hoping you'd tell me what happened."

He looked at her pleasantly enough, as if he had no idea what she meant or why she was there in his visitor's chair, and she began to stammer.

"Why I didn't—why you, uh—that is, I was wondering what I could have done—you know—to improve my chances of getting the job?"

He folded prim hands on his desk blotter and told her he wasn't accountable to her, but to the executive director and the board. Was she a member of the board and he hadn't heard? No? Then hadn't she best get back to work. He'd had to come up the hard way, and in time, so would she.

"I understand that."

He said in time she'd learn promotions didn't come because she wanted them. Or because she thought she deserved them. Promotions came after many hard years of work. And loyalty.

Claire said she understood that, too, but she thought her experience at the agency and her consistently favorable performance evaluations ought to make a difference. "My resumé—"

"Your resumé?" He fished it from a stack on the corner of his desk and waved it in the air. "Your experience?" Brandishing it, accusing her of something, but what? "Here's what I think of your experience." He crumpled the twenty-pound, cream-colored laid paper in his fist and, rising from his chair, turned his back to her. Then—flamboyantly, protractedly, comprehensively—he wiped his rear end with it.

You'd never get away today with the things Ray Hammond got away with then. But he had all the power, and Claire thought she was finished. How could she stay at the agency after he'd used her resumé like toilet paper? She'd have to go somewhere else, do something else. She held her frozen smile, her stiffened shoulders, her shredded dignity out of Ray's office, along the hallway and down the stairs to her desk. She even managed a facsimile of a lilt calling good night to the other clerks as they left for the day. Then Jessie showed up with a quart of Dewar's, a can of peanuts and a face aglow with expectation. "So? How'd it go?" she asked. Claire convulsed in sobs.

They killed the bottle. Jessie was gratifyingly furious on Claire's behalf, beating her fist on the desk while she railed what a jerk Ray was, and a lush to boot—counting off the hundred ways the man had alienated just about everybody. They drank at length to that and then moved on to the typical agency scuttlebutt, and after the peanuts were gone and they'd raided financial's refrigerator, ferreting out still-edible slices of salami and apple, they got around to talking about themselves, where they came from, where they grew up, how they'd ended up in Brooklyn working to make the world better, one prisoner's family at a time.

It was past midnight by the time they made coffee and sobered up enough to call it a night. Hours before, Jessie had phoned her husband and asked him to get Lisi to bed. Claire walked her home, and Jessie insisted she come inside. Henry brewed them more coffee and stood around scowling. He was mad as hell: women's lib be damned if it meant his wife staying out half the night carousing while the man sat home babysitting. It didn't help things that they kept breaking into giggles.

At a little table in Jessie's kitchen, they two swallowed coffee and dry crackers. It must have been around one thirty in the morning when Henry offered to drive Claire home. She didn't want him losing his parking space at that hour. She said it wasn't far to walk, but she'd take a cab if he was worried. No trouble, he insisted. He'd take her himself.

There was something gallant in his firmness, she thought. It struck her that Jessie hadn't said much about him that evening—or ever. Henry was a good father, liked his work as a veterinarian, was someone she'd known since the eighth grade. That was all the data Claire had on Jessie's husband.

In the car, he talked about Jessie. He said she'd been postpartum depressed after Lisi was born. Claire was feeling woozy and didn't realize she ought to stop him right there. He found Jessie a shrink, he said, who sent her out job hunting. And no, he wasn't looking for her to get depressed again, God knew, but this going off to work, it changed things. She was different, and Henry wasn't sure if, on balance, he didn't like her better the other way. At least he recognized her depressed. See, he just wanted the Jessie he knew, the woman he'd fallen in love with and married.

Wanting out of his confidences, Claire said, "Don't look at me. I've never been married." *But if I were, you can bet I'd keep my spouse's business to myself.*

"You're her friend. She respects you."

Friendship, respect: did he think she'd never heard that before? Such talk more often than not opened the way to a husband's entreaty: speak to her for me—make her repent her ways, make her apologize, bring her to heel. To Henry's credit, he never uttered such a plea. If he had, she'd have kept her distance, even cut off the friendship altogether rather than tell Jessie what he'd asked her to do. All the same, something inside Claire answered to Henry's unspoken appeal. Loopy as she was that night, she somehow knew she'd never leave the agency as long as Jessie was there. It wasn't a vow, nor did she foresee what they would become to each other. It was simply a fact that quickened into truth right there in front of her.

She did stay, for twenty years and more. Ray Hammond had retired long ago, right on schedule. She'd long since become CFO. And that old desk where she and Jessie got drunk and told each other their life stories—brief though they were back then—that desk still occupied the same airless corner in the old building, and for years now it had been Jessie's.

It was one of those small metal desks with a single stationery drawer above a single file drawer. The sides were scarred avocado-green steel, the legs battered chrome, the top wood-tone Formica, although when Claire went down there to clean it out, the top was hidden beneath a mess of papers and file folders. Above the desk, with its too-high computer and keyboard, was a bulletin board pinned with flyers and memorabilia: a postcard saying "So I haven't written in a while? So what? Neither has Shakespeare!"; an announcement for summer concerts at the city parks; a brochure for a conference on the computer debacle looming five years hence in the year 2000; photos of Lisi with Jessie's baby granddaughter, Natalie; and a beautifully hand-lettered poster, its curlicues, its vermillion and ultramarine reminding Claire of medieval illuminations.

The poster read "A tidy desk is a sign of a disordered mind." It had been a gift from one of "Jessie's Kids," a delinquent boy who, it turned out, was artistically gifted. Jessie specialized in the tough cookies, the incorrigibles, the worst of the worst, and somehow, every one of the troubled children she worked with turned out to be special—one skillful in computer repair, another golf, a third in quiet deeds of kindness. Sons and daughters of convicted criminals, their problems were complex, societal, yet the issues they struggled with, that cowed them in front of classmates and teachers, could be painfully ordinary. Asked *What are you doing this weekend?*, that casual, tossed-off, thoughtless question, what could they answer? *I'm taking a six-hour bus ride so I can see my dad in prison.* To the bitterness of their lives, Jessie brought an antidote that was stunning in its simplicity. Every kid needs to shine, she said: needs a place to shine, or a way to shine, or a person to shine for. Nothing big, just something that means something to the kid. In a nutshell, this was the secret to Jessie's magic with them.

4

From the second of Jessie's notebooks

The place: West Tulsa, Oklahoma
The time: Spring 1944

Once upon a time I lived with my mother in New York City. My mother is a raving beauty, everyone says so. Her dark hair is long and shining like Veronica's in Archie comics, only with millions of red highlights instead of blue, and her hands and feet are dainty and smooth. Uncle Jimmy says I am beautiful, too, but I think that is not the same as raving beautiful. My mother gave birth to me in Brooklyn at the Jewish Hospital, but Grandma says that's a happenstance and does not make me a Jew, and the less said about it the better.

I could just as easily have been born in the RKO Midwood, because my mother refused to leave until the end of the double feature. My father can't remember what the movie was that so interested her, and my mother says the whole thing is another one of his fabrications, but he says she slammed the popcorn right out of his hand when the first contraction hit her, and she spent the rest of the movie pressing her belly against the rail in the first row of the balcony, riding out her labor until the great swell of music that signaled THE END. By that time, the pains were maybe two minutes apart and they had to take a taxi, which was a big splurge in the Depression.

My father could afford it because he made antiques. He got his start as the wormer, making new wood look worm eaten by stressing it with a chain. Right away, he had the touch, never bruising the wood, just nicking it here and there with the tip of the chain, which was inked so that later, when the piece got stained, the edge would make up slightly blackened and look like some worm really had tried boring its way through. By the time I was born my father was a designer. He has a new family now, but I still have one of his old sketchbooks with patterns for fancy carvings and with his drawings of the front view, side view, and top view of chests and armoires and armchairs and even a lion-headed four-poster bed. When I am grown up I will have a giant four-poster bed.

My bed in the house on South Phoenix is not big, but it takes up most of my room, which before I came was a pantry off the kitchen with a door from the back porch so that Gramp, coming in with chicken doo all over his shoes, could bring the potatoes and onions directly in there to store in the root cellar, without having to mess up Grandma's kitchen floor. You can only get to the root cellar through the trapdoor in my room, and my bed covers the trapdoor.

If you took all the rooms in the house on South Phoenix, they still wouldn't use up the space in the apartment my mother and I had in New York City, not even the one on 59th Street, which was smaller than the place we used to have uptown near Carl Schurz Park. My bedroom looked out over the river, and I had two silhouettes on my wall, also a great big picture of a garden with lots of flowers and a lake with a toy sailboat like they have in Central Park. It was nice, but what I really wanted was a magnetic bulletin board with cherry-red magnetic letters and numbers that I could move all around and make words and sentences and names and do additions with. My friend Virginia had one, but my mother said I shouldn't covet my neighbor's things.

Ada gave me my lunch every day (except on her days off, of course) in the kitchen of the apartment on East 59th Street, where the window faced the orthopedic clinic and I faced the window. I could see across the air shaft into the window on the other side and wave at whatever patient was in the room that day. Ada never said it was impolite to look in someone else's window. But in West Tulsa, you dasn't do that. "Shoo, Jessie, look at you showing off yourself, naked to the world"—which I am not, hardly at all. But there are rules, and every evening Grandma goes around and polices the shades, pulling them down until the Ellises next door can't look one lick into our windows on South Phoenix.

The houses on South Phoenix are set way back away from the street with lawns raised three steps above the level of the sidewalk. Most of the houses have barns, and people grow things, but the barns mostly hold the family's car if they have one, and the growing is mostly victory gardens and things to put up for canning and maybe some chickens or a pig. The day I got thrown out of boarding school at Monte Cassino and Grandma and Gramp brought me to live with them in the house on South Phoenix, the first thing I saw when Gramp pulled into the driveway was a man sitting on the big white porch. The porch runs clean across the entire front of the house, with a gray floor and a swing that is gray and rail-backed and hangs suspended by A-shaped chains from the ceiling. The man was not in the swing but in a chair near the far railing. He was not regular aged, but the oldest man ever. He was shrunken to the size of a boy, and the bones in his head showed up so clear under his papery skin, he looked like if he died all you'd have to do is peel him and there'd be your skeleton.

We go inside, and Gramp says, "Give me your grip, child." Grippe is a name for influenza, but I am not sick, so I shake my head no. Gramp sighs and takes my suitcase from me and lopes away with it, his fringe of white hair hanging like a capital *U* on his round pink head.

You can see everything right from the front door: the living room you're in, the dining room just beyond it—wide open, not even hidden behind pocket doors so you might come to the doors and pop them open and have folks ooh and aah at the candles and gleaming silver and crystal. Beyond the dining room is the kitchen, and while you can't see more than the table and refrigerator, you can figure the sink and the stove are in there, too. On the other side of the dining room, you can see through a doorway right into Grandma and Gramp's bedroom, so the only surprises left are where is the bathroom and where will I sleep and why is the man on the porch called Sammy the Boarder?

Grandma says, "Jessie, you're such a pretty little thing. Come, let's set on the davenport and you tell me all about yourself."

I don't know which is the davenport—the lumpy, sunken old chair covered in faded flowers, or the funny chair that slides back and forth in a box, or the black arched-back sofa. Those are the only places to sit, unless you count the floor. Grandma lowers herself onto the sofa and pats the cushion beside her, so I sit down with her, and now I know a davenport is a sofa that scratches. The black is rough and prickly against my bare legs, and when I squirm to pull my dress underneath me, it is even worse.

Gramp comes back into the room. "What does Jessie have to say for herself?" he asks.

I'm not sure what they want to know. I know I want to know why they have a painting of a ship sinking and people swimming around and lifeboats that look overloaded to me, but I am not sure if it is polite to ask, especially since I am the one being asked to recite.

"I go to school. I'm in the fourth grade."

"You mean the third, honey. You're only eight." Grandma smiles and the fuzz on her upper lip shines when the skin pulls back to let her teeth show. Her teeth shine, too. They are very white teeth and very even, not like most teeth you see. Maybe Grandma keeps them that way by doing that thing with her mouth every little once in a while, making like she's chewing on something and trying to figure out should she swallow it or not.

"I can divide. That's fourth grade. Short and long division."

Gramp makes a noise, and that's when I notice he chews on his teeth, too, only way faster. He rocks and chews, his hands behind his back rubbing his backside like he was warming it in front of the fire, his belly sticking out round and tight like maybe he swallowed a medicine ball.

Once before when I visited here Gramp gave me his tea tin full of nuts and bolts and screws to play with. My mother says I was really little and can't possibly remember, but I do. I remember holding it and shaking it and hearing a scratch and a whisk and a clunk, and I remember seeing the blur of red and gold, and I remember when the top of the tin came flying open and tiny pellets shot out. They fell silently all over my dress and made tapping sounds on the gray porch floor. Some got wedged in between the floor planks, and I cried because I couldn't pull the tiny round heads free, and that's when Grandma came running out and grabbed me up and forced open my mouth and gagged me she was poking so hard inside and all around. Gramp brought a big black bar and waved it over the floor and all the tiny nuts and bolts and screws jumped into the air and grabbed hold of the bar. He swept the bar clear with his hand and dropped the pieces into the tin. Then he came over to me and pried open my mouth and forced the bar inside. It was so big it stretched my lips, and it tasted nasty. I tried my hardest to push it away, but Grandma said she might swallow something, she meaning me, and I tried to shake my head *no I didn't, I wouldn't,* but the bar was filling my mouth, and Grandma's tight fingers holding my head still. I was scared my teeth would jump onto the bar and Gramp would sweep them off into the tin and then I wouldn't be able to bite into the juicy purple plums Gramp said he grew just for me.

5

Claire

Hutchinson River Parkway, New York
April 1995

In her car in the Mobil Mart parking lot, Claire sipped coffee and stared at Jessie's notebooks and wondered how a world already in tatters could come apart again. Or more. Could come apart still more. Back in Brooklyn, the bereavement support group she'd joined was meeting for its fifth week. By driving around in the dark, she'd blown it off just when she needed it most. She hadn't meant to. Never the therapy type, she'd come to rely on its members in a way that would have been inconceivable before. Claire the support groupie was another one of the ways that grief had changed her so she didn't recognize herself anymore.

Everything was changed, everything different. The death of the person you love best in all the world does that. It plunges you into a foreign place that only looks like where you lived before. Nothing is as it was, and you find you've gone mad. They all had, all eight of them in the group: they thought mad thoughts, did mad things. To each other, they could say things unacceptable anywhere else. Maybe you'd developed a searing jealousy for every couple you saw, a rabid hatred if the two appeared happy together, worse if they were arguing, or sitting in a car at a stoplight grimly faced in opposite directions. When, in a small voice and haltingly, you admitted the urgent desire to hurl stones at the couple—rocks, heavy boulders, just for being still coupled—two-thirds of the group admitted feeling the same. So if Claire had gone stark staring bonkers over the edge, at least she was normal.

"Go with your gut," they told her. This wasn't permission to run out and stone random pairs of people in the street. It was about Claire's lost ability to plan. She was used to organizing the hell out of everything and everyone. "That's gone," she fretted. "I have no purpose. I make no plans. I carry out no plans."

"Forget it. Listen to your gut," they said. "What good are your plans, anyway? Man proposes, and God shits all over him."

"Old Yiddish saying: 'Man plans, and God laughs.'"

"No, man plans, and God shits all over him, and *then* God laughs. Claire, go with your gut."

Not that she had a choice. Going with her gut was all Claire had left. Sometimes her gut deserted her, too; sometimes when she listened, it wasn't talking. Though it had been loud and clear about Jessie's desk: *leave that alone*, it yelped, and she should have listened, because it had been right.

At home she'd managed to go through Jessie's clothes, photographs, jewelry, knickknacks, and to put them away or give them away or throw them away. All that accumulation winnowed out, disposed of. All that room now in the closets and drawers with only Claire's things inside. All that vacancy and no answer to the question: Jessie, why are you dead?

She'd closed Jessie's bank accounts, canceled the credit cards, even remembered to notify the DMV. All that paperwork completed, filed, finished. All the tough stuff done. And her gut telling her don't do the desk.

As the months passed, her boss, Gina Coletti, lost patience. She marched into Claire's office one day, Napoleon advancing on Borodino, and told Claire she couldn't hide behind that computer forever. She said it wasn't like Claire to leave things hanging. Gina was shrewd, but she picked the wrong time. Only that morning, hunting for an unsprung umbrella in the back of the apartment's hall closet, Claire had opened up a long box. Out leaped Jessie's collection of movie posters. Or to Claire they leaped, never mind that the whole roll of them merely laid there inert and dismal. When she pulled back the flaps, everything went reeling, and her heart howled. Her prostrate mind kept up some kind of shamanic incantation until she taped the box shut and shoved it back under the boots and canvas totes and spare wrapping paper—making as if Jessie wasn't gone forever, just temporarily on sabbatical.

Let Gina carp all she wanted that Claire sat at her computer for hours on end. You would, too, if you could inhabit small sectors of spreadsheets, where the fundamental classes of things were two, Personnel and Other Than Personnel: where revenue and expense could always be made to tally. She liked the realm of numbers because they were clean, sharp edged, comprehensible. She could lose herself in the games she played with numbers. Sometimes she even felt whole in their realm, among their secret systems.

Numbers numbed her. At her computer at her big desk in her big office lined with file cabinets, Claire could pretend the pain could be made to not exist. NUMBers, the perfect name. Numbers could be controlled. Numbers didn't erupt into harrowing nights in the hospital and boluses of morphine and chemotherapy that isn't working yet and cries and groans and a full commode and a harried nurse who does not come.

But finally the morning came, this wreck of a morning when Gina stood in Claire's doorway, all four foot eleven of her, clad in a bright-red suit, and said, "Felicia's waiting for you."

"Felicia? Why?"

"I've given her Jessie's caseload. She has nowhere to sit. She needs Jessie's desk."

Claire stared at her boss's scarlet high heels, which missed matching her suit.

"Today, Claire. With you or without you."

Translation: she and her gut were out of luck. If she thought it would do any good, Claire would have offered her own desk and her echoing office in the new building where senior administrative staff were housed; where board members were convened once every two months for lunch in the paneled boardroom next door, and if the reports were done right (and Gina made sure they were) the only sound heard was the thump of the rubber stamp.

Claire got the fancy digs and the big bucks because her work was about money. But everyone knew where the real work of the agency got done. It got done over there across the courtyard in the old building at desks like Jessie's—there and on the streets, in church basements, and in the dank, sterile, hopeless visiting rooms of jails and prisons.

So she went and picked up an empty carton from the supply closet and headed down to cope with Felicia. One of Jessie's favorite cinematic scenes swam in front of her eyes: *Zorba the Greek,* Madame Hortense breathing her last; women like raucous crows fly in and within minutes strip everything bare, leaving behind a piteous corpse in an empty room. Not that Felicia fit the part of a black-garbed Greek crone, waiting by the desk, her five foot nine, 250-pound frame sheathed in neon-blue spandex, her dark Latina hair bleached rusty yellow.

"I don't need any help," Claire told her.

Felicia shrugged. "No big deal. There's not all that much to do."

"Exactly. Thanks anyway." She maneuvered past the younger woman and set the carton on the gritty floor, all the while thinking *The body's not even cold yet*—though in truth, it had been eight months.

"I want to help for Jessie's sake. Okay?"

Not okay. Claire didn't need reminding that Felicia had been one of Jessie's Kids—a favorite, in fact—fourteen years old when Jessie took her on, a high school dropout barely able to read. The world had written her off. Jessie touched something dimly hopeful in her, something that didn't want the streets and the gangs, something that thirsted for all the things most girls take for granted, like it or not, as their destiny: husband, home and children, decency. Jessie coaxed her, coached her, cheer-led her through the high school equivalency exam and then community college.

Claire said, "She'd have been tickled, you know, that you're—" waving her hand at everything she didn't want Felicia to have.

"That I'm what?"

"Here. As a street worker."

"Yeah. Well, without Jessie, by now I'd be a street*walker*. Or dead."

Felicia turned away from Claire and lifted a stack of papers from the desk. "This here's correspondence," she said, flipping through. "Summer youth employment. Lining up openings, re-upping the kids, new sponsor requests. A bunch of e-mails here...let's see...recruitment and training, workshops, ecksetera, ecksetera."

Claire yanked at the top drawer. Twenty-six now, Felicia had a bachelor's degree and a full-time job with the agency. You'd think she'd have learned to pronounce et cetera.

The inside of the drawer was pure Jessie: a jumble of pens, pencils, rulers, stickies, gold stars, staples, clips, broken shoelaces, rubber bands, scissors, napkins, four pastel-colored golf tees advertising the quick-print shop down at the corner. Jessie didn't play golf. She didn't wear shoes with broken laces, either, but what she most of all didn't do was throw anything away. "You never know when it will come in handy," she'd tell Claire, and damned if she didn't find the most fluky uses for things: a bit of string to shore up a kid's drooping backpack or a slivered chopstick to walk a doubting child through the division of fractions, or a paper plate fashioned into a halo to thank a volunteer who'd stuck with a difficult youngster through a thorny period.

While Felicia separated papers to be saved for the files from those to be thrown away, Claire picked out items for her cardboard box—some photographs, the glass globe paper-weight that had belonged to Jessie's father, the magnifying glass she'd given Jessie a few years back, a Cross pen and pencil in silver, the set still in its original box. Cross doesn't make them in silver anymore. Jessie disliked the gold (too flashy), and she said the chrome with its greasy feel gave her the yiggles; so she'd safeguarded this set, not wanting to lose it. Here it was, like new, not lost. Jessie gone, lost forever. Vicious, the ironies.

Felicia opened the bottom drawer "The Lost Ark," she said, which is what Jessie had called it. A half-dozen or so letter-size box files were loaded up with papers, a trove of information Jessie had collected for her grant proposals. Claire watched as one by one Felicia extracted the files and dumped their contents into the trash.

All that time, all that effort to put together a coherent story in numbers: census-tract data, prison-population data for New York City and New York State, for other states and other major cities. Claire stared at the pages tumbling out of their order, like another death. Numbers of prisoners, percentage of the population, family members, income, recidivism rate, a hundred ways of measuring, quantifying, documenting human error and pain. These statistics, so carefully assembled, had gotten Jessie money for projects no one thought fundable until the grant-award letter came in.

"That's it, then," Claire said. "I guess we're done."

But Felicia had stooped over, her palm resting heavily on the desktop. "Let's see if Jessie really had any treasures hidden in there." In the tight space, she lowered herself to her knees, slid forward the drawer divider and poked her head into the dark cavern behind it. Jessie used to claim she could hide a winning lottery ticket there, and no one would ever go looking for it—most social workers falling back from a mass of tabulations like Count Dracula from a silver crucifix.

"What's this?" Felicia fished out a composition book, the kind with black-and-white marbled covers. "What's this?" she repeated, handing it up to Claire.

On the front, in Jessie's handwriting, was a title: *I'm Telling, Uncle Jimmy.* Claire riffled the pages. "Jessie's journal," she said. A lie. She had no idea what it was, but she'd caught a glimpse of a date and a place, so she'd improvised.

"There's more of them." Wide haunches shimmied in the air. Notebooks were transferred back, two and three at a time. When ever had Jessie done them, a dozen in all, each one filled with her handwriting, each one titled and numbered?

When the drawer was empty, Felicia clambered to her feet, crowding Claire in the small space. "Jessie never said she kept a journal." Chilly hint of accusation.

"No, they're from way back when," said Claire, making it up as she went. "The shelves in our apartment got too full, so she stored them here." It had a ring of truth. God knew, composition books like these hadn't changed since before the Flood. Felicia appeared satisfied. Claire knew the books weren't old, though. Jessie's handwriting had been rounder when she was younger and got jerkier, spikier only in the last few years. Skimming this page was like viewing an electrocardiogram. No matter what the date on them, these were recent. No matter what the supposed place and time, these were written by a middle-aged woman, in Brooklyn, in secret.

No secrets. That had been their promise to each other when they moved in together. *Secrets kill.*

"You want them?" Felicia asked.

"Of course. They're Jessie's. Of course I want them."

"Can I read them sometime?"

How could Claire say? She couldn't even tell what the thing was—memoir, fiction, or something in between—only that it seemed to be about Jessie's girlhood, a faux diary of her life as a child in Oklahoma. "Sure you can. Read all you want. Sometime, maybe."

It's about a teapot, she scolded herself, heading back home that night on the Hutch. You're getting yourself in a state over kitchenware. Jessie surely must have told you about her grandma's teapot. Over the years didn't we tell each other everything? Our best moments, certainly, but also our worst? Embarrassing things, painful things, about stupidity and meanness and shame: a falsehood entered into, a pledge unkept, a friend weaseled. Things we never told anyone else. The sex stolen. The ill-timed fart.

Scariest of all, they told each other the ways they thought they'd let each other down. And it was all right. In her quavery soprano, Jessie serenaded Claire with those lyrics from *Mame*, telling Claire that nothing she did was wrong. (*Nothing!*) And Claire joined in, telling Jessie in song how proud she was that Jessie belonged to her. Because they were together, it was all, all right. *No secrets. Secrets kill.*

From time to time, Jessie had talked about the year spent with her grandparents in Tulsa. Claire's impression was of an American idyll: a summer's day, the Oklahoma sun shining down, a bright golden haze on everything and nary a tornado in sight. A world innocent and uncomplicated, in which kids were left to grow up pretty much unimpeded, and where the hardest thing Jessie had to deal with was her unheated bedroom, a converted porch that got so cold at night, she'd wet the bed. Jessie described the softness against her skin of dresses her grandmother made out of flour sacks. She mentioned her grandfather teaching her how to take a bent nail and straighten it: how precious every scrap of wood or metal was, how you didn't waste anything, how everything was for the war effort, the whole community banding together for Our Boys. She described the redbuds blooming. Someone told her the trees' bare branches wouldn't flower until Cassino was taken from the Germans, and one day they bloomed in great clouds of cerise and magenta, and word came that Cassino had been taken, though the ancient abbey was only a rubble by then. She talked to Claire of all that, but she never gave a hint that she would write any of it down. And of this Claire was certain: Jessie never once told her about any Uncle Jimmy.

6

From the third of Jessie's notebooks

The place: West Tulsa, Oklahoma
The time: Spring 1944

Mrs. Ellis next door has a washing machine with two big cream-colored rollers that will squeeze your fingers flat if you aren't careful to let go with one hand before your other hand starts cranking the clothes through. Big-as-life Gene Autry pictures take up all the wall space in the Ellises' house, all except for John Ellis's room, which is covered in maps. Mrs. Ellis once almost married Gene Autry when he was just a yodeling cowboy on KVOO, but then she didn't. Gramp says that's because cowboys kiss their horses. I don't see Mr. Ellis kissing anybody, come to that, but he is the best I ever saw at spitting. He hits plumb center of the can every time. You never spy spit streaks on the wall around any Ellis spit cans, no matter when you look, so you can't say it's because Mrs. Ellis is a good housekeeper, which she isn't, anyway. "Lottie Ellis keeps enough dust in her house to weave blankets for the war effort," is what Grandma says. The floor of her washing machine room is covered in button halves from where the buttons got broke by the wringer.

Grandma says Mrs. Ellis is too lazy to pull the shirt out before the button flap goes through, but I don't think Mrs. Ellis can be real lazy because she's always sewing new buttons for the ones that got broke, which is a lot of work. When I lose a button on my dress Grandma safety-pins it closed, which is okay except for the time the pin popped open in the middle of the playground at the Eugene Field Elementary School.

Eugene Field is my fifth school, and I like it very much, maybe even better than Mrs. Grace's, because in addition to all the usual subjects I get to go to cooking and shop, both. Miss Forrest is the shop teacher, and Miss Glade is the cooking teacher. Nobody but me seems to get a kick out of their names, not even John Ellis, but it is a funny coincidence. I like coincidences. Seems like when you have a coincidence it is a clue to how the world all fits together, even though things may look to be wide apart.

Miss Glade is a square-shaped kind of lady, and she rocks back and forth when she walks. She is teaching us how to make toast in a skillet without burning even a crumb, so that when we are grown up and married, if we are ever stranded someplace where there is no toaster to be had, we will still be able to cook up a great pile of perfect toast and our husbands will love us and think we are smart. The boys are learning to make toast, too, so I will have to marry somebody who didn't go to the Eugene Field School.

John Ellis is only in the second grade, but he is very smart. I wouldn't want to marry John Ellis, even though grown-ups are impressed with him. He gives himself assignments to complete every day. One day it could be eight or ten books to read. Another day it might be twelve pages to color in twelve different coloring books without going outside the lines even once, or else he says you have to do it over.

John Ellis has a map of the European Theater of War, and every day he sticks pins in to show where the Allies are, especially the Americans, and where the Germans and Italians are. I tried to find Uncle Jimmy's village on John Ellis's map, but no villages are there, only cities.

Uncle Jimmy got yummy food when he was overseas, not in his rations, but after he was wounded the first time and recuperating in the little village near the hospital. He says the Italians cook real good when they have any food to cook at all. Some of them are starving, even the children, but if you can get them just a little bit of meat, they will do things with it I wouldn't believe, and the whole family will sit down to a feast. Uncle Jimmy says someday he will take me there to see for myself, after the war is over.

It doesn't matter what the meat is, either, or where it came from. Too bad the Germans shot his kidney to smithereens. That was the second time he got wounded, the time he saved his whole platoon and got heaps of medals and was sent home. Uncle Jimmy says if there'd been anything left of the kidney when the doctors got through with him, he'd have sent it right on over to the villagers. "They could have had a meal on me, right, sweet pea? Kidney in gravy, and call it the feast of Saint James." Then Uncle Jimmy laughs out loud at the very thought of being a saint at nineteen years of age.

I thought I might crayon the village in on John Ellis's map, using Crayola Carmine Red to stand for Uncle Jimmy's gallantry in the face of the enemy, but John Ellis told me I best not touch his map or we're not friends anymore. When he gets persnickety like that I leave him be for a spell and sit on the Ellises' porch and help his mama with the sewing. Except if Grandma sees me from next door and calls me in for a caution. "Don't you be wearing out your welcome there, Jessie." Wearing out your welcome is about the worst thing a body might do.

I learned to read at Mrs. Grace's, which was my first school. It was on 73rd Street in New York, and you had to go up three stone steps and through a big door painted red to get inside. At the front of the classroom was a gigantic chair with lion faces grinning out of the ends of the arms and eagle claws on the feet. Every day in the reading chair Mrs. Grace let us take turns sitting in her lap while she held open her storybook, a big book with letters that were big, too, so it wasn't even hard to keep them from dancing into each other. While

I was waiting my turn, I liked to sit on the floor and trace my finger along the crevices where the claw met the ball it held onto. Sometimes I picked the dust off and looked for wormholes that could have been made by my father.

My private name for reading time at Mrs. Grace's was cuddlesweater time, because Mrs. Grace's sweater was the unscratchiest wool ever, and I wished I could spend the whole day cuddled against her chest while her cushiony voice rolled the story through me and her fingers guided mine beneath the words. The sweater was fading from lime green to gray. It had thin spots on the front, and it was fraying at the elbows where she rested her arms. I guess Mrs. Grace was wearing out her sweater in the same way you can wear out your welcome.

I used to think maybe there is a fixed time for everybody's welcome, like fish before they stink, and you just have to know how long that is. Uncle Fred wore out his welcome with my mother, and I never saw him again. He never even came back for his hat, which my mother said wasn't a hat, but a pork pie. You have to keep a sharp eye on your welcome, is one thing. Like I could be talking to my mother some quiet Sunday afternoon and we'd be smiley and happy and then next minute somebody—Uncle Ben, maybe—would come in with his box of Schrafft's chocolates, and you could not even sneeze before you'd have worn out your welcome. Not that she'd say you had to go. But you'd know, and you'd rather be dried up like a dusty leaf that gets crunched underfoot.

See, everybody is different. Uncle Ben wears fedoras, which my mother said is a welcome change. "Pork pies'll be my ruination, the very death of me. Your papa wore one. Uncle Fred wore one. Mind, Jessie, don't ever get yourself involved with a man who likes pork pies." Grandma makes pies, mostly apple and cherry, never pork. But I try to stay away from pies, because you can't be too careful. Pie people wear out their welcome real fast, and I am already fast enough as it is.

Like the time we went to visit at Aunt Nedra's mother in Kansas a week or so after I got sent away from Monte Cassino.

Aunt Nedra, she's quiet in the car. The way Uncle Jimmy makes jokes and laughs a lot and likes to throw his head back and sing out loud, that's the way Aunt Nedra doesn't. She sits up front with Uncle Jimmy. I'm in the back watching out the window for roadside stands and Burma Shave signs. Uncle Jimmy recites the Burma Shave rhymes he knows from driving around on business. I sing "My Grandfather's Clock" with him while he makes the windshield wipers go tick tock despite the sun is shining. The road runs through green fields, mostly, and hills when we get to Osage country. Uncle Jimmy tells me the redskins have oil on their land and drive Cadillacs. "Oil is a dirty business, but that's all right when you end up filthy rich." I don't see any oil wells, just empty fields. I can't wait to get to Kansas, which I expect will look like in the movie *The Wizard of Oz*, kind of a brownish black and white. After a while I start drawing lines in the maroon carpeting with the edge of my shoe and then erasing them and drawing new ones.

How come when we cross over the state line, Kansas is the exact same Technicolor as Oklahoma? Aunt Nedra says the movie just showed it in sepia—spelling the word out for me—to tell you Dorothy's feelings about Kansas. She makes sense, I guess, even though I think Glinda the Good Witch is much more beautiful in the book, drawn in plain black and white. But the ruby slippers are a lot prettier in the movie. Wouldn't it be peachy to have a pair of those!

Finally, we get to Aunt Nedra's mother's farm, where they grow peanuts. There is a fat tree in the front yard and a porch with a brown floor, too wavy to play jacks on. Just inside the door, I pause and drop a small curtsy, which is from my second school, the lycée. Right then, I somehow wear out my welcome with Aunt Nedra's mother. The old woman gasps and squeals, "Get that wild heathen banshee out of here!"

"Mama," says Aunt Nedra, "this is Jessie. She's real careful...."

"I don't care. You get her away from me and my china teacups!" She looks like lumps of bleached-out prunes clumped together in the brown wicker rocking chair. Aunt Nedra lifts both her eyebrows at me in the way grown-ups have of letting you know they don't have any more power than you, sorry. So I go and sit in the car alone the whole rest of the visit until Uncle Jimmy comes out. Up to that minute he is still my favorite human being in the whole world, next to my mother, because he treats me like a grown girl, like he really thinks about what I say and like he really wants me to think about what he says, too.

The men who take my mother out on dates act like they liked me, but I've never thought they really did. And Uncle Chester, who married my mother, I think he really did like me, but he never knew how to show it or what to say. "My two girls," he'd grin, throwing an arm around each of us. "Look at my two girls," he'd say to the doorman or the maître d' in the restaurant. "Your finest table for my two girls."

Uncle Jimmy is more like a friend than an uncle. He seems interested in me, not just waiting for me to pay attention to him. Like at Aunt Nedra's mother's house. He comes out and climbs straight into the backseat of his car with me and pulls me over to him, and he holds me tight while I weep into his chest. I get gobs of tears all over the fish on his tie, but he doesn't mind. "Fish need water. Right, sweet pea? Nothing worse than a fish out of water, I always say. But if you're crying over Nedra's mama, it's a waste of those sweet, precious tears. The wheezy old battle-ax ain't worth spit."

"Aunt Nedra will be angry with me."

"Don't you worry yourself about that, sweet pea. Your uncle Jimmy's going to smooth everything over, you betcha. Aunt Nedra had no call to drag us up here, anyhow."

"She didn't?"

"No, sirree, and I told her so, but would she listen? No-o-o!"

I am in those last stages of shudders and hiccups that my cryings always end with. Uncle Jimmy starts rubbing my back, soothing, not patpatpatting the way most grown-ups do like they've forgotten all about you. "Understand, sweet pea?"

I sit back and nod and then manage to give him a washed-down smile, which is all I can get together though he deserves more, being so nice. He cups my face in his hand, thumbing the wet streaks away. "Oh, you pretty baby," he says.

"Am not a baby," I say, but he doesn't seem to hear. With his other hand, he pushes the hair off my eyes and forehead. "Such a pretty, sweet face," he murmurs. "Such a pretty, sweet, sweet girl," his voice cooing in his throat, like a pigeon. He leans forward and kisses my eyes—first my right, then my left. "Your uncle Jimmy would like to make you very, very happy."

I don't know what to say, but I know I can't go wrong with, "Thank you." My voice sounds funny, too—far away and small.

He kisses my cheek. "Oh, and are you ever soft!"

He isn't, though: I can feel the rough stubble of his face against me, and I pull away.

"No, no, sweet pea. Don't be frightened."

I'm not, really. But I want to go away from there. I don't like it in Kansas. I wipe my eyes and my face and smooth my dress, and Uncle Jimmy laughs. "I'm all right now," I say. "Truly I am."

"Well, that's my brave girl." His voice sounds normal again. "You remember you can always count on your uncle Jimmy if ever something goes wrong. Anytime you need a hero, why you just come to me, and I'll fix it up square, like that." Snapping his fingers. "And listen, sweet pea. You and me, we're special friends, right? So we got to keep mum whatever goes on between us. You remember that, too."

Special friends is what Uncle Jimmy made us when he came to take me out for a visit from Monte Cassino, which was my fourth school.

7

Claire

Brooklyn, New York
February 1995

At its first meeting, the bereavement support group's facilitator asked the eight of them to give their spouse's name and the basic circumstances of the death. Claire being the only "gay" member of the group, Donna could be forgiven for saying "spouses" and not mentioning partners or some other lame euphemism. When Claire's turn came, and she said she'd been together with Jessie twenty-three years, nobody around the circle so much as batted an eye. What a relief that these strangers should be so open minded.

But they must have thought she'd said Jesse, because there was an audible gasp when Claire continued, "She had breast cancer."

Someone whispered, "What?"

Someone else whispered, "Lesbian."

Claire detested labels. Any labels: morning person, night person; intellectual, flirt; flibbertigibbet, leader. Flattering or not, grain of truth or not, she loathed, abhorred and defied them all. The worst was lezzzzbian, with its ugly buzz there in the middle, like bees zeroing in on the sting, like kamikaze planes homing in for the smashup. The word fogged the truth, which was that Claire had fallen in love with Jessie because she was Jessie, and vice versa.

Had they gone gaga over mere packaging? Absolutely not! They fell for the selves they were deep down—the essential Jessie, the essential Claire. Whatever those selves happened to come wrapped in was very much beside the point. For a long time and fiercely they held that this made them Not Lesbians. Call it their womanhood-as-gift-wrap period.

Problem was, being a woman wasn't some petty happenstance, some tangential peculiarity like a sixth toe, and eventually they had to admit—or rather, to celebrate—that womanliness was integral, essential to the selves they gave each other. Loving Jessie, Claire loved a woman. And vice versa. Well, then, what defined a lesbian? Was it that she loved a woman (which each of them did)—or women (which they did not)? Desired a woman (oh, yes indeed!)—or desired women (emphatically no, never had)? Made love with one woman exclusively—or with women exclusively? So much seemed to hang upon the answers, but no answer definitively came. "Let's not think about it anymore," Claire said, still despising the word. Call it their ignorance-as-bliss period.

Time went by, and at some moment when they weren't noticing, it ceased to be important to them one way or the other what label they might be stuck with. Lesbian queer gay dykes or not, they just didn't care. They adored each other: what else mattered?

And so Claire stammered on past the whispers at that first meeting, staring into her lap while she told the group about Jessie's second bout with cancer, how Jessie said not to worry, bad things always came in twos in her life. Claire would see, it would be okay. Sure enough, Jessie beat that one, though what a close call it was. Then six months later, having survived two surgeries and a month of radiation and numerous appalling rounds of chemotherapy, Jessie was killed in a car crash by a forty-year-old DWI.

Alan, the lone widower there, asked, "What happened to the DWI?"

Claire drew a finger across her throat. "Killed," she said. "In the smackup."

"Good!"

"You think so?"

"Don't you?"

She swallowed and lowered her eyes to the floor, scuffed green vinyl tiles twelve inches square, black streaks slanting through them. Everything outside had gone silent, awaiting her response. She was supposed to say yes, it was good, the man deserved it, justice was served. Or else no, it wasn't good, his death couldn't bring Jessie back. She thought the old Claire would have said no, although it was hard to remember the old Claire, the one who died that summer day along with Jessie. It was even harder to fathom the woman sitting here now pretending ignorance of the answer boiling in her mouth. Of all things in the world unrecognizable since Jessie's last breath, Claire herself was the most.

At last she raised her eyes to meet the others', and her hands encircled the air. "I'd much rather have strangled the goddamn bastard myself," she snarled, her thumbs pressing into an invisible Adam's apple. The young woman to her left—too young to be a widow, but weren't they all too young, even the white-haired lady with the cane?—that young one blurted out, "You go, girl!" And everyone laughed, all of them, together. Gone were the whispers, the rustling, the politely blank faces, the limp smiles implying some of their best friends were lesbians. Loss was what defined Claire now. Loss defined them all, and loss is the same, no matter what label attached to your gender or politics or sexual history.

Not that loss was a term they all embraced. Alan, for one, protested when Donna asked him how he'd lost his wife. "I lose my keys, I lose my hat. I lose the bills that come in the mail. Sometimes I'm sure I'm losing my mind. But my wife? You're telling me she's just misplaced somewhere, stupid me, and I can't find her?" Eyes stabbing at the facilitator over his reading glasses. "Lois is dead. She's not coming back. What can I do about it? Nothing. Where can I go to get it changed? Nowhere."

"How did Lois die?" Donna amended.

Brain tumor. It began with headaches, and then her behavior got weird. Weird in what way, he wouldn't say. Two years it took her to die; the last six months were very bad. "So if you want to know who's lost, it's me." Thumb jabbing at his chest. "It's me."

"We," Claire said.

"We're all lost."

"No, that's not what I meant. I meant we've lost 'we.'" Claire and Jessie, Alan and Lois, and the rest of them: eight couples, uncoupled.

Across the circle, curled up in an *S*, sat a woman whose name Claire didn't know. Carol or Karen, Sharon—something like that. She wasn't wearing a name tag. "People tell me I look good," she said, "but it's like osteoporosis, you know? Like osteoporosis: the bone looks fine on the outside, but inside you're just a mess of holes." She said her husband had died of pancreatic cancer. His illness was swift and, until the very end, relatively painless. She said she was probably the luckiest one there on account of the peaceful time they'd been given together. But it was hard how other people kept telling her how good she looked.

"People say things without thinking. They mean well," Mary said. She had a shy way about her that Claire liked. Mary was the one with a cloud of snow-white hair billowing about her head. Slight and stooped, she walked with a cane, one of her legs in a brace. Her seventy-four-year-old husband had been stabbed to death in a mugging gone bad.

She'd come to the meeting with Emilia, her neighbor. Emilia had lupus, only recently diagnosed, and she said her husband had been gracious about it. Gracious? What a peculiar word to use, Claire thought. A week to the day after his sixtieth birthday, on the subway platform on his way home from work, Emilia's husband dropped dead of a heart attack, no warning. Now she worried who would take care of her when her disease got worse.

Sylvia, next to speak, said her husband hadn't been particularly gracious about anything in their thirty-five years of marriage. But they'd stayed together, and they were on the brink of one of those lifestyle retirements. True, he had diabetes, but they assumed they'd be able to travel, play golf. His kidneys failed. Now her friends were encouraging her to go on a cruise. Her friends said she'd have her memories to comfort her. But every day, even these empty days, brought with them new things that made new memories that didn't include him. And for that, she found she hated every new day.

Donna said, "Memories aren't always comfortable."

"No joke," muttered Helga, who might have been forty, though she looked older. Everything about her sagged: her skin, her hair, her belly and breasts and shoulders, her mouth. She said, anyway she had no time for memories. Her husband had died of heart disease, leaving Helga with four children under age ten.

Mary said her memories kept crowding everything else out. "Practically anything anyone mentions reminds me of something, and I wander off in my own little world."

Claire had to blow her nose, which was a kind of agreement. Sometimes it seemed there was nothing in the world that didn't connect to Jessie and their life together.

"People don't understand what they've said to make me sad," Mary went on. "I burst out sobbing and have to run to the bathroom to recover."

"Not here, though," Miller said. Here there were tissue boxes between the seats.

Miller told them her husband was a botanist who fell ill after a trip abroad studying jungle plants. Six vials of blood were drawn from his arm and shipped out express to a lab for exotic diseases. The test results were still pending three days later when he died, age thirty-eight. His widow was even younger, maybe thirty-four, a history teacher who seemed to have only the one name, like Cher or Madonna. The lopped-off singleness of it called to Claire's mind amputations, phantom limbs. Remnants, that's all they were, the eight of them there, phantoms missing the lives to connect to. Miller said she made it a habit to visit the cemetery every afternoon after school. "Gabbing with the corpse," her sister called it, and Miller hadn't a clue how to answer that.

It occurred to Claire that much as she loathed labels, she'd give a lot these days to find one that would fit her. Widow—except not. Lisi called her "my mother's surviving partner."

8

From the fourth of Jessie's notebooks

The place: Tulsa, Oklahoma
The time: Spring 1944

My mother decided I should go to Monte Cassino so I wouldn't have to feel bad about being a burden. She couldn't be home much; she was looking for the right husband, slow work the third time around. I didn't see why Ada couldn't take care of me, until I overheard my mother telling Ada she would have to let her go, money was tight.

I didn't like Monte Cassino except for the jungle gym in the playground where I could hang upside down and no one yelled about seeing my underpants because we were all girls. The kids made fun of me because I didn't have a uniform, and Joyce Webster stole my mother's picture from my bed table one afternoon and made me buy it back from her. I told Sister about it, but she told me that Joyce was a sinner and God would punish her. It was hard to figure out when God would punish you and when the sisters would, and which would be worse. The sisters taught you penmanship by hitting your hand with a ruler, and they made you go to classes even if you had a sore throat. You had a choice: you could go to class, or you could have your throat painted with Argyrol and then go to class.

Sister Ann Joseph was nice, though. She gave me an empty stamp album and some of her more common duplicates. Sometimes she took us to the woods to learn forest woodcraft, and sometimes we went with her into the grotto to plant bulbs and flowers.

It was pretty there in the grotto, a kind of secret garden, like an outdoor theater. The high, arched rocks made a kind of stage set for the Virgin Mother, her robes deep blue like late afternoon, her head tilted slightly, arms outstretched, eyes looking down on me with a look that told me she knew I was a good girl. Which proves it was only a statue, because after I did what was bad—not that I knew it was bad when Myra and Myrna made me do it—the approving look stayed sweet just the same.

You could only tell Myra and Myrna Daley apart because one of them had a left blue eye and a right brown; the other had a right blue eye and a left brown. Some of the girls said it was Myra with the blue right eye, and some said it was Myrna, and Myra and Myrna wouldn't say at all, so I got mixed up which was which. On Columbus Day we only had a half day of school because it was a holiday, and after lunch Myra and Myrna asked me if I wanted to go out behind the grotto with them and play. They said first I had to prove I was brave. "You're new here, so you don't know. But no one will ever play with you without you pass the bravery test."

"I can pass," I said.

"You'll have to climb up the back of the grotto—over on the left side, where there's moss—walk across the top till you get to the other side, then jump down and kiss the feet of the Virgin Mother."

I was wearing the new shoes my mother bought me when we packed for school. They were still slippery, and I didn't want to scuff the toes by pinching them in between the rocks, so I mostly used my hands to hold tight and tried to get my knees to support me more than my feet. I tore my dress a little when I got both my knees kneeling on it and had to tilt myself to one side and tug it free. But I made it to the top and I stood up tall, not even hunched over, almost like a real tightrope walker stretching out my arms and balancing my way across. I got to where I had to jump down on the other side, and it looked awfully far down to the bottom, but I knew it wasn't as far as it seemed. I knew because I learned to not be scared of high places by jumping off the stoop at Mrs. Grace's school, starting at the lowest step and going higher and higher and when that got easy, by jumping off the wall in Central Park clean over the bushes and onto the grass. So I took a deep breath and I jumped and I landed right under the smile of the Virgin Mother.

I no sooner kissed her cold, rough toes than Myra and Myrna started hopping up and down like they had to go to the bathroom and pointing their fingers at me. "Ooh, ooh, I'm gonna tell. Ooh, you're in trouble. You were on the grotto. Ooh, ooh!" And off they ran to find Mother Superior, zigzagging around the beds of still-blooming fall flowers.

But I could run faster. Even Teddy Draper, who is two years older than me—and a boy!—can't beat me when we race. So I got to Mother Superior first. At the door of the Convent House I stopped short, pulled my dress down from where it had gotten hiked up way over my knees and wiped the sweat off my forehead and from my cheeks and upper lip, using the backs of my hands and fingers so I wouldn't mix in all the dirt with my sweat and look messy. I didn't want Mother to send me off for a good face washing before I got to say anything, or she'd wind up hearing from Myra and Myrna before she heard from me.

I pushed open the thick carved-wooden door and stepped into the cool of the tiled rotunda. Mother Superior was in the library. She and Father Thomas were sitting in two high-backed, black-leather chairs that crackled when one or the other of them sat forward or leaned back. I tiptoed over to the doorway of the room and reached up and rapped the library knocker. Mother Superior looked over at me, smiled like she was copying the statue in the grotto, and held out her arm, beckoning me. I took a few silent steps on the thick Oriental rug.

Father Thomas watched me come, not looking cross or anything, and not puzzled either, really just nothing at all on his face except nice. I stopped and curtsied. Now, that's my specialty. I lift my skirts out like a fan with both hands, put my right toe behind my left foot, bend my knees and lean back, then slowly lift my head and chest and smile just ever so slightly. I am the only kid I know who can do it that way. I learned it from Mlle Dumas at the lycée back in New York and also to count in French and to sing "Sur le Pont d'Avignon" and "Au Clair de la Lune."

Being in a hurry, I could have done the short quick-dip curtsy, but anyone can do that, and besides, this was a formal occasion. I was in the Convent House, and that's not something you get to do every day.

"Yes, my child?"

"Mother Superior, excuse me." I stood very upright and looked her square in the eye and never fidgeted or twisted my hands or anything. "I just did something I found out afterward was a terrible thing and I wanted to tell you about it myself. I climbed the grotto."

"I see," she said, same bountiful smile holding there, outstretched arm maybe turning inward but only a smidgen. Her eyes looked over at the father's. My eyes traveled with hers, and they saw the left side of his lip curve upward and his eyes crinkle, just barely. He raised his teacup and took a sip. She looked back at me. I was still standing quietly without moving, still meeting her gaze. "Well, you didn't know. But thank you for being so honest with me. I'm very proud of you. You go on out and play now, you hear?" I nodded. "And try the playground this time. Instead of the grotto."

"Yes, ma'am," I said and curtsied again, a quick-dip this time. "Thank you, ma'am." With quick, tiny steps I headed into the rotunda.

The front door came crashing in, banging heavily against the wall. Myra and Myrna tumbled after it, breathing heavily, looking sweaty, their socks run down into their shoes. Myrna (I think) had a freshly bruised knee. She stuck her tongue out at me as the two rushed past me through the open library door. They didn't even stop to knock. They just burst in, shouting "Mother! Mother!" I heard sharp crackling from the leather chairs, and then I heard Mother in her deep assembly voice. "Just what is the meaning of this rude intrusion?"

"Jessie did something bad," said one of them.

"Real bad. A sin," said the other, whoever had the sketchier voice.

"This is neither the time nor the place—if indeed there ever is a time or a place—to run tattling after a friend."

"But she climbed the grotto. We saw her. She climbed up the back and walked across and then she jumped down."

"I see." Seconds of silence. I counted them the way my mother taught me. One Mississippi, two Mississippi, three Mississippi. "And you say you saw her?"

"Yes, we did."

"The entire thing?"

"Uh-huh."

"And never, at any time, did you do anything to stop her, to tell her—since she is new and probably didn't know—that it is strictly forbidden?"

One Mississippi, two Mississippi.

"Speak up!"

"No, ma'am," murmured one. "No, ma'am," muttered the other, and I slipped out the front door into the sunshine. I went back to the dormitory and wrote a letter to my mother. *How are you? I am fine. Would you like to see a beautiful statue? I can show it to you when you come visit. Also a beautiful garden with flowers the exact shade of your lilac dress with the peplum, the one I helped you pick out to wear that night you went with Uncle Ben to 52nd Street to hear Billie Holiday sing, remember? I hope you can come see them soon, because I know you will like them.*

Uncle Jimmy was wounded twice in front of Monte Cassino—not this Monte Cassino, but the real one in Italy. He was there fighting the Germans at the Rapido River, and he is a war hero. He gave his medals to Grandma. Two of them are

Purple Hearts. Two of them are ribbons, one with a disk attached and an eagle on it. Best of all is the Silver Star. When I turn it over, the words on the back say, "For Gallantry in Action."

Uncle Jimmy came to my Monte Cassino with an Italian letter to see if one of the old Italian nuns could translate for him. It was from the family Uncle Jimmy made friends with when he was getting over his first wound. There was only one old nun, Sister Maria, but it turned out Sister Maria was Spanish, and Uncle Jimmy understood more Italian than she did, so the nuns let him take me out for a ride in his car instead.

It was nice inside his car—the seats velvety, the windows big, so I could see out and didn't have to hike myself up on the armrest. I liked twirling the ivory knobs of the window cranks, so smooth they felt almost soft, soft down to the very center. I still love to do that. The only thing is I would rather ride in the back because I don't like the gearshift anymore, despite being a nice ivory, too. In the back I can cover my bare legs with the car blanket and pull it under my nose and let the fur tickle me like feathers. Now that I live with Grandma and Gramp, Aunt Nedra comes riding in the car a lot, and I get to sit in the back, but that day it was just me up front with Uncle Jimmy going out to visit Uncle Cubby and Aunt Cissie and their little dog named Clancy and their big old horse named George.

We came in the kitchen door and surprised Aunt Cissie, who was listening to hillbilly music on the radio and snapping beans. She was glad to see us and said I wouldn't remember her, which I didn't, but she said I spent some time there when my mother was at Grandma and Gramp's before Uncle Chester died. Uncle Chester was my mother's husband for a little while. He gave me a white fur muff once and put a ten-dollar bill inside it. His job was with the OSS. They say Uncle Chester died of pneumonia, which I think is a lie, because he was working in Jacksonville, and it's warm there. I think it's because he was a spy and was captured by the Germans like in a war movie.

Aunt Cissie has a soft kind of Southern accent, so what she said didn't come out stringy, in a twang, like Uncle

Jimmy's and Uncle Cubby's, and not like people talk in the movies, either, the way my mother does. Aunt Cissie's fluffs and floats up the way dandelion balls do when you blow them free. She gave us all some ham and corn bread and tapioca pudding, and then I went out to the barn with the men to visit George. Even though I was wearing a pinafore I got to ride bareback out across the fields. George has a back so broad my legs stuck straight out, but he moseyed along so slow it didn't matter. Sometimes he stopped to crop the grass, so I leaned back and watched the cloud shapes until he was ready to go on. I couldn't really steer him. George knew where he wanted to go and where he didn't, and he knew, when it started getting dark, to turn around and head on home.

Uncle Cubby and Uncle Jimmy were waiting near the barn, and I tried to get them to turn around so I could slide off of George without them seeing my underpants. They laughed and slapped their thighs hard, and Uncle Jimmy made like he fell over into the hay, it was that funny. Then Uncle Cubby spilled out what was left in his Dr. Pepper and helped me down. Uncle Jimmy got quiet and stood there not moving at all, until Uncle Cubby clapped him on the back and said, "Jimbo, time to get this little one back to her school."

It was cold in the car going home. I had come out without any coat or sweater, so I pulled my knees up under my dress. "Chilly, sweet pea?" Uncle Jimmy said. "I'll fix that." He pulled over to the side of the road and stopped the car. Then he reached across me and closed my window, though I knew very well how to do that myself, and he rumpled his nose up against my cheek. "Phew, Jessie, you smell like George," he said.

I giggled and pushed him off. "Then don't smell me."

He started up the car, gunning the engine, making it roar, squealing out onto the highway. Then he showed me how he could keep my fingers real warm if I held onto the gearshift knob and he covered my hand with his. He could drive with three hands, he said, two of his and one of mine. I liked the knob all right, the feel of the ivory. But I didn't like the way

Uncle Jimmy started moving his hand around on top of mine instead of letting go when he wasn't changing gears.

"I'm much warmer now," I said.

He made a quick grin, his lips rolling under like he was trying to hide them. "Got enough heat in me for a truckload," he said, but he didn't stop rubbing my hand. "You like games, sweet pea?" he said.

I love games. I know old maid and knucks, go fish and pisha pasha, and I've been playing checkers since I was four and my father unrolled his special checkerboard made of tiny felt-backed wooden tiles that smelled like the wood in Grandma's sideboard. My father taught me to play checkers, but I never could beat him.

My mother bought me my own set of checkers when I lived with her in New York, with a checkerboard that folded up, but we never played together. My mother doesn't play any games. She only smells nice and sometimes loses her stockings or her girdle. Mornings when she was dressing for the office, she'd say, "Jessie, you want to find Mama's lingerie?" or "Jessie, you think you know where my girdle's wandered off to?" I'd always find them behind a chair or under the bed. A couple of times I found a black sock there, too, with a design on it that she called a clock, even though it didn't tell time.

Uncle Fred wore socks with those clocks on them, and one time I told him I'd found his sock in the bedroom. He got all puffed up around the eyes, and his lips got fatter than ever. He shouted at my mother, and that's when she told him he'd worn out his welcome. It was Uncle Fred who taught me to play twenty questions, which I am pretty good at, although I can't decide whether radio shows are animal, vegetable or mineral. Movies, too. Would you say *White Cliffs of Dover* (my all-time best movie until *Meet Me in St. Louis*) is vegetable because the movie film is celluloid, or is it mineral, because that's what the cliffs are made of, or is it animal because it's about people? I asked Uncle Jimmy, but he didn't know either.

"I got a French game we can play," he said.

"I know some French songs."

"I'll bet you do, too, with that mama of yours. Well, go on. Sing me one."

I did "Au Clair de la Lune" and then I tried to sing the "Marseillaise," but I couldn't remember all the words. Uncle Jimmy knew the Marchons part, only he pronounced it March On like in English so we drove up the road with his window still wide open and the wind blowing his yellow hair around, and both of us going "Marchons, marchons, la la la la la." Every time Uncle Jimmy boomed out "march on" he punched the air with his fist, so I got my hand back from the gearshift knob and stuck it underneath me for safekeeping. I felt a little funny sitting down like that. At the lycée we always had to stand by our desks, backs straight and arms at our sides in respect for the national anthem of La France, but Uncle Jimmy said the Frogs wouldn't mind none and wouldn't take it for an insult, or if they did he knew how to beg pardon.

"Everybody makes mistakes sometimes," Uncle Jimmy said. "And everybody apologizes. We'll just tell them, 'Oops, pardonnez-moi.'" Mlle Dumas would have hunched her bony shoulders and searched the sky for help if she heard his accent. He shifted gears and then he made his hand fall against my leg and said again, "Ooops. Pardonnez-moi. Just like that, see?"

I knew I should answer "pas de quoi" or "ce ne fait pas rien," but I didn't want to. Besides, it was no mistake and no accident, because he went and let his hand slide off and brush against my leg a second time. I thought if I pretended not to notice, maybe he would stop. I said, "Is it a memory game?"

"Is what?"

"Your French game. Is it like geography?" I am very good at geography even when it looks like all the A-places have been used up.

He winked like I was in cahoots with him about something. "Why sweet pea," he said, his hand resting a little bit on my thigh. "This here is the game. It's a tapping game, like red light, green light or giant steps."

"That's stupid."

"Ooops. My French friends would not like to hear you say so."

"It isn't even a real game. Nobody wins and nobody loses." It was like a baby game where you didn't play against each other, you just did the same thing over and over.

"Sweet pea, a game isn't a war. In a war, somebody has to win and somebody has to lose. In a game, everybody can win." Then Uncle Jimmy said I should try playing it with him, but I didn't want to put my hand on the gearshift knob again because he might do that rubbing thing again, and for a minute I even wondered if maybe Uncle Jimmy hadn't made this whole game up just to get me to bring my hand out again. That didn't make any sense, though, Uncle Jimmy being a war hero, and the whole country proud of him because he kept fighting even when he was terribly wounded, and he saved his whole platoon from certain death.

When we got back to school, Uncle Jimmy stopped the car outside the main gate. He said, "We're special friends now, you and me. Right?"

"I guess."

"Well, I should say so. And I guess we don't have to tell anybody else our goings on, either. That's just between you and me."

"Like blood brothers?"

"Well, yeah, sure enough. Our own secret society." At camp I asked a boy if I could join their secret society, but he said no because I was a girl.

"Okay, sweet pea?"

I shook my head. "I can't say okay."

"Why, you're just hurting my feelings. I guess you don't like your old uncle Jimmy."

"I like you heaps and heaps," I said. He looked so awfully disappointed in me, his big forehead all furrowed, his mouth pouted out—and after being kind enough to take me on a visit. "But Sister says never use okay because it is a slang word and not acceptable in polite society."

Uncle Jimmy started chuckling, and then he threw back

his head and roared with laughter until I wanted to crawl under the seat because I thought he was laughing at me. At last he cupped my chin in his hand and said, "A lot that sister knows. Why, sweet pea, in the army everybody says okay. Privates, sergeants, all the way on up to four-star generals."

"Really?"

"Let me tell you. Over there on the Rapido River when we weren't yelling, 'Attack! Attack! Attack!' we'd be yelling, 'Okay! Okay!' Soldiers, buddies of mine, they died in the service of our country yelling out okay."

He moved his face close to mine, staring into me, his tarnished-copper eyes twitching side to side the way eyes do when you try to hold them still. Next he kissed my cheek and said, "You are a precious wonder, you are. You go and tell that sister every war hero in Italy says okay. If she don't like okay, she can go to the Krauts. You know what Krauts say?" I shook my head. His lips pursed out and his voice got toe deep: "Jawohl."

Of course, I couldn't tell Sister anything like that.

"Okay, sweet pea?"

"Okay, Uncle Jimmy."

After that Uncle Jimmy came to visit me whenever he was not on the road selling Dr. Pepper. One Sunday he took me to a magic show, and another time we went to a tent meeting to see the Holy Rollers, except it scared the bejeebers out of me when everybody started jumping up and down shaking their arms and screaming, "Glory, Hallelujah." Uncle Jimmy let me sit in his lap and told me he wouldn't let anybody grab me, and he circled me with his tight arms like a moat. He said he would be back the next week to take me to the rodeo, and I would see some real shaking and shouting, for sure. I waited for him all that day, but he didn't come, so he must have gone on the road. He didn't come the next week either, and neither did my mother, and I went on a nature walk with Sister Ann Joseph.

Then I got expelled and sent away. I figure it was for being a blasphemer. I was sitting at the back of the empty classroom writing *I shall not blaspheme* a hundred times when Sister Bernard, Mother Superior's assistant, came in. After a lot of whispered hissing with Sister Angeline, she made me bring my things and took me back to the dorm. "You'll pack your belongings and wait here," she told me and walked away. All the other girls kept staring at me, but they wouldn't talk to me.

I didn't mean to become a blasphemer. I thought we were having a discussion. At my other schools, you would read a chapter and then have a discussion. The chapter and verses were: "Upon this rock I build my church.... Whatsoever thou hast bound on earth shall be bound in Heaven; whatsoever thou hast loosed on earth shall be loosed in Heaven." Pretty much, I understood the words. I just didn't understand why Sister Angeline said the words made the Catholic Church the one true church, because Jesus established the church on Peter.

"That's just the way Catholics want to see it," I said, which is something I learned from Mlle Dumas at the lycée, which is a French Huguenot school and not Catholic at all. I thought it would be all right to say what Mlle Dumas said and not ask my real question, which was bigger.

"Blasphemy!" Sister's voice croaked like she'd just gotten a dose of Argyrol. "Plead forgiveness!"

The biggest questions are things nobody ever answers, like, how did Jesus get to be the son of God if Joseph was Mary's husband and God never was. I stayed my father's daughter no matter who my mother went out with, no matter who she liked, no matter who she married. Uncle Chester was a Desmond from the Philadelphia Desmonds, and my mother became Nancy Ann Desmond when he became her husband. When I got sent away to school, it was more convenient to call me Desmond, too, she said, rather than Friedman, my real name. "Less confusing, don't you think?" That way, if my mother called or came to visit me at school, no precious time would be lost in trying to figure out which little girl she belonged to. But even then, Uncle Chester didn't get to be my father. "Your father will always be your father," she said, and she should know, because Gramp never got to be her real father, despite she called him Pa.

I've never heard of Jesus having a last name. Just Jesus of Nazareth, which is where he came from, but not where he was born, which was Bethlehem. I could become Jessica Ann Louise of New York City. Jessie of Fifty-Ninth Street. But I could never be the daughter of Chester. And he was married to my mother, whereas God was never even Mary's husband, so I finally figured out for myself that it must be Jesus was the son of God the way we're all the children of God. But if Jesus was a child of God like anybody, then couldn't anybody come along and say to a friend, "I'm making you into a church and if you say a guy should go to heaven, that's what'll happen, and if you say a guy should go the other way, *whoosh*, ashes!"?

I didn't use exactly those words with Sister. I tried instead to have a discussion about how everybody in every religion thinks their churches are right, but the more I tried the more her face went purply against the tight white edges of her wimple.

"You," she barked, "are a blasphemer! An unrepentant blasphemer. I command you to be scourged."

Scourged didn't sound good.

"On your knees, ingrate. Beg for redemption of your everlasting soul!"

I shook my head. Someone in the row behind me gasped.

Sister Angeline picked up a ruler and shook it at me. "Beg, or you will burn in the eternal fires of hell."

I knew she was wrong there. "That's not true," I said, but I didn't get to explain about falling asleep without saying my prayers and not waking up burning in hell. She swooped at me and, one-handed, grabbed me up out of my seat. Everybody began talking, and some kids were crying, and Mary Ann Jameson shrieked. Sister smashed the ruler on the edge of the desk, and the room went dead silent.

I didn't want to have to beg Sister Angeline for anything. She wasn't even a good teacher. I was afraid of her face, so I stood there watching my feet and waiting for the ruler to fall on me. Years went by. When she dropped her hold on me and lowered the ruler, I looked up, and she was smiling like she'd put one over on me and wanted me to guess how. "There is no salvation for those who will not repent," she said, and she told me I had to go sit in the back of the room facing the wall and write *I shall not blaspheme* one hundred times.

After about ten times, I figured out a system that let me write the words without having to think of them in a sentence. They made a nice design on the paper. There were lots of tall letters that you could vary in height, and I could switch off between two different ways I knew to do the final *t* in *not. Blaspheme* had the only letter that went below the line. It was a tricky word to spell. Now that I knew how, I was planning to look up blaspheme in the dictionary back at the dorm, and find out what I'd done.

Except the kids in the dorm wouldn't talk to me, so I couldn't use the dictionary, because I couldn't take it without a monitor's permission, so I packed my suitcase, like Sister Bernard said. Every once in a while someone came near and dropped something on the bed. I acted like I didn't notice, but I marked it on the check-off sheet inside my head. Betty Sue Hollister put a mint one-and-a-half-cent Martha Washington down that she owed to me, since she licked the back of mine and stuck it in my stamp album without a hinge. Rosalind Waters gave me back the white Peter Pan collared dickey she'd borrowed, which she'd said she already returned to me, but I knew all along she was lying. Joyce Webster, her whole face red, and even what you could see of her head through her white-blonde hair, gave me back the dollar I'd paid her at the rate of a dime a week, my whole allowance, to buy back the picture of my mother. Lureline Davis pitched a half-empty box of Chiclets onto the blanket, and her sister put down my mother's lace hankie, still smelling like my mother. I hadn't even known it was stolen.

Their parade up and down the row of beds in the long room ended when Sister Bernard came for me and took me to Mother Superior's office, where Grandma and Gramp were waiting. Grandma was perched at the edge of the big visitor's chair looking a lot like my mother except with gray hair and lines in her cheeks and a little bit curvier nose. She was wearing the same dotted dress and small round hat as in the photograph my mother has of her and Gramp.

In the photo, you can't see all that much of Gramp's face because his hat covers the top part where he's bald, and in the middle part there's light shining off his glasses. The lower part of his face in the photo has a kindly grin, but he wasn't looking kindly at all in Mother Superior's office. He was standing in the middle of the rug softly slapping his hat against his knees. His forehead was sweaty and red.

I curtsied and tried to apologize, but Mother Superior held up her hand for silence. "You will go home with this woman," Mother said, not mean or cold, but like she didn't really know who I was. She nodded toward Grandma, who stood up and took my hand. She was sweaty, too. Tiny droplets glittered in the fuzzy hair on her upper lip. Grandma says that only horses sweat; ladies glow. She knows lots about being a lady, despite she comes from up north of Tulsa, where they still have outhouses and even the women chew tobacco. But still, she was sweating.

I figured I was going to get yelled at a lot for being so bad that I'd made them sweaty and red, so as soon as we got in the car, a green Packard from before the war, I tried to tell Grandma and Gramp how I got thrown out. It is always better to tell than to be found out, but as many times as I kept trying, they kept shushing me. Finally, Grandma said, "Enough, child. You try the patience of a saint. Bad enough I had to sit there and listen to that high-toned penguin tell me their charity doesn't extend to heathens and Christ killers."

Grandma called Mother Superior a penguin! That had to be worse even than being a blasphemer.

"What's a Christ killer?" I said.

"Hush now, Jessie. That's none of your concern. We're good Christians here. You, too."

9

Claire

Brooklyn, New York
April 1995

"I just wanted to get out," Sylvia was saying as Claire slipped in late for the meeting, the group's sixth. "I wasn't planning on buying anything. Just, the silence in my apartment was way too loud, you know?"

Exactly the reason Claire had been out to Long Island to the grand opening of that shoe warehouse. Not because she needed footwear or wanted it. The silence was why. The silence, with only a lily for company. She sat down next to Mary and crossed one leg over the other, revealing a pair of red ragg wool socks beneath the pin-striped gray trousers of her pantsuit.

"I wandered along Coney Island Avenue," Sylvia went on. "In and out of those odd-lot stores, not even paying attention."

Claire had been wandering, too. The place had been clogged with women who rummaged through tiers of boxes and then jockeyed for a try-on at the crammed benches. In the midst of their busyness, she felt slow and awkward, a ladybug lumbering through an anthill.

"Just something to do on a down day, you know? But then there was this jug that caught my eye, one of those rooster things. I've always liked them."

"Rooster things?" asked Alan.

"The spout is an open beak, a crowing rooster. Come, you must have seen them, Alan. They're French. Or Mexican, is it?"

"So it's a pitcher."

"Pitcher, jug—whatever. They're colorful. I always thought they'd be cheery in the morning."

He shrugged.

"This one had a really nice handle. Ear shaped." She scribed a curve in the air.

"And you bought it."

"Yes. No. Well, I—I left the store. And then I came back and walked past it six or eight times, trying to make up my mind. You know?"

Claire knew. She had stumbled, almost literally, into a tower of hiking boots in all shades and sizes and spent three-quarters of an hour limping to and fro in five successive pairs of ill-fitting rainbow-colored clodhoppers: sky blue, pink blush, cranberry, eggplant, two-tone teal. When nothing was left in her size but a pair of plain brown day hikers, she shoved into them unlaced and pivoted in front of the mirror. Hmm. Who'd have guessed? She viewed them from the back. Such accomplished-looking feet.

A woman awaiting her turn at the mirror gave an exasperated cluck. "You'll never get a decent fit with those trouser socks," pointing Claire to the hosiery aisle.

Proper socks did make all the difference. Claire found the raggs and for twenty minutes trekked through the store in the hikers, which felt fine, which felt good. All the same, Claire dithered. Hunkering down on the bench behind her mountain of rejected boot boxes, she told herself she didn't need hiking boots. When would she ever go hiking? Or if she did, wouldn't her old sneakers be more than a match for any hillock she might climb? She couldn't bring herself to buy them.

In the end, said Sylvia, she took the rooster jug to the counter at the front of the store and paid for it, eight dollars and ninety-nine cents plus tax. She bought it, and then burst out crying right there on the sidewalk in front of the store, her credit card still in her hand.

"Why?" said Donna.

"It's such a sweet little piece, you know?" Sylvia's eyes welled. "And Stu is never going to see it."

As to Claire, she'd fled from the boots, the store, its mobbed aisles, its bright lights, its grand-opening balloons and whiffling flags. She'd stopped at home just long enough to water the lily in her bedroom window and then come straight to the meeting, no dinner, the socks still on her feet. She'd shoplifted the socks.

In the week since finding Jessie's notebooks she'd shoplifted a small mountain of incidentals. She never knew she was going to do it. She'd be at a grocery picking up milk, or a hardware store getting plant food, and some other item would catch her eye and go right into her handbag. At a stationery store she'd taken a notepad—like she couldn't get all the paper she'd ever need from the office. Yesterday she'd ducked into a pharmacy to filch three pocket packs of tissues. And now these socks on her feet: you'd think someone would notice scarlet feet. You'd think someone would pose a question. You'd think the sock police would smash in the door, plunge through the safety of the circle and scowl down their muzzles at her.

It wasn't at all like what Sylvia did; it wasn't buying herself something new. She'd shoplifted, a secret no one suspected, and she ought to be ashamed of herself. Instead, she felt—well—gratified.

Miller, punctuating the air, said her sister had kept her on the phone the past three nights with the (air quotes) "Five Stages of Grief," telling her she was (air quotes) "stuck in Denial" and had to get herself to (air quotes) "Acceptance."

"She thinks it all proceeds on schedule," Miller continued. "Like I'm one of Mussolini's trains."

"Forget it. Your sister's a know-it-all," Alan said. Five stages? Five stages didn't begin to cover the ground, nor was any part of it phased, orderly or sequential. Pitched neck deep in dung soup was more like it. There they all were, splashing around, stunned. Every so often, a wave washed over, swamping them in their pain. "Let your sister try becoming a widow. See what she does then."

Donna said, "I understand about know-it-alls." The facilitator was a large woman with a waist like a tree trunk. Perfect strangers would stop her in the street to advise she go on a diet, as if she'd never thought of that and hadn't tried dozens of times. "Grieving takes as long as it takes," she said. "Alan's right. There's nothing you can do to hurry it along. But remember, too, that loss is common to us all. Sooner or later everyone experiences it, so you don't have to wish a loss on them. It's inevitable. It's part of life."

For you, maybe, thought Claire. For anybody else. But oh God, it wasn't supposed to happen to Jessie and me. She glared at the wall and pictured her hot fist slamming through it, the crunch of the wallboard scraping her knuckles, dust puffing from the hole.

"Let's talk about your spouses," Donna said. "What are you missing most?"

"Bickering."

The woman who sat curled up in an *S* and never wore a name tag said bickering. Claire exploded in wild laughter. See, this was a problem: she never knew when she was going to burst out laughing or crying or shoplifting or maybe putting her fist through a wall. But at least mirth wasn't inappropriate this time, was it? Bickering had to be a wisecrack, right?

Wrong. The woman was downright earnest. The staccato of squabbling had been the anthem of her marriage. She and Herb, they'd scrapped their way through life. And now, she said, with no one to battle out every last little thing on earth, the spice was gone from her days.

"What did you argue about?" Alan asked. "Politics?"

She snorted.

"Money, then."

Such a piker, her eyes said. "We could quarrel over temporary tattoos. We spent a whole afternoon once on the letter *p*. Not words starting with *p*, mind you. Just the letter itself." Her face aglow. Carolyn, Claire remembered; her name was Carolyn, and bickering obviously made her happy.

Go figure. Bickering, just the hint of it, made Claire itch all over. Not to say she and Jessie hadn't had their share of fights, especially in their early years together. They never bickered though: they shrieked, they howled, they threw themselves around, they acted (much to their chagrin) exactly like hysterical females, smashing plates, slamming doors. Claire had always thought of herself as controlled. With Jessie, she discovered a stunning capacity for excess, a capacity as unbounded as her passion for Jessie. She was nothing if not lavish in her misery, sometimes even tearing out her own hair. And after all, what had the fighting been about? More often than not, little more than the letter *p*. Some word, some common expression innocently used, untainted by any double meaning to the one who uttered it—but not to the one who heard it. The word "sure," for example.

"Want to go to the movies tonight?" says one.

"Sure," says the other.

Now, uttered faintly, that word "sure" is anemic. See, you were out of breath, you'd just walked up five flights of stairs, the elevator on the fritz for the umpteenth time. And how could you know that your word "sure," half-voiced like that, would be a dead ringer for a certain tepid "sure" that used to come from another mouth? In that other mouth, it meant, "We'll go, but if this film you want to see is a dud, you're responsible, and don't think I'll let you forget it if you insist on dragging me out for nothing." A single word from Henry to Jessie said it all: I want to go—unless later I find that I didn't, in which case you'll pay for it. For sure.

Old patterns die hard. Worse, when you're in the middle of the wild fear and screaming, nobody remembers what the exact word was that set the whole thing off. All you know at that moment is that you haven't said, would never say, "You'll play fast and loose with my goodwill once too often, my girl." And you won't tolerate being accused of it.

Getting to the bottom of it was always hell's own time. They had a rule never to stop until they got there, because once they did, the demon lurking inside the word vanished, *poof!* After a while, no bogeymen were left to fight over, but Claire could remember times back at the beginning when she and Jessie had to take the fight outdoors to the sidewalk for sanity's sake. Raving like madwomen is harder to bring off in front of neighbors on their way to the corner grocery for a box of oatmeal.

Mary spoke next. "I miss the yellow stickies my husband used to leave me...."

When it became clear she had trailed off and wasn't going to resume, Sylvia prompted, "What did he write?"

"Oh, I don't know. Nothing special. *Buy yogurt,* or *We're almost out of peanut butter.* That was on the refrigerator. He left them everywhere. On the dresser, on the bathroom mirror. Sometimes he'd draw a buttercup—" A gentle flush rose along Mary's neck, crossing her chin and cheekbones, her forehead. A small sound escaped her lips, barely more than a breath except that something in it reminded Claire of a puppy's plaintive yipping the first night away from its mother. "Buttercups were special to us," Mary whispered.

One white rose, Jessie brought Claire, each rose perfect, unblemished, or she wouldn't buy it. Every couple of weeks, on the kitchen table, there'd be a rose. "What's the occasion?" Claire asked, at first.

Jessie would say, "To let you know I was thinking of you."

Or Jessie would say, "To let you know I treasure you."

Or sometimes Jessie would say, "To let you know you deserve to be loved."

Once in a while, coming home empty-handed, Jessie said, "I bought you a rose today." She meant that she'd tried, but no white roses were to be had, only colors; or that she'd thought to buy one but didn't have the spare cash that day;

or that she'd have bought one but was too worn out to make a stop at the florist's.

Claire said she'd take the thought for the deed.

Once in a while, Claire bought Jessie a bunch of daisies, Jessie's favorite flower. But not often. Not even every so often. Every so often, she'd tell Jessie, "I don't love you well enough."

Her bemused Gioconda smile, upcurved lips. "Well enough for what?"

"For what you deserve."

Then Jessie's smile would broaden, and her arms would open wide. "You make me feel wanted and celebrated. You make me feel cherished and alive. You. You're the best lover in the world." And because Jessie said so, Claire knew it was true.

But I must have failed her somewhere along the line. Otherwise, why would she keep hidden from me what happened to her in Tulsa?

Helga, who was sitting next to Claire, said she missed watching her man diapering the babies. "Strong he was, with solid hands and bulging blue veins you could trace all the way up to the elbows."

No one uttered a word. Helga's husband had smoked "like a chimney," lighting his first cigarette before he got out of bed in the morning, stubbing out his last after the lights were out at night. He'd liked his drink, too. They all knew that, and because of it they were silent. The man had died young of heart disease, leaving Helga with four little kids, two of them still in those diapers he'd changed with the beefy hands and ropy veins she liked the sight of.

Bitterness hung in the air, but Claire, nonplussed, barely felt it. Claire hadn't imagined she shared the least little thing in common with down-in-the-mouth, down-at-the-heels Helga. Lo and behold, here it was: she, too, loved watching a pair of hands.

You never saw fingers less sensitive looking than Jessie's, stubby and block-like, the nails nippered off blunt; but each touch of hers was a caress, to which the world seemed responsive. Jessie took the world in through her fingers the way artists take in the world through their eyes, and musicians through their ears, or gourmets through their taste buds, savoring the sweetness of Spain and the tang of India. She touched everything—satin scarves, marble pillars, rush seats, plastic umbrellas. Where her fingers had been, the satin shimmered, the marble glowed. When Claire saw Jessie's hands playing across a burlap sack, her own fingers tingled with the roughness of it. If a concrete-block wall, grittiness prickled her palms. Something of a revelation. Something of a miracle, Jessie's hands running lightly over the world. And oh, when she touched Claire, Claire's skin turning to silk under a silken train of caresses—when she touched her, plain old Claire discovered enchantment.

Claire's fingers were just then torturing a small bit of paper wrapper from a straw, folding and unfolding and twisting it into smaller bits. Helga's hands lay stationary in her lap, fingers neatly laced. Helga said her husband could do anything in the house, while she couldn't even change a lightbulb by herself. "I'm like one of those riddles: how does a Polack widow change a lightbulb?"

"How?"

Helga shrugged. "She doesn't. Why bother anymore? What does it matter whether the light turns on?" The whole house could go to rack and ruin around her, she couldn't seem to care, except for dusting, cleaning and polishing the woodwork—the moldings and railings, all the paneling—because they were his, the work of his hands.

On Jessie's left hand, at the base of the pointer finger, there ran a thin, pale scar. A scant half inch in length and pale, it was scarcely noticeable against her freckled skin, unless you knew what it stood for. Henry had hounded and humiliated her, and she'd learned, in her marriage, to be silent under it. The scar stood for the day he took the browbeating too far, changing everything for himself and his wife and her best friend, who'd so carefully kept her distance. A fateful day, yet Claire couldn't remember now what Jessie said his ranting had been about, that time. The Good Mother, maybe.

You're supposed to be a mother. A mother doesn't let the table stay wet when a child spills juice. A mother is at home when her child gets home from school. You call yourself a mother? You call yourself a wife? A mother—fill in the blank: cleans the house, irons the sheets, straightens the curtains, keeps the oil changed in the cars, makes sure there's ice cream in the refrigerator, never curses in front of children, is never late, always puts her kid first, always puts her husband first, never puts herself first. Whatever it was that time, her husband hectored her past endurance, and Jessie went down into the basement of their house, among the clothes to be laundered and the immaculate wood shop, shiny new tools he never used, and she took up his hammer and smashed her hand with it, smashed and smashed and smashed until the hand was torn and broken, because she wanted to feel, to be able to feel anything. Anything but the pain of his contempt.

Was it his Good Mother routine? Or was it the time Henry accused Jessie of carrying on an affair with Ray Hammond? Cripes, Ray Hammond, of all people. Claire's erstwhile boss, retired by then, had confounded them all by hanging around as an office volunteer or sometimes playing basketball with the kids who were the agency's clients.

You fucked him, didn't you. I what? *You did. You fucked him.* I didn't, Henry. Not even close. *Not even close? How close is not close? A blow job? A hand job?* Never! How could you think it? *The grief you gave me over that girl in the swimming pool at Vail, just a one-time deal, meant nothing. Were you fucking him then? You were, weren't you? How long have you been fucking that asshole? All the time you were pulling my chain, milking Vail for all it was worth. What a sucker I am. What a life.*

There'd been a trip to the emergency room, X-rays, stitches. The hand was swollen and purple. By the time Claire saw her, she'd secured it in a homemade sling, coarse muslin diaper-pinned around her neck. They sat together in The Open Door's parking lot, in the car Claire had then, a rusted '68 Dodge Dart with sagging bench seats.

"Don't ever do this again," Claire said.

Jessie scrutinized Claire, not replying.

"Have you done this before?"

"No. Not really."

"Not really? What does 'not really' mean?"

She winced. "Don't cross-examine me, Claire."

In all the time they'd known each other, in all the time they'd been friends, Claire had never seen Jessie so pinched, so harrowed, so ragged and bitter. "I don't want you hurting yourself. Promise me you'll never do it again."

"Why? What difference does it make?"

"To me? All the difference in the world."

"I don't see why."

Did she understand how she was pushing Claire to speak, pressing with those sad eyes? "It matters. You need to promise me."

She searched Claire's face the way a child will. One time in the first or second year of their friendship, a lovely June Sunday it was, they had taken Lisi out to Long Island to Belmont Lake State Park, where they plunked around the lake in a rented rowboat, then picnicked on shore, lazily talking while Lisi played at the water's edge. Jessie's focused tension at this moment reminded Claire of Lisi after some sudden turbulence had stirred up the lake bottom. The child's small body became taut with anxiety waiting for the water to clear.

It had been that day, out on Belmont Lake, when Claire, watching Jessie work the oars, had suddenly thought, "I'd kill for you." It had struck her so absurdly that she'd instantly suppressed the whole idea, not understanding the least little bit of it then. Now, Jessie said, "Promise you? Why the fucking hell should I?"

Oh, didn't she sound fierce! "Jessie, don't hurt yourself, ever," Claire heard herself say, "because I love you."

The universe didn't go up in smoke.

The ground didn't give way, plummeting her into the second circle of hell.

Nobody even fainted. The quiet seemed unaccountably ordinary. Claire said, "Promise me you won't hurt yourself, because I'm in love with you."

Jessie, agape and blinking, could have been the Merriam-Webster illustration for "stupefied."

"I'm in love with you," Claire repeated, liking the sound of it better each time.

"How is that possible?"

She laughed. "How is it not possible? You being you?"

"But—we were friends."

"Still are, I hope." Clumsily, then, Claire explained how she'd been trying to keep her growing feelings under wraps, how she'd struggled to puzzle out what good could come from basing their friendship on a lie. How she didn't want to destroy the very openness they both prized. Couldn't Jessie see it was their friendship Claire was trying to preserve?

Jessie stared off, eyes welling. It was obvious to Claire she saw nothing. "Jess, until you came into my life, I never felt like—I never felt entirely at home in the universe."

"No. It's impossible."

"What is?"

"I'm so—" Jessie faltered. "So small."

"*Small?* Darling, you fill my world."

Lunch hour was nearly over. Every so often, a colleague passing by on the way back into work stopped and waved. Jessie looked queasy, and Claire was convinced she oughtn't to have started—but having once started, she couldn't end it there. More needed saying.

Turning all colors, her cheeks only burning hotter as she strove not to blush, she announced that Sex wasn't part of it. Haltingly she assured Jessie she didn't mean she desired her that way. Nothing physical involved. Nor was she asking Jessie to alter her life in any way. Nothing needed to change, Claire repeated several times, and nothing was required of Jessie—not even, sad to say, that she take better care of herself, though Claire dearly wished she would.

"It just means—" The hardest part done, why now was loss of nerve clamping her throat shut?

"Tell me."

"Oh, Jess, I hope and pray you won't make this the end of us."

That was on a Thursday. Not until the Monday were they able to meet again. It poured on Monday, sweeps of rain drenching the day. After work, in the dim compartment of Claire's car, fogged windows streaming, Claire gave Jessie a rose (yes, pure white—like those Jessie would later give Claire). Jessie, with her unmangled right hand, traced the line of Claire's ear. Claire tensed, then eased under her touch.

"No sexual desire, my ass," Jessie said.

After twenty-three years together, Claire missed everything about Jessie. She missed her milky roses, and she missed her exquisite hands. She missed the way Jessie's second toe jutted out longer than the others, and she missed the soft purr of Jessie's snoring in the dark. She even missed fighting with her. But what she missed most, and what she told the group she missed most, was Jessie's odor in the bathroom. Not the smell of her dandruff shampoo or her olive oil soap, those were easy to come by. What she couldn't replenish, what couldn't be replaced, or replicated, or created ever again was the smell of Jessie herself. The lonesomest thing in the world was using the bathroom day after day and smelling nobody's excretions but her own. Ridiculous but true, Claire wanted back the heavy, slightly spicy odor of Jessie's BM. How odd that that would be the thing you'd crave. How singular and unexpected and maddening.

Donna glanced at the clock on the wall. Claire's eyes followed. Ten minutes to nine, time to wrap things up. The session ended at nine, so bringing up a new subject now would be bad form.

"I want to visit Tulsa," Claire said.

A crevice formed above the bridge of the facilitator's nose. Postponing discussion until next week would be worse form. "Why?" she demanded.

Claire said she didn't know why. "Possibly, I need to go just to find out why."

Mary prompted, "Do you know anyone in Tulsa? Family? Friends?"

"Nope. It's where Jessie grew up. She always hoped to get back there one day."

Claire used to tease her: Oklahoma. Some destination. Paris had a better ring to it. Or Rio de Janeiro. As long as they were hatching travel plans, why not think big, do Rio?
"Because I want to see West Tulsa."
"Oh, West Tulsa. That makes a difference. How about West Africa? A safari could be exciting, no? West Timor? The West Indies? Key West?"
Jessie let her finish, then went right on talking about the house on South Phoenix with its wide front porch, the stores along Quanah Avenue, the swings and seesaws and ball field at the Eugene Field School.
One day in the hospital, she said, "I knew a man, Sammy, a drummer boy for the Confederacy. I talked to him in West Tulsa." Jessie's fingers stroked the sheet, the cotton blanket. She was in recuperation after her second surgery, and doing well. "A nineteenth-century man," she continued, wheezing the words out about this old-timer Sammy who used to sit in a sunny corner of her grandparents' porch. "And now a new century coming."
Claire nodded. "New millennium, too."
Her smile flickered. "Good chance—" she coughed, gasped, began again. "A good chance Nat'll see the twenty-second century." That morning, over the phone, her granddaughter Natalie, sixteen months old, had babbled baby talk to her, and she'd answered in kind.
Jessie's hand slowed along the bedsheet. Her eyes rolled upward, lids half closing. Claire hunched closer. A silence lengthened. Then she stirred. "We talk to each other, we reach across time," she murmured.

Was that Claire's hope now? Somehow, in Oklahoma, to reach across time?

Alan uncrossed his arms and pointed at her. "You say you'd like to see Tulsa. What does your gut tell you to do?"

"My gut says pack my bags."

"Then go with your gut."

"Trust your gut," Miller concurred.

It was at that point Claire thought she ought to tell them her gut also said steal tea bags and socks. But the time was already past nine o'clock. She'd already said BM was what she missed most, and there were limits to the strangeness you could own up to, even in a support group. Besides, she was already the Lesbian of the group; she didn't need to be the Kleptomaniac, too.

When she got home and went into the bedroom, the first thing she noticed was the table, bare. Then soil peppering the rug. Then the pot upended on the floor, the same nondescript beige plastic pot she'd found at her door the day Jessie was buried. Someone had left it for her, one gorgeous, trumpeting bloom, a translucent glow of white with a flounce of pink, tentative veins of chartreuse at its heart. A note, on handmade paper, small flowers pressed into the surface, said, "Please take care of Lily for me while I am too busy." It was unsigned. Claire had run her knuckle across the peaks and runnels and up and down the deckled edge, debating whether she could throw the whole thing into the trash, deciding she couldn't.

She brought the plant into her bedroom and set it near the window. Every few days, she watered it, but not overly—measuring to make sure. She cut off the dried bits as they appeared and turned the pot to keep the stem straight. When the flower declined, Claire wasn't surprised. Jessie had been the one to do whatever planting, watering, trimming and tending of greenery there was to do. Claire had a black thumb; plants knew it, and they would rather shrivel than be consigned to her care.

But the one flower, gone, was replaced by two. The two grew larger, and then a third came, and that very evening, when Claire had stopped off at home just to water it, another bud was opening its show: four magnificent blooms facing the four corners of the earth, trumpeting out splendor. Giving the pot a half-turn on her way out, Claire had said (out loud, talking to a plant!), "Lily, it may be I'm not a total incompetent after all."

And now, reaching toward the light in her window, Lily had toppled over to destruction. The sight on the floor of the strewn soil and lifeless petals undid Claire. "You goddamn bastard," she screeched, over and over again. At whom? At God? At the universe? At some brainsick inexplicable force that devoured beauty? A terrible rage seized her like a wind tattering a rag. She wept and she trembled. In her rising madness, she paced and she shrieked. She scratched and tore at herself and grappled herself by the throat and pressed as hard and as long as she could, irate for she'd been robbed, shame-ridden for she hadn't given adequate care. And frightened, oh so frightened.

For a brief while, a mote in time, a radiance had come into her life, now plucked away. Ah Claire, instead of whining for what has been taken from you, shouldn't you be thankful you've had it at all? Think how many never do. God, God, God, she *was* thankful, absolutely churning she was with thankfulness. But the flower! The flower was still dead. Too soon dead. Blasted, blighted, a gorgeous rarity that deserved above all others life and growth and—hugeness. Forgiveness could not, no, nor would not be granted for the heinous, untimely theft of all that might have been.

Dark spots blotted Claire's vision, and she slumped to her knees, still choking herself, desperate to her core. If, in her incandescent frenzy, if even then the obvious symbolism of all this was plain to her and she was sickened by it, nauseated by it—even then, even then, don't for a moment imagine she was any the less in anguish. Grateful? Claire was grateful for every nanosecond she and Jessie had had together in this world, but it wasn't enough. Not anywhere near enough. How could it be? How could it ever, ever, ever be?

When at long last the raving began to release its fervid grip, when at last it subsided and she could breathe quietly, when her legs would once again hold her, she got the broom, swept up the lily, brought it into the kitchen and propped its oozing stem against the wall. Then she stared at the phone. Then she called Mary. Mary was kind, and Mary would be awake: since her husband's death, she prowled the night, sleeping little.

"What's wrong, pet?" the older woman said at Claire's soggy greeting.

"I don't even want to tell you, it's so maudlin and trite."

"Grieving," Mary responded, "is maudlin and trite. Talk, I'm listening."

10

From the fifth of Jessie's notebooks

The place: West Tulsa, Oklahoma
The time: October 1944

I see an ad for a teakettle at the Times Square Stores, and I remember one of them somewhere way down Quanah Avenue. I figure I can start out early, go with Gramp when he opens the Rexall, then walk the rest of the way myself. Gramp will be okay about it. He never worries about the things kids can get into on their own. Once he let me eat mustard sandwiches all afternoon, never saying not to or that I could make myself sick. He just said, "It's your stomach. Seems to me you should know what to put in it," and went off to the henhouse to fix the roof. I got a swollen tongue and a bellyache that time. Grandma said I got a good lesson, too.

After Gramp crosses me at the corner, it's a straight walk down Quanah past the movie house and the Eskimo Pie. The movie house is not big and golden like Radio City Music Hall, and it doesn't have Rockettes or any live show at all, but it does have all the good movies—with Judy Garland or Margaret O'Brien and war movies and westerns, too. My friend Teddy Boy Draper likes Roy Rogers, but I like Hopalong Cassidy better, though I like seeing Roy Rogers because of Gabby Hayes.

Teddy always goes out for popcorn between the features, but I stay through and ask him to bring me popcorn. That way I get to see big episodes in the war like D-Day and the fighting in France. And I get to learn about grown-up diseases like cancer that can kill you. The health short comes on right after the newsreel. Then the lights come up and the ushers shake cans for us to put in what is left of our candy money before they show the cartoon. They've collected for the Red Cross and for TB and for polio, but never for diabetes. My mother has diabetes, which I have figured out is not a killing disease at all since nobody ever collects for it at the movies. Diabetes just means my mother can't drink pineapple juice anymore or eat ice cream, and when I get a cold I have to stay away from her so she won't get sick, because my cold would be her pneumonia if she got it. And she has to stick herself in the thigh with insulin every morning and remember to eat instead of just drinking when she goes out—or she'll faint. But it is just fainting, not dying, though it used to scare me every time she did it because I was afraid that this time it might turn into dying.

One time, my mother fainted when she had pneumonia, which I guess she got from me, though I was almost finished with my cold before she came back from her business trip. I was in her bedroom talking to her about Lucy Ann McIntyre who sat behind me in school and kept writing on my neck when my mother made me wear braids—so please, I begged, could I go without wearing braids? And my mother raised her hand up to her head with a headache from my whining and then, fast, her hand dropped down open, and she slid off her pillow. I shook her, but I couldn't wake her, not even when I screamed, "I'll wear braids, Mommy. Please!"

Ada came in and tried to shove me out of the room, but I wouldn't go. I huddled next to the closet, trying to keep out of the way as Ada pulled my mother out straight and stuck the smelling salts under her nose. "She just fainted, child," Ada said, shaking my mother alert enough to sip orange juice through the bent glass straw. "She'll be fine."

But Ada wouldn't allow me back near the bed, and my mother agreed when she could finally speak, "Go on to bed now, Jessie. It's best."

Ada pried me away from the closet door, picking first one curled finger, then the next away from the egg-shaped knob with its fancy carving, all the time repeating, "Don't be like this, Jessie. It'll just make things worse." I straightened my knees stiff but I knew enough not to let her pull me over. Instead I let her tug at me while I inched forward, my bare toes curled into the carpet. She could take all night for all I cared. But then my mother moaned. I stood straight, and Ada, with a quick pat against my shoulder and a hushed, "Go on now," went back to her bedside.

I could still see the two of them from my bed. The door that connected the two rooms always stayed open, except when Uncle Chester stayed overnight. Every night, before she went to bed, my mother would come and kiss me. Something about the candy smell of her always crept into my dreams.

She came in like that one night and let me hug her and closed the door. Later she came into my room and shook me awake and told me she wanted to sleep in my bed. She was crying, and she smelled like the scratchy-faced men who slept in the doorways under the Third Avenue El, not like candy. I rolled over to put my face away from her smell.

The store I thought was Times Square isn't; it is Tom's Square, painted with the same white letters on red background, and it doesn't sell teakettles. I walk home, dividing the walk up into little pieces: from the store to across the avenue from the Rexall, from the Rexall to Mr. Ketcham's barbershop, from the barbershop to the RC Cola store, from there to the general store. But from the general store, instead of kittycornering through the empty lot where everybody dumps ashes after they burn the garbage and then cutting through Teddy Boy's backyard to get home, I turn the other way and follow the railroad tracks for a while. From there I take a path that turns off across a field into some woods and leads me down to a creek.

I wander a long way all by myself until I meet another girl. She is standing in the creek holding up her flour-sack dress way above her knees. Her hair stands out curly all around her head and is held back from her forehead with a barrette. If Teddy Boy took his Brownie camera and snapped a picture of Shirley Temple and you looked at the negative, that would be this girl in her sack dress. I have seen her before, and I try to remember where.

"Want to come in?" she says.

She is a Nigra, and at the swimming pool they can't come in. I'm not sure why, but I figure it could be because the color will come off like dirt in the water and get on me. One time when I was much littler than now I licked Ada's dark cheek because I thought it would taste like fudge, and I cried when it wasn't the least bit sweet, it only tasted like skin. My tongue stayed pale that time, nothing came off on it, but all the same I'm thinking I oughtn't to take chances, so I tell the girl no thanks, I want to stay dry, so she comes out and we play. Her name is Hetty.

"You live here?" I ask.

"Naw. Up in Greenwood with my grandmother."

"I stay with my grandmother, too."

Now I remember where I've seen this girl. It was on a night so hot we were all out on our porches, Grandma and Gramp and Sammy and Mr. and Mrs. Ketcham and John Ellis and his mama and everybody else up and down the street, even old Mr. Davies who never leaves his front room ever no matter what.

Teddy Boy and I were making paper fans for everybody. I was just finger-nailing the folds of mine when Uncle Jimmy pulled up to the curb. Aunt Nedra wasn't with him. As I got up to go inside, he shouted, "Who wants cold watermelon?" To my surprise, everyone yelled, "Me!" including even Sammy. So the grown-ups piled into Uncle Jimmy's car and the Ketchams' car, and John Ellis and I got to ride in the rumble seat even though we are never allowed without a grown-up, and we drove way out into the country to the watermelon stand, where an old man in a starched white apron will bring you a great big watermelon and slice it up for you, and everybody can have just as much as they want.

I hold my breath when he cuts it open. I am startled every time by the color. John Ellis says it looks like the best candy, but to me it's the pink I see when I close my eyes and wish hard for something, and my wish comes true. It's the bright, juicy color of people keeping their promises. And the sweet taste, too.

I was on my third helping, and Gramp said if I kept it up I might turn into a watermelon. My skin was already turning pink, he said. It was, but not from eating watermelon. The whole sky was glowing from the sun going down, and everything was rosy, and I started thinking how it would be if the whole world turned to watermelon. The trees over yonder with that sliver of white light above them could look like rind if you squinnied up your eyes, and all the people could be pits if they would stop moving, the big ones talking and laughing, the little ones playing tag in between the tables.

That's when I saw Hetty standing quite still in the colored section over along the side of the building, where they get their servings from a little window high up in the wall. She stared at me and I stared at her, but we didn't say anything, just looked. Nobody on our side ever lets on they see anybody on the other side, it's not polite. There isn't any wall or fence along the edge of the building, no brass stands with swingy velvet ropes like at the movies, not even a line marked out on the ground to separate our side from theirs, but all the same the line is there. And even little kids know you dasn't cross over it.

I asked what would happen if Charlie Chan came for watermelon: which side would he go on? Nobody answered me. Instead, Grandma said poor Mamie Carter's son—who used to sing in the church choir?—came back from the war a changed man, just sits around, won't even look for a job, and Uncle Jimmy said best to stay away from guys like that, especially when they're angry. I tried asking my question again, but Grandma said she heard Clara Morgan's boy, Nelson, got himself hitched to some swishy-hipped number from the USO. So then I got into a pit-spitting contest with John Ellis and another boy. I thought it was too bad the dark girl couldn't come over and team up with me. I figured we might put the boys to shame.

Now I show Hetty how I can bend all my fingers at the top joint, except for the pinkies, I'm still training them. She shows me how to make a whistle out of grass. We chase after squirrels and chipmunks until we're out of breath and sweaty and have to flop down under a tree and talk awhile in the shade. Her mother is a laundress, and her father is a hired hand. They don't live with Hetty, and they don't live with each other. It's just like me, except her mother and father aren't divorced, and Hetty says they like each other. Hetty is allowed to go and stay with her mother sometimes, and that is when she can come to the creek.

She is half Indian of the Cherokee nation. I am part Indian, too. My mother's grandmother's mother was Cherokee, so that makes us blood sisters. We go Indian file through the woods, and I show Hetty some of the pioneering skills Sister Ann Joseph taught me, like marking a trail with stones. We come to a clearing and make a fireplace and build a small tee-pee fire, but we don't have any matches, and rubbing sticks together doesn't get us anything but dirty.

After that I go in the creek with her, though I make sure to stay upstream of her at all times just in case.

When I get home, my room smells like feet after a day without shoes, and my bed is moved, which means Grandma is down in the root cellar. I'm not scared to sleep right above the trapdoor. John Ellis once told me to be cautious and listen in the night for breathing, since every cellar has a monster in it who lives on the spiders and other creepy-crawly things down there. No such a thing, I told him. He said is so, and don't ever claim he didn't warn me.

Uncle Jimmy is in the living room lounging on the dav-enport and smoking a cigarette, which he would never do if

Grandma weren't down cellar. "Hi there, sweet pea," he booms. Aunt Nedra is nowhere around that I can see. Maybe with Grandma.

Uncle Jimmy wiggles his hand at me to come on over. His knuckles are knobby, and they stay bent even when he straightens out his fingers. He holds the cigarette between his thumb and pointer finger and cups it in his palm like he is hiding it from somebody. He doesn't wave it in graceful curves like my mother. She started smoking when she was a young girl and didn't know what to do with her hands, and now she's hooked.

"Looka here, sweet pea," Uncle Jimmy says. "I got a surprise for you."

I stay where I am and ask Uncle Jimmy if he started smoking to have something to do with his hands. He smiles crooked like, with one side of his mouth, and says, "In a way, sweet pea. In a way." Then he shows me how he can blow the biggest smoke ring ever, bigger than a hotcake, bigger than the tam my mother bought me to match my plaid winter coat the year we went to Connecticut for Christmas. My mother never blows smoke rings because it's not ladylike, but someday I am going to learn how, even if I only do it when I am alone. Then I will show Hetty how to do it, too, since she can't be a lady, being colored and all.

"C'mon here," Uncle Jimmy coaxes. "I got a little surprise for you."

I go two steps closer.

"Aw, sweet pea, what's the matter?"

"Nothin'."

"Aren't we friends no more? 'Cause if not I'll keep this nice new game for someone else."

I don't like his games, but I dasn't tell him so. "We're friends."

"And I know you ain't a-scared of your Uncle Jimmy. Right?"

He's the one who should be scared—of Grandma if she heard him saying *ain't*. He crooks his finger at me, so I move to where I figure I'm just outside his reach. Over the arm of the davenport I can see a checkerboard, except instead of the squares being red and black they are white and black. On the Bible table are bunches of black-and-white figures carved out of wood. The figures look like people, except they don't have any faces or clothes.

"Is it chess?" I say. He's been promising to teach me chess so we could show everyone I am a genius. I try to get a better look, and Uncle Jimmy grabs my wrist. He puts his arm, with my arm, too, around my waist, and he pulls me tight in against his thigh. "You're real pretty, you know?"

I squirm, trying to get free.

"Now, sugar. Forget your manners? I said you were real pretty."

"Thank you, sir," I say softly, squirming a little bit more.

His fingers release my wrist, but his arm still locks me against him. "You are a good little girl, aren't you?" I can feel his other big knobbly hand moving up my back, spreading out across me. "How come you're wearing these old coveralls?" He moves his fingers inside the straps.

I wiggle like he's tickling me, even though he isn't. He laughs, but nothing is funny. I try to pull away again, and this time there is no tug of war. Uncle Jimmy drops his arm and draws one leg up onto the cushion, letting the other sprawl straight out so I'll have to climb over it to get by. I put one leg over, and then he hikes his leg up and catches me between my thighs and sort of rubs at me. I make myself fall over sideways, and he drops his leg. "So? Why you wear those dumb old coveralls? Don't you know you're a girl?"

"It's Saturday. I got to save my dresses for school, is why. And I like coveralls." I like blue jeans better, but Grandma won't let me wear them. She says they're called dungarees because of where the cowboys go in them. I don't know where that is, but I always nod and say, "Yes, ma'am."

"Jessie. Yoo-hoo, Jessie. You there?" Grandma is calling from the cellar. I clamber up and go out back to my room.

"John Ellis and Teddy Boy were looking for you. I told

them you went down Quanah with Gramp, and they said for you to find them at John Ellis's house when you came back."

"Can I go, ma'am?" And I know instantly I've made a mistake.

"If you're able you can, miss. If you get permission, you *may*."

"Yes'm. *May* I go?"

"You may. Mind though, you be back here by the lunch whistle." Noon, every day except Sunday. Sunday, the church bells tell you instead.

"Yes, ma'am. Thank you, ma'am."

Like a dummy, I forget to go out around the back way and I get caught by Uncle Jimmy as I go through the living room. "Hold on there, sugar. Did I hear right that you were way down on Quanah this morning?"

"Yes, sir."

"By yourself?"

I nod.

"And just what took you down there all by your lonesome?"

I don't want to say it out loud, but I don't want to go any closer. If I go closer he might catch me again, but if I don't, Grandma might hear me answering, and the surprise will be spoiled. So I have to take the chance. "I was trying to buy Grandma a teakettle for Christmas," I whisper. "I saw an advertisement and I thought that was a Times Square Store down Quanah, but it wasn't."

Uncle Jimmy doesn't touch me, even though I'm bending toward him with my hands cupped to his ear. "Heck, honey," he says. "Why didn't you ask me? I can drive you. There's a nice big Times Square over on the east side. I can take you there this afternoon, easy."

"Take her where, Jimmy?" Aunt Nedra is suddenly standing here, her face looking like maybe I am bad.

"Hi, sweetie. How's the candling going?"

"Where are you planning to take her, I asked."

Aunt Nedra smells like salad. "To the Times Square," I tell her. "For the you-know-what I want to buy Grandma."

"We have chores to help with here," she snaps. "You can't be driving this girl all over." They must have come over to give us a hand with the extra eggs. The War Food Administration wants everybody to wipe them with vinegar and store them in vats of boiled, cooled water until a shortage. But I can't think what I have done to make her so cross, when I haven't even been here all morning. Though sometimes grown-ups get cross over nothing. Other times you find out you're bad even when you think you're being good.

Like the time Grandma told me not to walk in the dining room—Uncle Cubby had just finished waxing it. I had to go to the bathroom, and Gramp was plucking a hen for next-day dinner in the back tub. The way to the other bathroom was through Grandma and Gramp's bedroom, which meant crossing the dining room. But I could do that and never touch the floor. I could squiggle onto the side chair and from there get onto the sideboard, then walk the length of the sideboard on my knees till I got to the other side chair, and from there push off and land in the bedroom. I'd done it a dozen times on hot summer afternoons when Grandma was working at the war plant and Gramp was at the Rexall or busy in the barn. I played snakes, where the floor is covered with them, and you have to get across. I'd gone around the whole room, in fact, never touching the floor even once, but Grandma didn't know about that. She heard the toilet flush, and when she called "*Jessie,*" I answered "Yes, ma'am" from behind the closed door of the bathroom. She got so hopping mad she clomped clear across the dining room to give me a face-to-face tongue-lashing. I didn't explain. I guess I figured even if I hadn't been disobedient I'd done something wrong, because the whole idea was to keep feet off the floor till the wax dried, and somehow I'd managed to get Grandma's feet on the floor, and they'd made all those dull, squishy spots, like galosha prints in the snow.

Over at John Ellis's house, we are making scooters out of his roller skates when the noon whistle blows. I no sooner hear it start than I am off. The noon whistle is a kind of hiccup followed by an ear-piercing scream, and you don't want it to finish before you've got yourself where you're supposed to be. You don't ever want to be late for Grandma's lunch and see her standing there in the middle of the kitchen with her mouth all pinched up like you'd caused her a deep hurt to see the food going cold on the platter. She'd ask if you have to be reminded that it's the early bird who catches the worm. "No, ma'am," you'd say. "Sorry, ma'am. It won't happen again." And she'd tell you to see that it doesn't.

One time, instead of saying, "No'm," I asked, "What does the late bird catch?"

"Hell," said Gramp. He wasn't late, but that's what he caught from Grandma for saying a bad word. Whenever Gramp comes late to the table, Grandma tells him, "Land sakes, Doc Langley, I don't know but you'll be late for your own funeral." And he winks at me and says, "That's what I'm aiming for." To which she says, "Don't encourage the child."

This time, I stop though, and risk being late. I stop in front of Uncle Jimmy's car, staring at it. The headlights stare back, and the chrome grille grins at me in a not-nice way. *I have your number girlie*, it seems to say.

In the pocket of my coveralls I finger the nails I have just straightened. They're the leftovers from making our scooters. I test their sharpness against the soft pad of my thumb.

Don't try it. You'll be sorry.

I pull them out and look at them, four slightly wavy, dull-gray, two-inch nails.

Practical jokes always backfire.

It isn't a practical joke I have in mind, exactly. It's a way to stop the car from taking me anywhere with Uncle Jimmy.

I played a practical joke on my mother once, and it backfired. Just before she married Uncle Chester and went to Florida on her honeymoon, she took me away to the mountains. "Just us girls," she said. "A weekend in the country all by ourselves." From the guesthouse window you could look out over the lawn that curved down to a dirt road. The road was red, not brown. It made me wonder if the dirt all around us was red, so I found a shovel and went halfway down the lawn and dug a hole as big as Grandma's dough bowl. Sure enough, red.

"Jessie, I have a surprise for you," my mother said that afternoon. I was in the window seat, watching the sky turn dark, and my mother was having her cocktail.

"Mommy, I have a surprise for you, too," I said.

"Guess who's coming tomorrow morning to be with us? Uncle Chester. Isn't that grand?"

I said, "You have to close your eyes for my surprise." To my amazement, she immediately set down her drink, folded her hands in her lap and shut her eyes. "Now stand up," I directed.

"Where are you taking me?"

"You'll see."

My idea was to show her the red hole, but as I led her by the hand a new plan jumped into my mind. I took her in zigzags across the lawn and in a wide figure eight around the hole. She was humming "Don't Sit Under the Apple Tree" under her breath. I kept silent. I walked her straight toward the hole, and she went right into it. Her foot twisted, her leg crumpled under her, and her eyelids flew open as she fell squealing to the ground.

"Mommy, are you hurt?"

She said no, but her eyes were full of hurting.

I never expected her to fall, that was the thing. I never expected her to trust me like that right into the hole. Just like I never expected we would really have the whole weekend all to ourselves.

Afterward I didn't like practical jokes, but like I said, the trick I have in mind isn't a practical joke. It's a plan to get out of going for a ride in the car with Uncle Jimmy.

One nail is all I figure I'm going to need. If I prop it up against the front face of his rear tire, then all he'll have to do is go straight forward, and he'll have a blowout, and that will be the end of our ride. I stand at the curb on the passenger side of the car and glance up and down the street and up to our porch and across the street, too, to make sure Mrs. Davies isn't peeking out her window like she often does. The coast looks clear. From my other pocket I pull a pretty pink rock I found on my way home from the creek and am saving to show Hetty next time. I toss it in the air once or twice, like I'm playing, and then I toss it and clap my hands before catching it, and then I pretend clap too late, and the rock drops to the ground. When I kneel to pick it up, I quick poke some nails up against the tire, hoping at least one of them will stand pat like a soldier at attention, prepared and waiting to puncture the rubber when Uncle Jimmy jolts forward.

In the kitchen, lunch is on the table. Grandma has made fried-egg sandwiches with Wonder Bread. I slip into my chair and unfold my napkin. She frowns. I duck my head and mush in the center of the yolk. I like to see the yellow stuff ooze out and soak into the bread, and then the bread tastes good, too. Wonder Bread helps you grow strong in twelve ways, the radio says. Twelve ways is hard to figure. Two hands, two feet, two arms, two legs, so far so good. Your head, your chest, your belly and your behind? Or do they mean bosoms? It is not polite to say anything about a woman's bosoms, especially not that she has beautiful bosoms or good bosoms or kind, generous bosoms, but it is a fine thing to say there is something good and beautiful and kind and generous deep in her bosom. I don't understand why if you say my bosoms swell with pride it is dirty, but if you say my bosom swells with pride it is clean. And I don't understand why if Wonder Bread helps your bosoms grow, why would a boy want to eat any? Unless for boys they mean his thing. But there's two bosoms to only one thing, so any which way you count up, it doesn't come out even.

Uncle Jimmy helps himself from the platter. He presses his fork down into his circle of yellow, and it breaks, yellow moving over the fork tines and Uncle Jimmy laughing down in his throat like he does those times I don't like in the car. He nudges me with his elbow, and all at once I don't want any lunch. I stare at the wall above the sink, at the picture of the boy carrying home a bottle of milk. He is watching his little dog chase a butterfly, and the bottle of milk he holds at his side is spilling out behind him, but the boy isn't paying attention. By the time he gets home, there will be no milk left. Whenever I ask, Grandma says it's little Uncle Jimmy carrying the milk, and if Uncle Jimmy is there when I ask, he ducks his head and says, "Aw, Ma." But I don't ask about the boy today, even though I am staring at the picture instead of eating my sandwich.

"Jessie, stop playing with your food," Grandma scolds. "Eat up now, child."

I try. The egg is halfway on the bread and halfway on my plate, and I slide my fork under the eye of it, trying to drag it more onto the bread, but yellow leaks out all over my plate, sticking itself like wax to the carrot. I scrape the drying yolk with my fork. I push my thumbnail against it, trying to get it off the carrot. It crumbles onto the plate like baby yellow mouse droppings. I wipe my hands, then stick my finger into a fold of the napkin and dab my mouth properly. "Excuse me, ma'am. May I please be excused from the table?"

So fast I don't see it coming, Uncle Jimmy plants his big hand on my stomach and shakes it. "Full already? Must be something to have such a petite little tummy." I stand at the side of my chair, waiting, easing away from under his hand.

"You may be excused, Jessie, but I'll thank you not to fill up on Miz Ellis's oatmeal cookies next time."

"Yes'm. I mean, I won't."

"Sweet pea," Uncle Jimmy says, grinning like he's going to suck his tooth. "You'll want to put on a pretty dress now."

"I don't need to today, sir," I say.

Aunt Nedra lets out her breath, real sharp, and Grandma says, "What's this?"

"Why, Ma, I'm taking my girl out this afternoon."

Aunt Nedra shakes her head.

"Well, Nedra," Uncle Jimmy says, "you got the rest of those fresh eggs to candle for Pa and then packing them in the vats. That's going to take all afternoon."

I say, "Let's help out, and then Aunt Nedra can come with us." I would even be willing to put on a dress if Aunt

Nedra will come. I'll sit in the back of the car, and Uncle Jimmy won't be dragging his hand over my naked knees every time he shifts gears.

"Now, aren't you just the sweetest heart ever? But sweet pea, even if we started candling this very second we'd never be done in time. I got to take Ma to the plant for the four-to-midnight shift." He salutes Grandma the way he always does when anyone talks about her work at the war plant. I don't know what she does there, only she has to wear pants and a hairnet to do it, and Uncle Jimmy salutes her because of it, but I don't think he means it.

I try to catch Aunt Nedra's eye.

"You be back here to get me by three?" she says.

Uncle Jimmy leans his chair back against the wall and laces his fingers behind his head. "I don't know as I can promise that. The little lady and I, we got errands to run might take us some little time."

"You be back before three," Aunt Nedra says, and the silence afterward says, if you value your life, James Abner Anderson—but nobody says that out loud, and Aunt Nedra's face is fallen like the time we went to Kansas to visit her mother and she had to make me wait in the car.

Grandma lays out my change of clothes and giggles as she fusses over my hair. "Your uncle Jimmy always did like the womenfolk to look like ladies." She doesn't make me wear the dark-red silk dress, the one with all the tiny green flowers (talk about backwards!), the one without even a collar or sash. My mother sent it from New York, and I have to wear it every Sunday for church, which is the chief reason I hate to go to Sunday School. In the midst of all those other girls who have puffed sleeves and smocking and round collars and sashes, I have a saggy, limp dress that crawls all over me whenever I try to raise my hand or stand up to recite.

Maybe Grandma figures that dress is only for Sundays, because she lays out one of my school dresses and white socks and saddle shoes. School clothes on a Saturday, and for what? For Uncle Jimmy, because he likes dresses?

If I really thought we'd be going anywhere in the car today, maybe I'd ask for the red silk dress, after all. It is so long, below my knees, that when I sit down I am covered clear to my ankles, which is good if I have to be alone with Uncle Jimmy. But all the while Grandma is picking out the clothes and brushing out and rebraiding my hair, I am imagining the tire and the nail and the surprise I have in store. I am imagining Uncle Jimmy grinning sidewise at me as he turns the key and the motor chug-chugs to life. "Off to the races, sweet pea," he's going to say. Maybe he reaches over and tugs my braid, like we're having so much fun together, but I don't know whether to believe him about finding the teakettle, or whether he's going to head away from downtown out toward Red Fork, like he did last time we went for a drive.

Only he's not going to have a chance anyway, because I can see what happens when he sets the car in gear and steps on the gas. The tire begins to turn, the car moves forward, and the nail rips at the naked rubber. It tears, and the air whooshes out, but we don't hear it, because Uncle Jimmy is singing "John Jacob Jingleheimer Schmidt" at the top of his lungs and just getting ready to quiz me why don't I join in when he hears a sound he doesn't like, plum-DUM, plum-DUM, and he pulls the car over to the curb just past John Ellis's house, because we haven't even gone half a block. "Flatter'n a pancake. Wouldn't you know it." And I go skipping home.

Or maybe he does hear it right away. Maybe when the nail bites the tire, there's a huge bang like a balloon when you pop it, so loud it startles me even though I've been expecting it, and I scream, and Uncle Jimmy doesn't even turn the car off, just snaps the gearshift and slams out of the car, tight-lipped, and runs around the back to look at the damage.

It's not until I'm all dressed and ready to go and heading through the kitchen with its picture of little Jimmy spilling milk that another possibility crosses my mind. What if the nail buries itself all the way up to its head in the rubber, and the rubber moves aside to make room for it like people in a full subway car make room for another passenger? What if the tire just sucks in that nail and keeps on going, or what if the air comes out around the nail but slowly, like it can leave your cheeks when you puff them up? What if my practical joke turns out to be on me, and I get stranded with Uncle Jimmy way out somewhere with nobody around, like almost happened once before at Red Fork Hill?

"Ready to go, sweet pea?"

He is already by the door, jingling his keys in his hand. "She looks real pretty, Ma," he tells Grandma.

I need time to think. "Wait a second. I forgot something."

"What did you forget?"

"Um. My money, Uncle Jimmy. I have to get it from my room." I give him a knowing look—at least I mean it to be—about how we are in cahoots on the present for Grandma. "You know, in case I want to buy a souvenir or something?"

He shakes his head. "If you find something to buy, I'll lay out the cash for you, and you can pay me back when we get home." He takes my hand, and there is nothing I can say. We go out to the car.

Uncle Jimmy opens the passenger door, and I start to step in. Then, as if my eye has caught a glint of something on the ground, I pretend to look more closely. "Oh, what's that?" I say. I kneel down, being careful not to drag my skirt in the dirt, and make like I've found two nails in the gutter. Did I put three there? I don't see any others, and I can't take long searching around for something I'm not supposed to know anything about. So I straighten up and show the two nails to Uncle Jimmy. "Wonder how they got here," I say. He squints at me like he's trying to look inside past my eyes, into someplace deep where my secrets are kept, but he doesn't say anything, and neither do I. We get in the car, and he starts it up, and in my mind I keep repeating *I hope I hope I hope. I hope I hope I hope. I hope I hope I hope.*

I hope there is no other nail. Or if there is a nail I hope it will flatten the tire right away. Or if it doesn't flatten the tire right away I hope he will really take me to the Times Square Store and not for a drive out past the dairy farm. That's where he took me the last time, out past the dairy farm where Gramp and I sometimes go to get raw milk. Uncle Jimmy drove me past that farm, past the two big oil tanks that look like they're guarding the road into town, past all the stores and houses, all the way out to Red Fork Hill.

I knew it was Red Fork because my class had once taken a trip there. The bus had driven until the rocks got too big and close together to have a road anymore, and then we climbed up the winding trail. It was shady and so nicely paved with pine needles that some of us on the way back down had gone sledding without the sleds or the snow, just our dungarees. That was the one and only time Grandma ever let me wear dungarees, an old borrowed pair from Teddy Boy.

But no one was climbing Red Fork Hill the day Uncle Jimmy drove me out there and pulled off the road close the trail. "Sweet," he said. "Cool and sweet," touching my knee nearest to him. At first I thought he meant the trail, until he said, "Are both your knees so cool and sweet? Swing 'em over here, like a good girl, so your uncle Jimmy can see if your other knee is as cool and sweet as this one." When I didn't budge, he walked his fingers—his thick-knuckled, heavy fingers—across my thighs, leaving little white dents behind as if maybe he might need a track to find his way back if he had to retreat.

But he didn't stop and he didn't retreat.

I pushed my free right knee as far away from his hand as I could so he couldn't get it and even though he leaned way over, he couldn't reach, and I thought I'd won—until his fingers arched back, looking like monster-head snakes searching for someone to strike, and found the inside of my thighs.

He's going that way, I thought in a panic, *up and then over and down till he gets my knee.* I tried to pull back still more, move away, but my leg was pinned by his forearm as his fingers kept moving—reaching, searching, higher and higher.

"You are so soft and so smooth. I declare, was ever anyone in her whole life as smooth and soft?" He had that funny voice again, like he was gargling his words. "Ooh-eee, looka here. She's got cotton underdrawers."

He shifted his arm slightly, to wedge one of his fingers under the elastic rim of my panties, and I pulled my leg free from him and drew them both up so I was almost on my knees and leaning tightly against the car door. "Uncle Jimmy, stop. You're hurting me."

"No, sweet pea. Uncle Jimmy wouldn't hurt you, of all people."

Knuckles rapped on the car window. "Something wrong?"

Uncle Jimmy sat up straight and cranked down the window. "Officer," he said in his Dr. Pepper salesman voice. I could hear the smile in it. "My little niece here is from New York City, and she wanted to get a closer look at our local mountain."

"That's real nice, sir, but with those tires of yours, I'd keep off these rocks, lest you wind up with a puncture."

"Absolutely right, Officer. We'll follow you out." He turned to me. "Sorry, sweet pea, but we'd best be getting back now. Wouldn't do to get stranded out here all night, only a lap robe to keep us warm."

So now today, as Uncle Jimmy starts the car I am worrying and hoping and worrying again, all because of a nail I have straightened and set in place under the back wheel on the passenger side of his car.

"Off we go, sweet pea," Uncle Jimmy says, vroom-vrooming the motor in loud roars before he shifts into gear. He begins humming "Off We Go Into the Wild Blue Yonder," and I know that will be our song for the afternoon. My heart sinks.

It doesn't sound like what you might sing on the way to the Times Square Store.

It sounds like something you might sing on the way to getting stranded all night way out somewhere like Red Fork Hill, with only the lap robe to keep us warm in the dark.

I don't see Grandma running across the lawn, waving her arms at us. I don't see her until the car is starting to move, and she is suddenly right alongside my window, knocking at it, and then at the back on the car itself. Then Uncle Jimmy brakes, and she's at his window. "They need me at the plant," she says. "Now. Soon as I can get changed. Three ladies went home sick, and they're short-handed, and they can't reach anyone else."

I watch Uncle Jimmy turn the motor off and rest his forehead against the palm of his hand. "Another time, sweet pea."

I am already half out of his car.

11

Claire

Cincinnati, Ohio
April 19, 1995

The young woman who shared row G with Claire on the flight out of Kennedy exchanged the usual pleasantries: visiting a sister in Cincinnati...a nice town, cleaned-up riverfront... restaurants, parks...so important, parks. Making conversation, this was called, familiar to Claire, and not hard to do exactly; but foreign to Claire now, like playacting, like claiming to be a Rockette or Oscar de la Renta's design assistant. At home she was grateful for people who knew her and her story and either deferred to her grief or tiptoed a wide berth around it. This young woman didn't at all seem to notice the fact that Claire was only half a person, her better half gone. So if Claire kept up her side of the chitchat for longer than strictly necessary, it was because she apparently struck this stranger as having the room inside herself to give a hoot about parks making or breaking a city.

She was so glad she hadn't invited Lisi along. There had been a moment, just before Lisi said, "I'd like to ask you something," when Claire had almost confessed the notebooks and the trip. Lisi, sitting cross-legged on a cushion on the floor of her Bronx walk-up, freckles across her nose, a bump in it just like Jessie's, and Claire tempted to tell her all and ask her to come along. Claire had brought Lisi some things of her mother's—old scrapbooks, a buffalo plaid jacket Lisi liked, a statuette of a man praying at the Western Wall, a valentine on a doily with Lisi's name in crayoned, twig-like letters. There was that moment, and then Lisi's narrow, ungenerous mouth crimped itself like Henry's and grimly said, "I'd like to ask you something."

"Ask away."

"If you wouldn't mind."

"Go ahead."

She chewed at the inside of her lip. She gulped air. "Do you think my mother wanted me to succeed?"

"I think she wanted whatever you wanted for yourself." This was old ground.

"You know what I mean. American success. Like, to graduate from college, meet a rich man and have two kids in a nice house in the burbs?"

"Lisi, I've told you what I think. What I know of your mother." Quavering at the last. *What do I really know?*

"Come on. Didn't she want me to turn my back on all that? After she failed so miserably at it?"

Lisi had done a year of college and then dropped out. She'd worked on and off as a waitress, a dog walker and a teacher's aide, and now was dabbling at being a seamstress. She had talent with a needle. Five minutes earlier she'd been chattering about her new dream of breaking into high-end fashion design—in a year or two, as soon as Natalie was established in kindergarten. She lived with an unemployed Sri Lankan man twice her age and half her intelligence. Not the child's father. Claire said, "Here's how Jessie defined success: being most fully yourself."

"Exactly!" Lisi cried, fervidly slapping her knee. "Exactly what I mean. Thank you, Claire, for not pulling any punches."

"You're very welcome." Why this ardent response, she hadn't a clue, but if Lisi was satisfied, so much the better. Claire could put on her jacket and go home, file closed, no harm done.

But how could it be she'd been thanked for exactly the opposite of what she'd done? When everything inside her begged to float like a butterfly and sting like a bee, she'd pulled her punches. She wanted to tell that blind kid how Jessie loved her so much she'd gladly have put them in debt up to their eyebrows to see her right through college and graduate school: *Wham!* She ached to comment on the paradox of Jessie helping so many luckless kids claw their way out of the most vile circumstances, while her own favored, talented daughter sashayed through life, evidently satisfied to be the least she could be: *Wham!* For the impudence of the little twit turning her nose up at the life Jessie had chosen, condemning as a miserable failure the love they'd shared: for that alone Lisi deserved to be whammed against the ropes, battered down to the mat, left broken and bleeding on the canvas—had she not been Jessie's daughter.

But she was. And if Jessie's daughter imagined she had dibs on explaining away her own mother, that only made her like every child in the world. Claire didn't want to hear it, though, which was chiefly why she felt glad not to have Lisi next to her on this flight. Her own reasons for hopping a plane westward were unfathomable, but she knew they didn't include having to wrest ownership of Jessie from some Lisi-made chimera. Nor did she fancy being pushed into substituting for it some clay image of her own making.

The day she'd found Jessie's secret notebooks, she'd lost everything she thought she knew about who she and Jessie were together and what they stood for. As she read, her confusion only grew. Things niggled at her—little things, but still they niggled. Wonder Bread: Claire could vividly recall (since she'd watched *Howdy Doody* avidly on TV) how Buffalo Bob looked her square in the eye, convincing her that Wonder Bread built strong bodies eight ways. Eight ways, Jessie—not twelve, as you wrote. True, the fifties were not the forties, and maybe Wonder Bread's advertising had been revamped; but corporations were not in the habit of downsizing their claims over time, quite the opposite. Inflation being what it is, Claire would have expected twelve ways to kick in sometime in the sixties, then twenty ways by the seventies; and by today, there'd be more ways of building than bones in the body.

And Times Square Stores? They'd been in New York, but had they ever been in Oklahoma? Oh, now look where her craziness was taking her—straight away from where she wanted to be. She wanted to be rid of these futile questions. They upset her out of all proportion to their worth. On this trip, it was not her wish to nitpick Jessie's credibility. On this trip, it was her hope to rediscover Jessie: her Jessie, the Jessie who simply, wonderfully, was.

She would go anywhere for that, twice around the world if necessary.

Somewhere west of the Alleghenies, the plane suddenly swooped. Gravelly words—the captain's—crackled overhead, calmly announcing they'd hit a bit of turbulence. A bit? Why, then, was there nothing in the cabin not rattling? Why did the two stewardesses practically sail their breakfast cart to the rear of the plane and hastily strap themselves into jump seats in the kitchenette? The plane gave a sickening lurch and then plummeted again. Three rows ahead of Claire, a locker door jounced open, disgorging coats and carryalls onto the strip-lighted floor. Up and down the cabin, bleating people fished into their seat pockets for airsickness bags. The young woman next to Claire retched. Claire's stomach bucked, and sweat trickled down her temples and between her breasts. Mind you, she wouldn't at all have balked at falling out of the sky and dying. Just don't make her have to throw up first.

Ah, Jessie, where the hell are you? You should be here—you, and not me. This so-called bit of turbulence would subside before long, but oh, how Jessie with her iron stomach would have enjoyed it meanwhile. "Comeuppance," she'd be punning while everyone else was filling up bags, and some desperate few were raking through the seat pockets for more. Comeuppance: we humans getting reminded where our shiny Tinker-toys rank in the grand scheme of things.

To Jessie, untamable nature represented everything we can't prepare for and can't know. Gargantuan forces and mysteries delighted her. Sudden unforecast storms would send her running out in the wet, coatless, hatless, heedless of danger. They'd be tucking into cheese calzones at the pizza parlor on the corner, licking at the oil that ran out of the pinched bottom edges into their hands; or in the middle of reorganizing for the umpteenth time the self-sowing papers that overran every inch of their apartment, stacks of mail, of magazines and books; or on the Belt Parkway heading down to the Jersey Shore, first day of summer, beach gear in the backseat reeking coconut oil—when she'd point a finger at the angry-turning sky. "Not again, Jess. Not this time," Claire would moan, eyeing the clouds as they turned from white to gray to pink. Then she'd full-out plead, keening, "Je-e-es-s-s."

Jessie would only grin. And the moment the clouds went lemony, she'd grab Claire's hand, and they were out the door of the pizza parlor, the door of the apartment, the doors of the car, which she'd have summarily ditched on the parkway's narrow shoulder, passersby honking and flipping them off. And she'd be romping under the heavy plops of rain, Claire with her, dancing and squealing like five-year-olds. Claire never could refuse her, no. Because it was in the middle of just such a storm that they first made love.

Jessie had engineered the elopement, Henry out of town on business, his mother minding Lisi for the weekend. They were ready, they told one another—oh, more than ready. Seven weeks they'd been waiting. It seemed only moments since the revelation that they loved each other, yet it seemed like forever ago, and the pent-up need to touch each other made them both giddy, made them both wild. Three whole days alone together at her friend's cabin in the Adirondacks! And on that Thursday when they packed the car, each one of them was so more-than-ready.

The cabin stood at the top of a rise. They came up to it late in the afternoon through piney woods, a Craftsman-style green bungalow surrounded by birches and maples.

Gray rooftops of other dwellings showed through below, and beyond them a glitter of lake. It was the perfect spot for a tryst.

Thursday night, Friday morning; Friday afternoon, Friday evening, Friday night; Saturday morning, Saturday afternoon: nothing. Nothing happened. A day and a half they'd been hidden up there together, feigning ease in the cabin's capacious armchairs. Together but apart, increasingly solemn, increasingly terrified. They'd taken hikes; they'd affected a lively interest in every bird and wildflower, in fungi, the lichen on the boulders, the tiny mushrooms along the trail. They'd claimed exhaustion: "Wicked stuff, this mountain air." "Unbelievable."

How painfully polite they were with each other that Saturday afternoon, the longest in history. How meticulously decorous, though still goggling moonily at one another. No question they'd have returned on the Sunday without even getting past first base, but for the unpredicted summer tempest that blew in about four o'clock.

One minute, the sun was shining; the next a heavy dankness descended, muffling sound, muting color. The dark air stirred and then spun. A pattering began, and Jessie went to the cassette deck and turned it on. Claire followed her out onto the covered porch to watch the storm. They stood under the scant protection of the roof, not touching, Beethoven banging away full blast from the speakers as the wind flew in all directions, catching at their hair and clothing, thrashing the dark trees. A chittering in the red leaves nearby, some bird or squirrel, then heaven cracking open, the *Eroica* drowned in thunder. Nature gone all aslant, warm rain driven sideways, wetting them through. Close by, lightning strikes a branch, loud crack of wood. Everything shivers, and a hard surge of drumming deafens them. Downpour, it's the downpour, it's ravishing. Claire kisses Jessie's soaked lips. Jessie drinks of Claire's mouth, eyes, ears, wrists. In the torrent and fully of it, at last at long last they forget to remember their scared selves. *Her nakedness. The curve of her belly.* Reaching out blindly, reeling and reeling, they find their way to oneness, ablaze in the rain. An outcry, crowing, jubilant: Jessie.

In Cincinnati, there was no accordion thingy to connect fuselage to terminal—sky tunnel or whatever those ad hoc walkways were called. Instead, when the plane landed Claire followed the queue down a wheeled staircase into a brilliant morning, chill and crisp. It was the kind of spring morning people said made you glad to be alive, the sun still low but offering promise of warmth.

She crossed the tarmac to the terminal, which swallowed her. A vast, high-ceilinged cavern of a room it was, impossibly jammed from one end to the other. Waiting knots of travelers were leaning against every vertical surface. Luggage stood anywhere, blocking aisles, children zigzagging through, running into people, knocking over their bags. A warehouse, a passenger warehouse, that's what it was, stuffy and overheated, with what looked like a million gates lined up chockablock. What was she doing there?

She moved toward an archway for no better reason than that it seemed best to keep moving, to jostle rather than be jostled. Through the arch was an equally crowded rotunda of kiosks and eateries, where she bought herself a buttered corn muffin. She chewed standing up, weaving her way back into the great hall, scanning the aisles for the telltale gatherings-up of anyone getting ready to relinquish a seat. Her flight to Tulsa was scheduled for shortly before eleven a.m. eastern time, a two-hour wait, assuming an on-time departure. She could have been back home, could have been in her office crunching numbers, analyzing data, planning. Planning was what she'd always been good at, not this flying off into unknownsville.

Half a row away, she spotted a man collecting his things. She raced for his seat even before he stood and, beating out a traveler coming from the opposite direction, sandwiched herself in between an earnest fellow who was hunched over one of those new PDAs and a coed who was reading sociology and tapping her feet to the beat from her Walkman earphones. Perched on this hard-won wedge of vinyl, Claire partway managed to unfold a map of Oklahoma from the AAA in New York, opening it enough to find the inset of Tulsa: a bit of geography to master and nowhere to go for a while and no choices to make and nothing at all to do but study the map.

Soon enough, maybe even later today, she'd be following this map across the Arkansas River out of Tulsa into West Tulsa. She would drive up to 2212 South Phoenix and park her rental car at the curb fronting the sidewalk and the postage-stamp lawn. Half of her hoped to find 2212 South Phoenix utterly unchanged from Jessie's memory of it. She'd rest herself in the porch swing and listen to the chain creaking against the wood. She'd scatter feed for the chickens in the barnyard and toe at them as they pecked in the dirt. She'd lie down in Jessie's small bed and read aloud from her notebooks. Nestled there under the quilt, she'd listen to Jessie's words go leaping into the air, alive as girlhood. For Jessie's sake, she'd seek out any present traces of the past: Jessie's house, Jessie's school, Jessie's family. That world was all there in the notebooks, which were stowed in Claire's suitcase, stacked and wrapped in her cotton nightgown between her denim skirt and her four pairs of rolled-up underwear. Twelve identical soft-cover composition books—a treasure, of sorts, though one that angered her. A message of sorts, just not the message Claire craved from Jessie. The other half of Claire wished she'd never heard of 2212 South Phoenix.

Going with her gut had brought her this far—and when had Claire Bramany ever been a gut kind of person? Up until eight months ago, she'd have sworn she didn't even have a gut, at least not the kind that registered gut reactions and sent up directives you were advised to go with. But that was then. Jessie's death had catapulted her into a different place, a different country, some kind of mirror image that only looked the same as where she'd lived before. In this country, planning was as unknown and futile as would be skyscrapers in a two-dimensional Flatland. In this country you tried to take it one day at a time, or one hour, or one minute at a time. One second. The next second.

Time was the dimension that ruled in this country, and time could be a cruel taskmaster. In the old country, before

Jessie's death, time had been nothing, a commodity, strictly back shelf—in short supply, certainly, but just as certainly something benign. You vaguely wished you could buy more of it, provided what you bought would be time together. Then had come three final hours: three brief-and-crawling, terrible-and-precious hours together, the nurses and doctors standing back, giving them room, time mutating into something monstrous.

When Jessie's breath ceased, time sprang into hideous life. A lumbering brute it appeared at first, and Claire, wrangler that she was, tried gamely to rope the beast. Time was ruthless, though, and it never for a single moment let up in its ceaseless demand: *What will you do with yourself now?* She ran herself ragged, going back to work three days early, volunteering on weekends for any cause and every event, driving herself way past endurance, way past exhaustion. But no sooner did she let down her guard than time spat at her again. *What will you do with yourself now?* Its hot breath rank in her nostrils. *And what now? And what now? And what now?* A perpetual taunt. A choice to master every moment for eight long months, and every choice meaningless without Jessie.

Here in this airport, though, here in this seat among this mass of captive travelers, there were no choices, nothing to do but wait. From the way people drummed their fingers on their kneecaps and jackhammered their heels into the floor, it was obvious that the waiting was driving them nuts. Yet Claire found herself finally relaxing her stiff back into the seat, letting the map fall to her lap. A slow smile curved her lips, probably the first genuine smile since Jessie's death. For it had dawned on her that there was one thing and one thing only she could do here.

Kill time.

It seemed a disturbance that had nothing to do with her. A sound passed through the Cincinnati terminal, a collective moan. Claire woke from a kind of reverie and glanced up to see all the estimated departures on the monitor in a rolling change, turning one by one to Delayed. A noise louder than the moan rippled through the crowd, emerging here and there, in spots and eddies throughout the cavernous room, until it finally reached her aisle. A stifled scream, and people stood up, trying to make their way out of the hall.

Somebody said, "Something happened in Oklahoma City."

At the federal building there, a bomb.

Still in something of a stupor, Claire searched her map. Oklahoma City? Was that anywhere near Tulsa? Would it affect her?

Strangers who a moment before had averted each other's eyes were now huddling together, hungry for news. "Why Oklahoma City?" a woman behind her asked. No one knew.

"When did it happen?"

No one knew.

From Oklahoma City to Tulsa, three-quarters of an hour by car, maybe. Hard to tell. Could be half an hour. Not all that close. She concluded (wrongly, as things turned out) that this thing wouldn't impact on her personally.

"Who did it?"

"Terrorists."

"But why Oklahoma City of all places? Why the Murrow Building?"

"Not Murrow. It's Murrah, the Murrah Building."

Claire elbowed her way out of the aisle but couldn't get anywhere near a spot to watch, much less hear, what was going on. In the rotunda, clutches of people were crowding the few available TV monitors. Rumors flew. They'd caught the bomber, an Arab. The FBI had blocked another attack, in Missouri. Rescue teams were helicoptering in from all over the state. One was down there already.

The man to her right bent close to her ear, sneering, "What makes them think anybody's going to survive?"

Right then, she lost it. If there were going to be deaths, she didn't want to hear about them. She already knew all she ever wanted to know about dying. Man proposes and God dispossesses: the ones left behind in Oklahoma City were only beginning to learn that, and she didn't want to think about them. She about-faced and pushed her way out of the crowd, fleeing down a near-deserted arcade of shops.

At the Hoffritz counter, the weeping saleswoman whispered, "Those poor people. They never had a chance to say good-bye."

"Why would they want to?" The question popped out before Claire could stop it, and the woman gaped, chin drawn in, shoulders bunching up. A cold piece of work she thought Claire. Let her. Let her be shocked, let her be scandalized. Saying good-bye? What sense did that make?

When Jessie hung on, through the ordeal of rescue after the crash and then the ambulance and the ER, waiting to see Claire, needing to see her, it wasn't good-bye she wanted to say, it was hello. Good-bye would imply some summing up, some ultimate truth that got handed over, a final transfer of loving wisdom, and that's not at all what happens. What happens is you're quiet together, and soon you find yourself saying yes, the sky is clearing, humidity down. I saw an egret by the shore this morning. I saw a brown squirrel. The neighbor's son lost a tooth. You say I love you, and it sounds the same as always. Only the tears in it are new. A comfort to shed, those tears, but they didn't mean good-bye, and they didn't mean God-be-with-you, which, if Claire remembered correctly, was the origin of good-bye—and the only way "saying good-bye" might possibly make any sense at all. Even when Jessie was wheeled out of the ER to the surgery from which she never regained consciousness, what they said, gripping hands, was, "See you later," and Claire had to believe someday they would.

Later, in recovery, watching Jessie's breath go out and in, out slower, in shallower, then not; watching Jessie's breath go out and in, even then there was no good-bye, because hope clung on every breath: surely the decree would be lifted; surely all would be well; surely, Death, today of all days thou shalt die. Even afterward, the hope persisted that she would come walking through the door, alive. For how could she be dead? Impossible: the world was not constituted without Jessie in it. Jessie was so real, how could she be there one minute, the next not? The world could sooner not be. The world was full of make-believe and masks, pretensions and mistakes. Illusions. A tree might fall in the forest and make no noise. The Hindu god Vishnu might waken from dreaming his dream of the world. It wasn't hard to fathom the tree not existing, the forest not existing, all reality just an idea in the mind of God, and God not existing.

But Jessie, she existed, exists, will exist always. *Come to me, Jessie. I'll take you anywhere, do anything for you. Only please, please don't say good-bye.*

The saleswoman asked stiffly, "How may I help you?" She offered a tissue and waited while Claire dried her cheeks and blew her nose. The woman's stiffness helped. It lent an air of normalcy to their dealings, she retreating stolidly to the role of shopkeeper, Claire going along, portraying a customer, scanning the bright display and asking to see the tray of pocketknives.

Onto the showcase, arrayed before her, came row on row of folded-up knives in assorted sizes and types and colors. Claire picked up a green one and held it in her hand, trying its heft. "A Gerber," the saleswoman said, her lips curling around the name, pronouncing it with the kind of flourish that said Claire must recognize its reputation for excellence.

She liked the way the knife curved, the way it nestled into her palm. A small knob, a nubbin on the side of the blade, got her attention. Clumsily, she gave it a nudge. *Thwick.* The blade snapped open, four inches of gleaming steel, serrated partway down.

"Gerber makes a great gift for a hunter," said the saleswoman.

Claire folded the blade back in, one-handed. She busied herself with the knob, using her thumb against it this time, the blade locking into readiness, a soldier springing to attention, keen for further orders. She thumbed it shut, flicked it open.

Very like a switchblade. Again and several more times,

until the motion was easy. Then, setting it aside on the counter, she toyed with the other knives in the tray until the saleswoman finally went away to the far side of the store. And then Claire slid the green knife off the counter and into her purse. "Thanks so much," she sang out. One more clean getaway.

On the morning of April 19 in Oklahoma City, someone set off a bomb, and as a consequence, in Cincinnati Claire Bramany shoplifted a Gerber hunting knife—though shoplifting, in this case, might be something of a misnomer. Shoplifting suggests some modicum of choice in the matter, and Claire had the peculiar impression that the knife had chosen her, rather than the other way around. Certainly, she had no expectation of needing a hunting knife—well, no more than she'd needed the chamomile tea bag. She had no intention of using it, either—no more than she'd shoplifted those ragg socks with the idea they'd warm her feet as nothing else did in bed on chilly nights.

When she got to the gate where her flight was boarding, the line was hardly moving. A woman in a blue uniform was detouring some of the passengers over to the side, where a man in a blue cap rifled through their things. Claire hung back, looking for a pattern. Did they check every third person, for instance? Were they homing in on some specific trait? Dark skin? Nervous eyes? Was she a candidate? Claire began working herself up to protest: she'd cleared security at La Guardia; plainly, she posed no danger to the airline; it was an outrage, she wouldn't stand for it.

If they found the knife, they would not understand that she had no intention of using it, ever. They would not understand, nor would it matter to them, that a hunting knife wasn't the point, wasn't what she wanted. It was *taking* the knife that she'd wanted: just grabbing it because it glinted, because its weight felt right and good snuggling in her hand, like an extension of her will. Because her gut said, "Take it," and when her mind objected that taking it was a harebrained thing to do, her gut demanded she take it anyway. Because her mind didn't have the strength any longer to keep separate what made sense from what didn't.

Who would believe her if she gave that explanation? On this morning of life and death in Oklahoma City, she wasn't sure she believed it either. She did know, for sure, that having a hunting knife on you doesn't necessarily mean you own the knife. It might mean the knife owns you.

Claire hung back until the flight's last call. As a few stragglers stepped forward, she held out her ticket. The stewardess waved an arm, herding her and the others aboard. No one so much as blinked at Claire's renegade purse with its stolen treasure. The airline needed to get things moving now, time being money.

12

From the sixth of Jessie's notebooks

The place: West Tulsa, Oklahoma
The time: November 1944

When I was little and didn't understand about holidays, I thought the flags and parades on Armistice Day were all for me, because November 11, Armistice Day, is my birthday. It's neat to have a holiday on your birthday. Bands march down the street and ladies hand out red paper poppies and everyone smiles and waves, and even though you know better, you still can't help feeling some of that fuss is for you. The morning of my ninth birthday three soldiers come from the American Legion post in Tulsa, which is almost the original and oldest American Legion post in the whole entire country. They are wearing uniforms that Gramp says are from 1918. Even after all this time, their trousers still look sharply pressed, and their sleeves are barely frayed at all. Mostly, their jackets look too tight for fighting in, though.

    The men help Sammy down the porch steps and into an open car draped with red, white and blue bunting. Sammy is wearing his gray cap from when he was in the Civil War, which he calls the War Between the States. Sammy was a drummer boy, but he never had a war wound, and he is not a hero like

Uncle Jimmy. Uncle Jimmy can play drums, but he didn't march into battle beating a drum, because they don't do that anymore. I have on my brown-and-white-checked gamp with a white blouse underneath that Grandma has starched till it crinkles. I'm waiting for my mother to come and take me to the parade like she promised, but it's way after breakfast and I've been waiting for hours, and she still hasn't called to say when her plane or train or however she is coming will arrive.

Grandma tells me to find some way of keeping busy and out from underfoot. "But mind, Jessie, don't go getting dirty." I sit in the porch swing for a while, and when I get tired of that I decide to walk around the block and count the steps it takes.

I have gone clear around, no kitty-cornering, and am coming up past the last corner in front of Mr. Harden's house, where Teddy Draper and I like to watch the ants, when Grandma hustles toward me down South Phoenix, her mouth puckered into a wrinkled line like Gramp's seersucker jacket. I've gotten to 17,321 by the time Grandma stops dead in front of me.

"Jessie, I declare. Where have you been?"

"Keeping busy," and under my breath I am repeating *seventeen thousand three hundred and twenty-one.*

"I thought you were waiting for your mother."

I nod. It's easier to hold the number in my head if I don't have to talk also.

"I looked out and saw you gone, so I thought you'd gone off with her to the parade." She wheels about and starts us for home, pushing me forward. "You may have missed her, you know, with your 'keeping busy.' I declare, a body's got to keep you in sight every second."

No, I couldn't have missed her. I walked in the direction she'd be coming from. That's why I walked around the block the way I did, starting past the Ellises' house. Seventeen thousand three hundred and twenty-seven. I stop. "She'd wait, wouldn't she? She'd have come in and asked where I was, wouldn't she?"

"Lord, girl, how am I to know what your mama would do if you're not even there to greet her? Hurry up, now, or we'll be late to the parade."

I keep counting.

"Come along, Jessie. We don't want to miss seeing Uncle Jimmy. Your mother will be here sooner or later, I'm sure."

It's exactly seventeen thousand three hundred and forty-one steps around the block. If you're nine.

Aunt Nedra, next to me in the backseat of Gramp's car, says, "Look over to your right, Jessie. See the bands forming up?" Each time we pass through an intersection, I can catch glimpses of bright uniforms and flashes of brass before another group of buildings blocks my view again. Downtown is filling with people and cars, and Grandma frets we started out much too late. "We'll be way off at the back of the crowd and won't be able to see a thing." But then Gramp finds a perfect spot to park, and we're in luck. We get ourselves a place right up front near the reviewing stand so we know we will have a good view of Uncle Jimmy and Sammy in the parade.

The reviewing stand is empty until just before the parade begins, when some men go up there and shake hands all around. One is wearing an army uniform, and another a navy one, and the rest have on coats and ties and hats. I recognize the minister, Mr. Howard, there in the back row, and Aunt Nedra tells me the man up front smiling and waving is Mayor Flynn.

The high school band plays, and the men in the reviewing stand settle down. The Shriners and the Owasso Fire Department march by, and representatives from the five civilized nations do an Indian dance. Grandma points out the seven-sided star of her people, the Cherokee; mine, too, she reminds me, through my great-great-grandmother. Grandma says part Cherokee is what all the best people are, which I know is true because Will Rogers was part Cherokee. He has a movie theater named for him, with the letters of his last name spelled in lights down the side of the building.

An Indian dance is not at all like a ballroom dance. The braves and squaws kind of hop and stamp and shuffle around in a circle, not touching each other at all, and they sing loud.

The braves' moccasins have little bells and other jingly or clacky things attached. The squaws have big turtle shells fastened around their legs that rattle *tchhh-shhh tchhh-shhh* as the women dance. I think they must be strong and stalwart to stamp so hard in their soft moccasins. I try it and the pavement feels hard as bones even through the soles of my shoes.

After the dancing, Mayor Flynn makes a speech about the fine heritage the Indians have contributed to the great city of Tulsa and the great state of Oklahoma, and Grandma pokes me and says, "See, now, Jessie, life is not so short but there is always time for courtesy." And then suddenly here is the car, a gleaming black Buick convertible with its three holes in the side, and in the backseat, on our side of the car, Uncle Jimmy beaming and waving. Uncle Jimmy in the very first parade car! When he sees us, he stands up, pulls his army cap off his head and covers up his chest with it where the medals and ribbons are, making a bow toward us. Aunt Nedra waves, Grandma claps her hands and cheers, and Gramp says it is a show not to be missed.

Sammy's car comes much later. We wave good and hard at Sammy, too, but he never waves back. Gramp says he's dozing right there in the car in the middle of all that hubbub, and dreaming he'd never left our front porch.

My mother doesn't show up at the parade, even though we stay till the end. When we get back to the house she isn't there. After lunch, Grandma sends me with Gramp out to Aunt Cissie's to pick up the chickens Uncle Cubby killed for us in the morning.

Two fat hens, plucked clean and pink, are covered over in a pan ready to go into our backseat, but I dillydally as long as I can. I race Clancy, Uncle Cubby's wirehaired terrier, around the house. I whoop past the hen yard, scattering all the chickens. I go out to the field and feed George a carrot. I help Aunt Cissie make baking powder biscuits.

Finally we have to go home, back to Grandma, and I don't want to because I know my mother won't be there, because she never is. She put me in boarding schools and didn't come to see me, not when my composition on Benjamin Franklin won a prize in the assembly, not when I had the part of Massasoit in the Thanksgiving pageant, not when I made wee in my bed every night and had to wear the wet, cold pajamas afterward. And she sent me to camp and didn't come to visit me on visiting day when every single other parent came, and even when I got locked in the stable all day and all night by mistake and I cried and cried for years until I fell asleep—even then, she didn't come till long after they found me in the middle of the night and I was safe again and in the infirmary. Then she came—after I was rescued.

So when we drive up South Phoenix and I see someone standing on the front porch, someone with a glossy mink coat hung over her arm and a huge box—a box so big and covered with so many ribbons you almost can't see her—I open up the car door and shout and have my legs leaning out and Gramp is yelling at me to come back inside and I'm yelling at him to hurry, and he no more than slows down to make the turn into the driveway than I jump out. I could skin my knees real bad if I landed on the gravel, but I fall on Mr. Ketcham's grass, and I scramble up and go running into my mother's arms.

She kneels down so she can grab me tight, and we just hug and hug. She doesn't yell out or anything. Grandma and Gramp are doing that for her aplenty. She just laughs and coos, "Jessie, sweet Jessie—ooh, ooh." And I just keep saying over and over again, "You promised. You promised."

The huge box turns out to hold a brand-new bicycle, a red-and-white Schwinn with a horn built right into it that honks when I press the button. Grandma and Gramp give me a new pair of pajamas for my birthday, and Uncle Jimmy and Aunt Nedra come over with a pair of roller skates. Of course, I love the bike so much better than the skates or the pajamas, but I don't want to hurt anyone's feelings or make somebody mad or make them think I don't care about their present, so I put on the pajama top and the roller skates and try riding the bike with them on. It works okay, all in all. I can get the middle part of the skate across the middle of the pedal, though not exactly flat on it, and I have to get on the bike in the gravel driveway, where the wheels won't roll, and then pump hard to get to the sidewalk. On the sidewalk I can't stick my foot out to stop, even if I'm just barely moving—when I try to, I only roll more—so I have to get the timing just right to bring the bike to a dead stop with the pedals and then get the skate carefully to the pavement before the bike falls over.

John Ellis comes out to watch me and ask what I think I am doing.

"A new game."

"What's it called?"

"Ride..." I say—"ride-n-skate."

I've made it up right that minute, but John Ellis has to believe me all the same, so right that minute it becomes real, and John Ellis wanting now to play it because it's a game he never tried before. I turn around and look hard at Uncle Jimmy up there on the porch, smoking a cigarette because Grandma doesn't like them in the house and passing the time of day with Sammy, all the while watching me, watching me so hard I felt him even with my back turned. In my head I can hear how he laughed in the car. *It's a tapping game. Oops, pardonnez-moi.* And I know something about him I didn't know before. I know now he could make up whatever games he wants to play.

"Can I try, Jessie? Please?" John Ellis says.

I let him use my skates, but not on my bike. I don't want his dents and scratches the very first day of owning it. He says he doesn't care about riding any old girl's bike, anyway, so we're even. I ride the bike and he skates, and then I ride while he holds onto the back fender and I pull him along on the skates. And then my mother calls me home and tells me to freshen up and put on my dressiest dress, because we're all going out.

"It's my only daughter's only ninth birthday. A time to celebrate."

"What's this?" says Grandma.

"Dinner and dancing. My treat."

"But I've just fried up those chickens for our supper."

"They'll keep. I've already made reservations, so it's settled. C'mon, everybody, shake a leg. Places to go and things to do."

———

The restaurant downtown is just like a New York nightclub, with long white tablecloths and big gold menus and waiters in tuxedos and a glittery chandelier over the dance floor and a band with a singer named Patti something. My mother gives the waiter a five-dollar bill and tells him she must have her martinis very, very dry, and keep them coming, and for the young lady (which is me) a Shirley Temple with extra cherries. Uncle Jimmy says the steaks here are like butter, even Grandma and Gramp can eat them. My mother tells the waiter we'll have the biggest steaks on the menu, all around. The band plays, and Gramp takes Grandma out onto the dance floor. They try to dance together, but his belly gets in the way.

Uncle Jimmy dances with everyone. Except Gramp, of course. Wouldn't that be a funny sight! When Uncle Jimmy dances with my mother, they stand wide apart with their arms and chins raised like Irene and Vernon Castle in a movie I saw about them once, except they talk to each other and he never dips her. He dips Grandma, lots, and each and every time she grabs at his arm and sticks her leg out straight and laughs, and then as soon as he straightens her up she twitches her skirt and laughs again and then waves at us. She soon gets out of breath, so they have to stop. Aunt Nedra dances with her head against Uncle Jimmy's chest. They know a lot of steps and travel around a lot on the dance floor.

My steak comes, and it's good, but it doesn't taste anything like butter.

"Did you notice my new brooch and bracelet?" my mother asks, touching herself with her red fingernails.

I'll say. You couldn't hardly miss them. The pin is big and silvery, with lots of curves and swirls like the Arkansas River the time I walked there with Hetty and we kept trying to skip rocks across it but couldn't get the knack. My mother says the man who used to make jewelry for the Ziegfeld girls made this set as a special present to her from an admirer. She waggles her wrist in the candlelight, and the bracelet gleams. It has a silver part like the pin, but it is mostly beads, black and shiny as ink when you fill your pen from the bottle—which we are just learning to do in school.

"Are they still wet?" I ask, reaching out to touch one.

Everyone laughs, and I feel a million hot prickles of blushing.

"No, silly, they're jet. Costume jewelry, for the girls to wear with their costumes."

What's jet, I ask, and my mother, taking a pull at her drink, shrugs. After swallowing, she says, "I don't rightly know, looks like polished Bakelite. Pretty, isn't it?"

Grandma says it couldn't be Bakelite. She remembers her Aunt Mariah had a jet pendant back before Bakelite ever got invented. 'Course, she could be wrong. You're never too old to learn, that's the truth.

Aunt Nedra, taking her seat, says, "You're not wrong. I've heard jet was Queen Victoria's favorite."

"May I have this dance, sweet pea?"

As politely as I know how, I say no thank you, I don't care to just now, maybe I will later.

It doesn't work.

"Don't be shy. I'll show you how. Nothing to it, really." Uncle Jimmy poses, one hand in the air, one on his stomach, and twirls himself around. "I'll have you cutting a rug in no time flat. Scout's honor."

My mother shoots me a wink and a purse-lipped grin. "Jessie can dance," she says. Then, pushing her fingers at me like she's shooing chickens, "Go show Mr. Astaire what you can do."

I can do the waltz. I can do the box step in a fox-trot. I can even do it in a rhumba if I concentrate. They aren't playing any rhumbas, though, and mostly Uncle Jimmy wants to swing me in the air. He spins me around like he's doing it to please me, but he is squeezing me in a way I don't like. "Please don't hold me there," I say.

"Don't hold you where, angel?"

"My behind."

He raises his eyebrows like he's amazed, but I know he's not. "I got to hold you from behind. That's the way to dance. I guess you don't know much about dancing, after all."

"Do so."

"Well, then." Like there was nothing left to say. He swings me around so hard my neck hurts.

"That's not dancing," I say. "Not with your hand on my... backside." You can say backside out loud in company if you really must.

He laughs. "Sweet pea, do you see any man here dancing with his hand on the lady's front side?"

There are two other words, but I can't say them. They are only polite if you mean something else altogether.

"I'm the man, I have to lead. That's my part. You're the lady. You have to be able to follow."

The two words are butt and ass. You can say cigarette butt, and no one will think the worse of you, and you can say ass if you mean donkey, even in church. Yet it is very bad, like a curse, to say butt or ass if you mean backside. Either which way, you spell and pronounce the words exactly the same—butt, ass—the only difference being what you're thinking of when you say them. Maybe it's the thinking of that part of your body that makes you bad—except that's the same part you think of when you say backside or behind. So there must be some other connection between the thinking and the saying that I haven't figured out yet.

Uncle Jimmy sets me down, and I step with the wrong foot and bump into him. "Oh, sorry," I say, but he tells me not to apologize because it is never the lady's fault. The man is supposed to lead the lady by pressing his hand against her back, like so, and if he does it right, the two people will move like one. His big hand slides over my neck, and his fingers press into my spine, and I step with my left and trip over his foot. "Whoa, let's try that again," pulling me even closer. "Just relax and follow the man's lead. If he's really a man, you'll know what to do."

Finally the music ends, and we go back to the table. My mother is laughing. She laughs at anything anybody says. Like when Grandpa tells her, "Nancy Ann, eat some of that steak. It's a sin to let good meat go to waste," my mother whoops and Uncle Jimmy snorts. And then when Uncle Jimmy asks Aunt Nedra to dance again, she says no, the dessert is coming. "Oh, baby," he says. "Oh, sweet honey cake. You going to make me beg for it?" My mother laughs very loud. Aunt Nedra says she thinks Uncle Jimmy has danced quite enough, and maybe he ought to think about acting his age. My mother says she'll dance with him.

They don't move crisply like before. The band plays a jitterbug, but they keep doing the fox-trot. A curl of my mother's hair is hanging out from her hat where it should be tucked under, and her left arm slides down until she is holding Uncle Jimmy's elbow.

On their way back to the table her foot seems to twist, and she stumbles into her chair. Then she looks up above my head and smiles, and the waiter sets down in front of me the hugest chocolate-frosted cake with ten burning pink candles, nine and one to grow on. I make a wish that every day could be my birthday, and I get the candles out all in one breath, and when Uncle Jimmy starts singing happy birthday everyone in the whole restaurant joins in.

The cake is delicious, chocolate almost all the way through, chocolate frosting, chocolate layer cake, raspberry jam filling between the two layers. Even the flowers on top are a light-chocolate color, though the leaves are green. According to Gramp it must have used up all my mother's ration stamps for a month. The waiter cuts slices for everyone, but my mother waves hers away, a big, loose wave like the tennis counselor at camp demonstrating how to follow through on the backhand. "Ooh," I say quick so no one will take it away, "may I have that piece, too?"

"Jessie," Grandma says, "it's not polite to eat and not cover your mouth. A lady covers her mouth when she talks at the table."

I know Grandma is wrong about that one. I know I'm not ever supposed to put more food in my mouth than I could push over to one side if I absolutely, positively had to say something necessary and important. Better yet would be to swallow it before I say anything at all, because it's not really polite ever to talk with food in your mouth, and putting your hand up is no excuse. I look over at my mother, because it was my mother when I was really little who taught me never to cover my mouth to speak, it's low class—but she isn't looking at me. Her eyes are half-closed, and her beautiful high forehead looks rumpled and oily. I run to her and kiss her cheek. It feels cold and damp.

Gramp tells the waiter to bring some orange juice right away. Grandma tells Uncle Jimmy to take me home and put me to bed.

"No. I want to stay."

"Go, now, Jessie." My mother's lips have gone slack, her voice flimsy. "It's very late. I'll see you in the morning."

Uncle Jimmy is rattling the car keys next to my ear. "Let's hit the road, sweet pea."

Aunt Nedra grabs the keys right out of his hand. She'll drive, she says, Uncle Jimmy's had too much to drink. She's staring hard at him, and Uncle Jimmy tries to stare her down, but she wins. "You're coming with me, Jessie," she says.

"I love you, Mommy."

"I'll see you in the morning," my mother repeats. But I sleep too late, and when I get up, she's already gone back to New York. She's left me her black jet bracelet.

13

Jim

Oklahoma City, Oklahoma
April 19, 1995

On the morning of April 19, about the time Claire landed in Cincinnati, Jim was on his way to the YMCA for his morning round on the exercise machines. As usual, he stopped for coffee and a chat in the greasy spoon just past the Journal Record Building. There was a nicer coffee shop across the way, on the fourth floor of the Alfred P. Murrah Federal Building, run by a blind man named Ray. Good guy, Ray. Here, though, you could sit all day with a newspaper and a cold cup of coffee if you had a mind to, and nobody was going to bother you. The coffee was bitter, the sticky buns were sweet, and the grill hand remembered how you liked your bacon fried. It was that kind of place, down in the basement but right off the street where poor suckers went rushing to and fro, harried in their morning-sharp suits, their ties noosed up tight against their throats, and Jim could lean back in his chair and gloat along with the other regulars, glad he was out of that rat race for good and all.

He'd arisen at seven that morning and taken his usual care with his personal appearance, shaving, trimming his nose hairs, rubbing Grecian Formula into his hair and combing it flat against his skull. The oil stained his hair a sad burnt yellow, the color of barn piss that's gone cold and iced over, but better than white. Just before leaving his apartment, he put in his hearing aid. Then he rode the elevator down and stepped out into a beautiful spring morning. Above the cluster of government buildings across the way, the sky was endless blue.

In the downstairs snack shop, the center table was at full wrangle.

"That's bullshit!"

"God's honest truth, Harve."

"Nah. You don't know *B* from bullshit."

"Bull's *foot*," Ed corrected. "The expression is '*B* from a bull's foot.'"

Harvey, once a long-distance trucker, chewed a bit of sausage, his pale eyes gazing as if he had a long, vacant stretch of prairie road in front of him, instead of a retired school teacher with the face of a terrier and a temperament to match. He shrugged his heavy shoulders. "Still bullshit, Ed," he said.

Jim lowered himself into a chair next to Chappy. "This one's a comer," Chappy said, smiling broadly. Chappy himself never argued a point, keeping his opinions, and pretty near everything else, entirely to himself. No one knew a single fact about the thick-bearded, slouch-hatted, lame-gaited old guy, other than he showed up every morning, ate his short stack slathered with grape jelly, and invariably set the other men at loggerheads.

"What's it about today?" Jim said.

"O.J. Simpson. Trial of the Century. Stick around, Jimmy Boy. Fireworks afoot."

"Don't ever call me that."

"Hello: don't call you what? Don't call you Jimmy? Or don't call you Boy?"

"Just don't."

Chappy nodded. "Suit yourself."

The Y could wait, Jim thought. He'd been feeling a little creaky, anyway. He ordered fried eggs, bacon and grits. Nothing was wrong with his heart, or his liver or the one kidney, but maybe, to make up for the breakfast, he'd do two circuits later. Take care of the body, and it'll take care of you.

It was 9:05 by Jim's watch when he came up out of the snack shop onto the sidewalk and paused to check the time. The watch was fast. Actually, it was 9:02 a.m. in Oklahoma City, and glorious morning light was reflecting off the broad glass front of the Murrah Building across the street. The nine-story federal building was almost entirely glass, supported by four stout columns. The soaring atrium formed by the columns and the glass was, to Jim's mind, the best sight in the city. The first time Jim ever entered the building, on his way to the Social Security office to ream out some stupid cow of a clerk who'd been impossible to deal with over the phone, he'd been stopped dead in his tracks. For his money, there wasn't a better spot this side of heaven.

At 9:02 on the morning of April 19, 1995, the spot ceased to exist. As Jim stepped off the sidewalk, a Ryder truck loaded with thousands of pounds of ammonium nitrate fertilizer and fuel oil erupted, blowing itself, and the building it fronted, to pieces. The explosion tore upward, disintegrating the walls, destroying the columns, ripping the building apart. It lifted Jim off his feet and threw him backward onto the pavement. A blue-orange fireball bloomed above him. The earth shook beneath him, and the air flew in shatters and shards around him.

Other citizens caught in the rumbling blast thought earthquake; Jim's mind shouted *artillery*, and it may be that he screamed the word aloud, curling into a ball and shielding his face and head. Six feet in front of him a green Ford Explorer burst into flame, flipped over and slid toward him, trailing great plumes of black smoke. "I'm a goner," he whispered, scrabbling backward away from it. Something whomped his thigh.

Ten seconds after the enormous blast, there was a second boom, the concussion caused by massive movements of matter and air into and out of the vacuum created by the explosion. The bomb had blown out the second and third floors of the Murrah Building. Now, a deafening roar arose as the fourth, fifth, sixth, seventh, eighth and ninth floors pancaked on top of each other. Inside the noise, inside the thick, swirling air, Jim watched the car slide within three inches of him and then halt in a slice of fractured pavement. He rolled away from it, his leg a sudden searing thing as he turned.

People poured out of buildings onto the street, frantic, their clothes ragged and spattered. Jim was only dimly aware of them. A four-inch metal shard was lodged in his thigh. He pulled, and blood poured from the wound. He grabbed at the tatters of his shirt and ripped two strips, a long one from his left sleeve, a wide one from his left chest panel. One he used to mop the wound, the other to fashion a makeshift tourniquet. The blood stopped gushing, and he inspected the gash as best he could. It had gone into the muscle, but not deeply, and it had missed his groin by a handsbreadth. Lucky bastard.

The building he'd just exited looked like an enormous tornado had hit. Arrowheads of Murrah glass had shot straight through its concrete walls. In the basement coffee shop—though he didn't yet know it—his cronies were dead.

Disoriented, exhilarated, unaware of or unheeding the wail of sirens approaching, Jim got to his feet and wove, crouching, through drifting smoke into what had been the parking lot, now a mess of raining dust and papers and photographs, of mangled file drawers, legless chairs, topless desks, shredded plant life. The gleaming Murrah Building was gone, replaced by a seething heap of wreckage. Things swung as if caught in stiff breezes—wires, insulation, waving like arms signaling. Or was that really an arm, someone signaling? He moved toward it and stumbled on a foot lying in his path. Just the foot, torn away at the ankle, a woman's bare foot, with scarlet pedicured toenails. He turned from it perplexed and found a child's cap in the filth, a small pink baseball cap with a yellow duck embroidered on it. He bent to pick it up. It was torn, and on the underside of the peak were clots of grayish gore.

Jim knew the Murrah. He'd visited the Social Security office, had business at the Office of Veterans Affairs, even stopped once or twice at Army Recruiting to see if he could lend a hand. He knew that building. And he knew the day care center. Ears ringing, blood still oozing through his ripped pants leg, he was already climbing the steaming heap by the time the first police vehicles pulled up at the scene, clawing bare-handed through precarious mounds of carnage and rubble looking for small, trapped survivors.

A massive search-and-rescue effort got under way. Firefighters formed up volunteers from the area into squads. A janitor, an account executive, and a personal trainer joined Jim in the still-cascading debris. The building shook and shimmied as they crawled through unstable caverns of concrete, steel and wire. Insulation that was red meant someone nearby, maybe alive. Body parts lay everywhere, and most of the victims they unburied were mangled beyond recognition. Jim had an eerie instinct that told him where to dig. He unearthed a girl who was nonresponsive but breathing, squatting on a corpse to do it.

Ten a.m. More than fifty people had been brought out alive, six of them children. Jim labored without pause. Survey crews came and rescue specialists with their cranes and backhoes and gas-powered tools, their acoustic equipment and fiber-optic cameras. But bare hands did the work. And when they wouldn't let him dig anymore, he formed part of the line, the bucket brigade that passed debris back. And when they no longer let him do that, he talked to survivors, talked to the families who had gathered tight-faced at the First Christian Church, waiting for word.

He poured coffee, he went out and directed traffic, hundreds upon hundreds of cars bringing blankets and food to the site. At some point, they made him have his wound attended to. At some point, someone discovered that he couldn't hear much of anything, his hearing aid having been blasted into nothingness, and they got somebody to get somebody to get him a replacement from God-knows-where, but somehow an audiologist showed up over at the Methodist church, which had become a temporary morgue, and fitted him with a new one that worked twice as good, so he said.

And when he was all done in, and they told him to go on home and get some well-earned R & R, then this TV fellow asked him to do an interview, and he was doing his best to duck it. Not because he was publicity averse. He didn't mind playing hometown hero. But the guy was some kind of turkey. Most newshounds were. They got the stories, alright—just never got the stories all right. That's what Ed Decker used to say down in the snack shop, breakfast mornings. Now he was dead. Sometimes Jim wondered why so many others died and he went on living. Too mean to kill, he'd opine, grinning.

The EMT said he hadn't bled much, all things considered.

"Not much blood left in my veins, sugar," he said. "Mostly piss in there, and vinegar. I'm too full up of piss and vinegar to die."

She gave him the once-over. "From the looks of you, I'd guess that's right," she said.

14

From the seventh of Jessie's notebooks

The place: West Tulsa, Oklahoma
The time: November 1944

Mrs. Vincent pronounces Ponce de Leon with an *s* sound and no *e* at all, not like Sister Theresa, who used to pronounce the *c* like *th* and the *e* like *ay* and make the whole name glamorous: *Ponthay day Layown.* As I write the name out, I whisper it under my breath, listening to the sweet, rhythmic pulses of the syllables. I am writing Ponce de Leon on the test paper when the classroom door opens and Cal Winters, the tallest sixth grader in the school, comes into the room with a folded note for Mrs. Vincent. "Wait," she commands. She has to do that every time with Cal, because there might be an answer she'd want him to take back, but he can't seem to remember from one time to the next. Cal is as short on brains as he is long on legs, is what Grandma says—then she adds, "But he's polite as a mortician," which is what his daddy is.

Cal shifts nervously in the front of the room, his hands hanging way far out of his sleeves, wrist bones and arms showing beyond his shirt cuffs halfway to the elbows. Mrs. Vincent looks up from the note, eyes scooped wide open so she can see above the top of her half-glasses. "You. Jessie." She waves the note out at me. "There's someone come to see you. In the main office. Mr. Olsen"—the principal—"says you're to take all your things and 'proceed forthwith.' So bring me your test paper, take your wrap from the cloakroom and get along with you."

Cal is waiting for me outside the room. "Do you know who's come for me?" I ask, hoping it's my mother. Praying she's come just as I wished for, when I wished every day could be my birthday.

Cal shakes his head.

"Is it a woman?"

He shrugs.

I skip ahead of him and turn so I can be facing him. "Did you see any strangers in Mr. Olsen's office?" That should get at it. If it was Gramp or Grandma come about something, he'd know them, so it wouldn't be a stranger.

Cal shrugs again and then slows, remembering something. "It did smell good from the doorway, like perfume."

Yes! My mother! Hiding behind the door and waiting to surprise me. Yes!

I rap on Mr. Olsen's door. A somber "Enter," and I turn the knob. The thick odor of shaving lotion. Uncle Jimmy in the leather armchair for visitors.

"Hi there, sweet pea," he grins. "Surprise!"

From behind his desk Mr. Olsen holds out his arm as if to push Uncle Jimmy back in his chair, even though Uncle Jimmy hasn't moved except to uncross his legs. "Jessie, are you acquainted with this man?"

"Yessir. I am, sir," I fairly mumble, but not quite, because you can get in trouble for really mumbling.

"Whom do you recognize him to be?"

"Uncle Jimmy."

"That's just what I told you, right?" says Uncle Jimmy, slapping the arm of his chair and rising like the slap has burst him out of his seat. "C'mon, sweetness. You and me, we're outta here."

"I trust conditions will remedy themselves," Mr. Olsen says.

Uncle Jimmy nods. "I trust, too."

Must be Uncle Jimmy has come to get me because something is wrong. When I try to ask, he puts his finger across his lips and looks hither and yon like he expects spies behind every cabinet and door in the long school corridor.

No sooner do we get outside, though, than he bursts out laughing. "I fooled 'em good, Jessie. Sprang you free and clear, and now we got the whole day together."

"No. I want to go back inside, or home. You make me come with you and—and I'll tell, Uncle Jimmy, I swear I will."

"Tell?" He is still smiling, sort of. Only his teeth don't look friendly anymore the way they used to back when he was nice—really nice, I mean, not pretend nice so he can get me alone and make me do things I don't like. "What'll you tell, sweet pea?"

"You know," I say, trying to play cagey.

"I know that I took you out of school. Terrible sin. The smartest kid in her class, and she can't afford to take half a day off now and again?"

That's not what I am threatening to tell, but I have no words for what I would say, and I have plenty for this, so I go along with him. "You lied, though. You lied to get me out. You said there was something the matter, didn't you?"

"I said there's been an accident and I need to fetch you. That's not a lie."

"What accident?"

"We accidentally ran out of time the other day, didn't we? And never got to the store for your teapot."

"You're going to take me to the store?"

"A promise is a promise."

"Straight to the store? Right away?"

"Now, sweet pea, isn't that what I just said?"

The Times Square Store takes up the whole corner of the block. You can come in the front door if you are walking or are parked on the street, or you can come through the back door if you are parked in a special parking lot they've made just for customers. Uncle Jimmy says these men are a new breed. I shiver. If they are some kind of Indian, even a new breed, that's a good omen. My mother sent me a beaded Indian collar and purse from an Indian craft store near Times Square in New York City, and here I am about to use money she sent me from New York to buy a teakettle from a Times Square Store run by Indians in Tulsa, Oklahoma. A weird connection like that says the world's topsy-turvy but connected, so it's all going to be okay someday.

When my mother used to take me shopping in New York City, she would look and ask and fiddle through things, and sigh and shake her head and smile. Of course, she always said, "Thank you," in her jelly voice to the salespeople behind the counter, and they always said, "You're very welcome, I'm sure," in their jelly voices, but I still thought they must be angry because she'd take up their time and mess up the little drawers they'd put out on the counter and then not buy anything, like she would have if they'd had anything good enough but, oh, such a pity, they didn't.

In this store you don't have to go to the counter to ask for anything. You can go in and out of rows of shelves and pick up what you like, check the tag for the price and decide if you want it or not, and not bother the salespeople or make them angry.

I spot the teakettle at the end of the second row, and it is exactly what Aunt Nedra promised—well, not promised, just described, but it's exactly the idea I had about it, and I don't want to let go of it, even to pay. I have five dollars saved up from collecting pop bottles and oiling Gramp's tools, added to the money from my mother and the dimes I won from Uncle Jimmy after he taught me to play acey-deucey. We wagered—Grandma says nice folks don't bet, but Uncle Jimmy said what she didn't know wouldn't change her opinion of us none, and anyway, we weren't betting, we were wagering.

I'd be happy to take the kettle home just the way it came off the shelf—no box, no wrapping, no nothing. Not that the Times Square does gift wrapping, a big sign says not, but Uncle Jimmy crooks his finger at the man behind the cash register. "How's about a little old sack for this little missy's purchase." His voice doesn't go up at the end, so I know it isn't a question, even though if he had to write it on paper it would look like one.

Back in the car, Uncle Jimmy begs to remind me that I need the sack to keep the teakettle a surprise from Grandma.

"But she's working the early shift so she's not home to see anyway."

"Don't you be sassy. Besides, you don't carry things out of a store without that they be wrapped. It's not decent."

I make myself busy, rustling around inside the bag, taking off the pom-pommed whistle, blowing into it. Mostly I get spit in it trying to make it whistle, but I expect to wash it and set it out to dry when we reach home. I can feel Uncle Jimmy glancing over at me every now and again as he drives, but grown-ups always do that sort of thing. So I hardly pay him any mind except to keep on doing what I'm doing, making sure it somehow stays cute.

The teakettle is rounded and my eyes look extra big in the shiny surface. I hold the kettle between my legs and with my fingers pull my lips wide apart. I stick out my tongue and waggle it. Uncle Jimmy laughs at first and then grows silent and then clears his throat a couple of times the way grown-ups do when they want your attention but want you to think they're too nice to order you around.

"Want to see something special?"

I look up at him, curious. But he has that ugly smile, so I go back to the teakettle and start shining it up with the sleeve of my sweater.

"You just keep on looking at that pot of yours, and your uncle Jimmy'll make something appear like magic."

I like magic shows, and Uncle Jimmy knows it. He's the one who took me to the first magic show I ever saw, at the Baptist church. "Don't you tell nobody," he said. "Ma'll tan both our hides she finds out we set foot inside the Baptist church." Grandma is a Methodist, so I never told about the magic shows, figuring it'd set her off.

But if Uncle Jimmy can do magic.... I stare at the teapot, peek around the sides a bit. A thick pink finger wiggles at me. I scoff, "That's no magic." But when I look at Uncle Jimmy, he's got both his hands on the wheel. I quick look back at the pot, and that finger is still wiggling at me.

"How'd you do that?"

"Magic."

And then I recognize what it is. It's his thing. Not a little thing like Teddy Draper's when he wees against the back of John Ellis's barn. Not all floppy and wrinkled up like the one that boy who lives across the street from Teddy once tried to show me when he said we should play married. I would have played school with him, or even library, but I didn't want to play house—for one thing, I haven't played with dolls for years, and I said so. He told me I was just a dumb kid who didn't understand squat, and he scrunched his thing back inside his pants and buttoned up his fly. Naturally, I told him I was no baby goat. I was very civilized, not an Okie like him. He slammed my head against the corner of the back steps and I screamed and he ran off when Gramp chased after him. Grandma said I shouldn't call anybody an Okie, because it is a term of terrible disrespect. Though even so, she guessed that riffraff boy deserved it.

"Want to feel something nice?" Uncle Jimmy says. He's got one hand off the wheel now, reaching for my hand. I shrug away from him, squeezing myself tight against the car door, trying to put as much distance as possible between us. He's looking back and forth between me and what's out on the road. I fix my stare ahead, searching for something to talk about, some old man's long johns flapping on a clothesline, some barn kneeling down it's so worn out and rotted. Off to the left I spot the Indian lodge with its big sign saying Souvenirs.

"Looka yonder," I say, being careful not to really point. Ladies don't point, Grandma always says, though I can't figure how sometimes it isn't more convenient than a whole lot of describing that may take so long you're way past what you wanted to point at. I keep my fingers tightly curled into a round fist and gesture, not point. "Can we stop awhile and look at the trinkets?"

I remember to add, "Please, sir?" but still Uncle Jimmy snatches at my outstretched hand, grabs it tight inside his and brings it toward him. "Pointing's not proper, little darling. You got to remember you weren't brought up in a barn. And your grandma wouldn't be too happy if I told her you said 'can' when I suspect you meant 'may.'"

I nod and mutter as to how I'm sorry, but he doesn't slow down any for the Indian lodge, and we just keep driving farther and farther out past anything I can even see of people living there.

I try to slide my hand out from inside his. He holds it up close to his face and won't let it free. He starts in rubbing at it with his thumb and telling me how sweet I smell, and he does that breathing in and out real deep. My arm grows tight from being stretched out like I was doing a Heil Hitler, but I'm not going to budge from where I'm wedged in next to the door.

Eventually, he has to let go my hand because he needs to downshift. The car is slowing, and Uncle Jimmy pulls off the road, and we're bumping our way toward an empty billboard half overgrown with brambles. Uncle Jimmy stops the car in back of the sign, and I hope it's because he has to go to the bathroom, though usually when Gramp "feels the call" he'll park on the road side of the sign and go around the back for privacy.

Uncle Jimmy doesn't get out of the car. He starts talking. I watch his face, which is pointing straight forward like he's looking for someone in the scrubwood. "You are a precious wonder, you are, " he says, low-like, the words burbling out of his jaw. He sounds like Sammy the boarder telling me stories about the Civil War. He'll suck in air, but before four words are out of his mouth the breath will be gone and all you'll hear is a burbling hum.

Uncle Jimmy is doing a kind of rocking thing now, his arm moving and his body moving, though just a little, like he can't really sit still. Grandma'd be on him real quick. "Quit your fidgeting," she'd say. "That's no proper way for a gentleman." I

am still sitting pressed up against my car door, not doing anything bad, when he reaches out his arm like he might be going
to smack me. "You gonna hunch there, stiff and sour faced?"

I don't answer.

"I'm talking to you, girl."

I shrivel closer to the door, close as I can, pulling my
legs up to where I can get my back flat against it. Uncle Jimmy's hand trails down, fingers piano playing along the front of
my dress and coming to rest in my lap. "You know your uncle
Jimmy would never do anything to hurt you. Don't you?"

I shake my head.

His fingers begin twiddling my dress.

"Stop. You'll wrinkle it, and Grandma'll be put out."

"Mustn't put Ma out," he teases, smoothing the material.
"Mustn't make her miffed at us." Now he turns his whole body
to face me. "Jessie, you are the prettiest little thing I ever did
see. Whoo-ee. Your uncle Jimmy sure does love you a lot."

His right knee is pulled up on the seat, and I can see the
gap in his pants and his thing is sticking out. He's not supposed to open his fly and take it out until he's in private, ready
to wee. Teddy Draper and John Ellis both told me that's an
A-number-one rule, like not picking up your skirt and pulling
down your underpants in public is for girls. His thing is fat and
stiff, especially after he puts his fingers around it. I'm scared
he is going to pee right there in the car.

"You know all the nice things your uncle Jimmy does for
you?" he says, like it's a yes-or-no question that I have a choice
about, but I know I'm supposed to say yes. I'm staring down at
my fingers, working at the piece of cuticle I forgot to bite off
neat. I shake my head no.

"No?" Like his eyes must be popping out of his head.
"You don't recollect all the times I've saved my Lucky Strike
packs so you can peel off the silver foil for that ball you and
Teddy Boy are entering in the war chest contest? Or me teaching you acey-deucey and letting you wear that cap I won off
a sailor and showing you how to fold it so you could stick it
in the back pocket of your coveralls? You don't have a single

remembrance of how I'm using my gas stamps to cart you around looking for your teapot? No, Jessie?"

I recollect I have a remembrance. But I want to go home, right now, and starting to cry, I say so.

"Sure, sugar. I know. We're just having a nice talk, private-like, is all. I was just reminding you how much your uncle Jimmy loves you." His hand inches up across my shoulder and he tries to pull me close to him. The padded bumps of car door press against my back. His hand on my neck tugs harder, and I'm pulled over, my cheek grazing the roughness of his pants. "Hey, that's nice. You want to put your head in my lap, maybe take a nap while I drive home?"

We're going home? I struggle to get up, but his hand won't let me. My left eye is closed shut against the ribs of the serge; my right eye is looking at his shoe, at the circles and ovals punched out on either side of the bracket that marks the tip. Two burrs have got themselves fixed to the inside of Uncle Jimmy's pants cuff. Maybe they will stick him before he finds them and pulls them loose.

Uncle Jimmy lets go of my head, and I try to sit up, but quick like anything, he's got his hand on my hip, moving toward my panties. I try squirming, and Uncle Jimmy sidles over so somehow I'm closer to him than I was before, and he's got his legs up on the seat, one on each side of me. His arms have both gone around my back and he's holding me tight against him and trying to work his hands down inside my panties. There's no way I can roll off and something hard is pushing at my pant-ies in the front, rubbing against my belly button and getting caught in it, like the pommel on a saddle one time when I tried to get down all by myself.

I try arching my back to get out of his grip, and it works, at least enough for me to free one arm. "I want to go home, Uncle Jimmy. Please."

He laughs at me, but nicely. "I know, sweet pea. Soon." He closes his eyes, and his hold on me loosens. I use my free arm against the steering wheel and I'm up even if there's only a teeny ledge for me to sit because Uncle Jimmy is still lying sprawled across the whole seat.

"You gonna do up your pants now?" I ask. He smiles, his eyes still closed. "Sure," and he drags his hand up from the floor where he's let it flop, across his lap until it finds his thing, all stiff and fat and angry-looking. He opens his eyes and looks down at himself. "Darn shame, sweet pea. All this is for you. I could show you just how much your uncle Jimmy loves his little darling."

It twitches; it looks alive. I try to turn, reaching for the door. His hand grabs mine. "Just touch it. Feel it. It wants you so much it hurts. Did you know that? Did you know how much your uncle Jimmy hurts from loving you?"

I don't want to hurt him even though he is not my friend anymore. It's because he is not my friend anymore that I know how much loving can hurt. But I am shaking my head and fighting him while he forces my fingers against him, clamping my fingers around the hot, damp piece of him and moving my fingers up and down, trapped inside his paw-like fist. And so fast I don't even know it, he's grabbing my head and pushing my face down, forcing my mouth against him, forcing his thing inside my lips, inside my teeth and I want to bite him but I'm scared he'll wallop me—then deeper in and then it rams the back of my throat and I gag. And he shouts, "Oh, baby. Oh, yes. Yes. You love me," and I'm crying and all this salty stuff comes squirting into my mouth. He must be pissing in me, and I try to pull away, and I'm crying and he's pushing me down harder and harder, and I can feel him bumping up into me, and I'm crying and he's still shouting—only it just sounds like "Aaaaargh."

———

Uncle Jimmy slows the car up on Quanah, outside the Eskimo Pie. "Want some ice cream, sweetness?" I don't want to open my mouth, not even for ice cream. He opens the car door and gets out. I don't budge. I just stay staring down at the floor, twisting the top of the paper sack with the teakettle inside. Uncle Jimmy opens my car door and reaches in his hand. He touches the soft spot under my arm, and I shudder.

"Well, come on then by yourself. Come on."

I shake my head back and forth, back and forth.

"We're going to have a sundae or a malt together. Like on a date. Wouldn't you like that?"

On hot summer afternoons, Gramp'd sometimes take me to the Eskimo Pie. It'd be even more of a treat almost to sit on the high leather stool and twist around and always stay cool than to get the ice cream.

Uncle Jimmy is waiting. "You're gonna sit there, ain't you? Not say nothin' and spoil our day." He straightens up, sore at me, and I flinch because I know he's about to slam the door. "Women!" Shoving it shut with all his might. For the next couple of minutes I don't know where he has gone or what he is doing. I don't look up or anywhere, except at the crumpled-up top of the paper sack I am holding. I work at rolling the top edges of it tighter and tighter, thinning them down into skinny threads like bits of clay. Then I hear him get back into his side of the car. He stretches his leg out to step on the starter. I roll the edges between both hands. His foot stops. I look up, straight ahead.

Everything looks normal, ladies holding hands with their small children, standing on the corner waiting for the traffic light to change. A man in a black-and-red-checked wool shirt and baggy brown corduroys pulling a load of newspapers in a red wagon. Art Nickerson at the Sinclair station fueling up a maroon Buick.

"So, sweet pea, you got your nice present for Ma, you happy now?"

I shrug.

He waits.

"I guess."

"Hold on. Didn't Uncle Jimmy take you all over to buy this here present?" He flicks his finger at the sack, and I let go of it. "Didn't he?"

Why do grown-ups want to call themselves by name when talking to kids, instead of simply saying I? "Yessir."

"Yes, indeed. And isn't that what you wanted? To get Ma her present?"

"Yessir."

"Then I should think you'd be happy and grinning."

"Yessir."

He bends around, like some tall, dark swan, and pushes his face up close to mine. "Oh, sweet pea, are you scared I'm gonna tell our secret?"

I shake my head.

"You know I'm no tattletale like Doc. You know that, don't you?"

Murmuring, I allow as how that's true.

He looks satisfied. "I can see," he says, settling back into his place again, "that you put big stock in the high art of keeping confidence."

I know what all the words mean, but I don't quite know what they mean all together. I shrug again.

"You and me can trust each other, isn't that right? To keep quiet about our goings-on. Right?"

"I guess."

"That's my sweetest thing. You and I'll just keep this whole afternoon our little secret, right? 'Cause if you was to tell Ma just one little part of today, she'd want to know it all—she's like that—and soon she'd have the whole story out about the teapot. And we wouldn't want that, would we, sweet pea? Not and spoil the whole surprise."

South Phoenix is deserted when Uncle Jimmy drops me off home. I get out of the car the instant it pauses in the driveway and run toward the front porch.

"Hey," Uncle Jimmy calls. "Hey, you forgot something." He's stretching across the front seat, holding open the door, dangling the paper sack.

I walk back slowly and take the package from him. I watch him sit up and put the car in gear. I shut the door, and when he gets the car rolling, I pitch the sack, teakettle and all, just behind the rear wheels. Backing up, the car makes a kind of hiccup as the rear wheel hits the sack and then again as the front wheel squashes whatever life was left inside it.

Uncle Jimmy stops and stares over the steering wheel at the crushed sack. He rolls down the window. "Ah, sweet pea, now look what you've gone and done. Why'd you go and spoil your nice surprise?"

I'm silent. I pick up the remains of the teakettle and I walk it to the refuse burner out back and I drop it into the trash can. Gramp will burn it, and nobody will ever know my shame.

15

Claire

Tulsa, Oklahoma
April 19, 1995

Quanah Avenue didn't exist. Neither did 2212 South Phoenix. The street was there, South Phoenix, but no 2212. A housing project circa 1970 filled the block where the house might once have stood. *Did* stand, Claire amended—did once stand. Quanah she kept looking for, uneasily convinced she was lost again.

The clerk at the rental car counter had given her good directions from the airport to the motel downtown. She hadn't stopped at the motel. She'd gone straight past it over the bridge, to someplace where tumbledown shacks knelt in the dust.

West Tulsa, when she found her way there, gave signs of having once fared better. She happened on the Methodist church, a narrow façade of handsome grayish-brown stone. A staircase at the side of the building led down to what must be basement classrooms. Try as she might, she couldn't imagine Jessie descending those stairs in her too-long dress. The place looked wrong. Just wrong. It should have been grander, more imposing. It was too small, and the Eugene Field School a few blocks away was also too small, a single story of dour maroon brick, its shadowy windows festooned with gay paper cutouts of tulips and rabbits. A Lilliputian playing field was tucked alongside the school, sparse grassed, bare of any equipment at all. No swings, no seesaws.

The area in West Tulsa where Quanah should have been had all been torn down, no sign of a movie house, a barbershop, the Rexall. Quanah itself was among the missing, hypothetically swallowed up by a dusty, potholed Southwest Boulevard and by the Red Fork Expressway, a desolate highway as dun colored as the road that had brought her down from the airport.

In the terminal, at the sight of a New York driver's license, the rental car clerk had chirped, "Welcome to the Southwest," as if Claire had arrived someplace radically new and singular, and wasn't she in for a treat. But so far, nothing about the city struck her as peculiarly southwestern. Even the gorgeous sunset, scrumptious sky streaked pink and violet, hadn't obscured the fact that not a single watermelon stand dotted the rosy distance all the way into town. Golden arches flashed by instead, neon donuts.

About the best she could say for the ride: it was fast. A quarter of an hour and she was in city streets a-rush with cars. She sought among the scatter of pedestrians for any hint of local color, ten-gallon hats, bolos. In vain. The men wore conservative business suits, spread-collared shirts and pastel neckties. Welcome to the Southwest.

That rental car clerk hadn't the least hint of a southwestern twang in her speech either, more like a drawl, asking Claire, "How are you today?" A curtain of straight black hair framing her face, high cheekbones you'd trade your mother for. "So, what brings you to Tulsa?"

Too travel worn to figure out an evasion, Claire automatically responded, "I'm chasing down a—" and then stopped. A what, Claire, exactly? A ghost? A figment? "Chasing someone down."

The girl giggled, candy-cane-striped fingertips at her mouth. "Geez, me too." She'd followed her boyfriend here all the way from Atlanta, she said. Atlanta, that was her hometown.

She typed Claire's information into the computer, watched it process, then pulled the three-part form from the printer and set it on the countertop. Claire declined the insurance for no better reason than that Jessie always had, and initialed the paperwork where the clerk indicated. "How's your chase going?" Claire asked.

She tapped the naked fourth finger of her left hand. "Any day now."

"Good luck."

"You too," handing Claire the keys. "I'm sure he'll come around."

Eight months ago, Claire might have said, "What makes you assume it's a man I'm after?" Now she was tempted to say, "What makes you think it's someone living?"

"Just keep at him." Luminous blue eyes like bits of morning, she had. "You'll see. Men come around, sooner or later, if you don't quit."

Claire almost laughed. There was only one man she could even think of chasing down, and that man would be Uncle Jimmy. If he ever "came around," she'd wring his godforsaken neck. Or worse.

All the same, she wondered about Uncle Jimmy. If he still existed, James Anderson would be an old man by now. She pictured him seventysomething, a shambling codger in a pair of stained overalls ogling little girls from his grimy window at some trailer park. She saw him slick back his thinning hair with the palm of his hand. She saw the leer on his face. She saw him give two thumbs up to the girls as they passed, and one little girl waving tentatively back at him.

Why should all this come so clearly to her mind's eye, yet not Jessie rising to answer a question in the basement of the Methodist church, just down that cream-colored wooden staircase, a thin slip of a girl squirming inside a clingy red dress?

It was all so small, that was the problem, such a little piece of the world, and an unremarkable piece at that. Jessie's notebooks painted this neighborhood end to end with so much color and vitality, it had to be bigger. Either fifty years had rendered the place limited and stale, or else the problem was Claire herself. Anyway, she couldn't go wrong putting her trust in Jessie—so she went on walking the nondescript blocks in widening rectangles, searching for railroad tracks and a stream, discovering none. At last she settled herself wearily into the Chevy she'd rented and headed back the way she'd come. Jessie was not to be found here, among everything lackluster and paltry, the school, the church, the street, the neighborhood.

She was backtracking her way to the motel, or so she thought, along uniformly dinky avenues. A wrong turn in the now-full dark, or the one-way street she was forced to detour around, brought her without a shred of warning into the abrupt shadow of the oil tanks. Claire braked and stared. Had the traffic been any heavier, she'd have been rear-ended. Craning upward, she pulled the car over. Rotund cylinders rose before her, their tops alight. This was more like it: the wide, blue-gray bulk of them every bit as staggering as Jessie reported. They blotted out the landscape and the sky.

The chubby assistant manager who checked Claire in at the motel had a gold ring in his earlobe. His lapel pin pronounced him Andy, hailing from Cairo, Illinois. The room he gave her on the third floor had two double beds covered in a blue-and-beige print, a dresser with TV and a writing table, both of dark-colored wood. Beige-draped windows overlooked the parking lot. She might be anywhere, she thought. So much for the lure of tourism in the wild-and-woolly West.

If the familiarity was meant to make her feel at home, it failed. She felt edgy, anxiety humming in her chest. The time on the bedside clock stood close to eight p.m. but the last thing she wanted to do was eat dinner; and though she was exhausted, she knew it would be pointless to lie down. A dark staccato troubled her when she tried to rest, deep cellos and basses vibrating along her nerveways, like the sound track of *Jaws* playing through every frame of her life.

She double locked the door to her room, unzipped her suitcase, and from an inside pocket removed a palm-sized plastic pouch full of clear liquid. After Jessie's second surgery, someone on the hospital's pain management staff had mistakenly left it behind on Jessie's bed. On the verge of notifying a nurse, Claire had reneged, then taken it home and put it away against a life without Jessie: a time inconceivable to her then, but if too awful to bear, she had her insurance in that nocuous fluid. Every so often, she held the soft, pliable bag in her hand and gently squeezed its nipple-like protuberances, wondering just how much of the oily-looking drug would be needed to accomplish its work, uncertain whether it was drinkable, whether she'd be able to keep down all 250 mL of morphine, terrified of waking up incapacitated but not dead.

She took the pouch with her into the bathroom, washed her face and stared at her haggard eyes in the mirror, a buzzing beneath her skin, like a nest of mad hornets. These jitters of hers, what sense did they make? The worst had already happened. Let a whole army of hornets assail her, they'd count as so many pinpricks compared to the pain she carried in her heart.

Too much time had elapsed since the morphine came to her, promising deliverance. Printed on the label was an expiration date, now two months past. Had the drug lost its potency, or did she have a grace period? There was not a soul to ask. Even had there been a Quanah Avenue and a Rexall drugstore somewhere along that avenue and a potbellied old guy with a fringe of white hair at the counter at the rear of the store offering help—even then, you could hardly stroll in and inquire whether the medicine you held in your hand was strong enough to kill you.

No, you couldn't ask anyone. But you could check it out yourself. There was some sort of library. She'd been given information about it when she checked in: not two blocks away from the motel, and it stayed open until nine o'clock. She might find pharmaceutical information; or she might find some record of Jessie's family. Or find nothing. All she knew for certain was, she had to get out of the motel room.

Tulsa's Central Library turned out to be a substantial four-story building fronted by a broad plaza that reminded Claire of Lincoln Center. Where New York's fountain would have been, a silent circle of people stood holding candles, a dozen or so men and women and a handful of children, their somber faces flickering in the gloom. As she approached, the tallest of them brandished a fistful of flowers, oddly menacing. Someone began to hum, an Asian woman, wet cheeked, crooning something low and tuneless. Someone joined in, a mountain of a woman, sound leaking from her mouth, her feet planted wide as if at any moment the pavement might start quaking and erupt.

It was a vigil for Oklahoma City. Claire had almost forgotten. Virtually every car she passed had a yellow ribbon tied to its antenna, yet she hadn't realized, hadn't put it all together that every ribbon was a manifest prayer for the victims of the bombing.

Had Jessie been there with her, they'd have stopped and lit a candle, adding their own small offering of hope for the survivors and remembrance for the dead. A grief so raw and new deserved that acknowledgment. Claire merely straightened her shoulders and marched right past. Something odd had happened to her in the two-block walk from the motel. Her jitters had switched off, vanished, along with every other trace of feeling. As if some filtering membrane had slipped into place—or out of place—she was permitted to see and hear, but nothing else. In this breezy plaza beneath the purplish sky and rising moon, she might just as well be separated by walls and moats from those other people for all the commonality of loss she felt. Stopping to burn a candle with them would be a sham. Their life might just as well be a movie she watched on a screen, except that the illusion seemed to be not them, but

Claire herself watching them. Even her sorrow had become depthless and flat, her loss lost to her. Dumbfounding to be so suddenly relieved of pain. Or rather, bereft of pain. Lacking it, she had become the shadow of a shadow.

A cramped and slow-moving elevator took Claire up to the library's third floor reference desk. Behind the computer waited a platinum blonde who told her the library owned little in the way of medical reference—she'd do better over at the university. A large round button, red letters on a white background, was pinned to her ample bosom. It read, "Ask me about local history." To Claire, this was a directive straight from Jessie, so she asked.

Who is as lonely as a reference librarian? She took Claire by the arm. "We're a trove of local records," she said, and toured the floor, showing Claire shelves of old phone books and drawer upon drawer of newspapers, maps and archival material.

"Did you build this collection? It's amazing," said Claire. Lame, but she had to say something.

"Me? No." The blonde's plump lips making soft, plosive sounds of pleasure and deprecation. "Actually I'm an émigré from Northern California, been in Oklahoma only a little over a year. This here is my baby," she said, her arm sweeping to encompass an entire wall of wooden card-file drawers. "It's a necrology file." In the drawers was information about tens of thousands of deceased Tulsans. She'd gone back as far as the sixties she said, and would someday complete it back to the 1880s. She hoped to capture everyone who'd ever died here from the early days of "Tulsey Town" right on up to yesterday.

If there was an exact moment when Claire's reason for being in Tulsa crystallized, it was in front of this enormous card catalogue as she confronted the drawers. Still viewing herself, movie and moviegoer all in one, she discovered her first impulse was not to hunt for Amos Langley or Lula Anderson Langley. Not for a moment did she scan those middle rows looking for the *L*s. Instead she veered left to the first row, homing in on the surname of Lula's children, though without a clue whether she'd prefer finding James A. Anderson dead in the file, or whether she wanted him alive. All she knew was how willingly she'd sacrifice her morphine—her way out of this life—for the pleasure of watching Uncle Jimmy die. The realization should have shocked her, but didn't.

The drawer was missing. At a nearby table, flipping through cards, sat a shaggy man in a faded denim shirt. She sat down across from him and nodded when he glanced up.

"You waitin' for this?"

"If it has through the *A-n's* I am." She tried not to stare at the black eye patch he wore, the elastic crossing his furrowed forehead at a jaunty angle and disappearing into a snaggle of longish, graying curls. He ought to make up his mind which walking cliché he wants to be, she thought: Marlboro Man or Long John Silver.

"Well, I was about done, anyway. Tracking down an old sweetheart. You know how it is," he drawled. An honest-to-goodness, real southwestern twang, at last. *About time.* He slid the tray toward her across the table, and she got busy at once, distractedly thanking him while she fingered the cards. *Alvarez, Ames, Amsterdam.*

"This here's a great place. Know what I mean? A great resource."

"Uh-huh." *Anastasi, Anchor. Anders.*

"Found my old army buddy here."

Anderson, Horace. Anderson, Martin. She pushed the drawer back toward him. Uncle Jimmy wasn't in there.

Alive, then. He was alive, James Anderson. Well, let's call it provisionally alive: James Anderson might not be his real name. Jessie could have remembered it wrong, or disguised it, or made it up out of whole cloth, for that matter. Jessie had once mentioned Lula's failed marriage to someone before Doc, and a father Nancy Ann hardly knew; but Jessie hadn't said the father's name, not that Claire could recall. Though even if Anderson was genuine, Jimmy could have moved out of town and died elsewhere.

And even if James Anderson had up and died right here in Tulsa, as close as that YMCA flophouse she'd passed on her way over, he might not have a card in the file. Suppose he died in the 1950s, shot dead by the irate father of some poor girl, and the librarian hadn't yet gotten to his record. Or else just this morning, so very recently he wouldn't show up yet.

The patch-eyed man, seeing her gather her things, circled the table.

"Are you Tulsan?" Claire asked.

"Born and bred."

"Your name wouldn't be James Anderson, would it?"

He made a little bow, arms bent across his waist front and back. "Norman Winchester, ma'am."

"I have to go now."

He moved closer. "That buddy of mine, they gave him an autopsy, you know how it is." His stale, humid breath enveloped her.

"I have to go."

"His heart was all wore out."

She avoided the elevator, bolting for the stairs. He followed her down two flights to the main floor. In the lobby, he clutched her arm, his fingers narrow, his nails thick and yellow. "Ma'am, if you have anything you want to do, you better do it right now. Know what I mean."

"Believe me, I do."

She fled the library and hurried across the night-dimmed plaza, empty now save for hollows and echoes. He didn't trail her, but fear did. Here it was, she could feel it again, the fear dogging her every footstep. She could hear it again chittering in her ear, familiar and new. The motel marquee became her beacon, the lighted lobby her haven and her beige, unaccented room a welcoming nest. She threw herself on the bed, hugging the pillow with one hand. With the other, she grabbed the phone directory from the open cubby of the night table.

Two James Andersons were listed. On the bedside notepad Claire jotted their addresses and phone numbers, then checked under Andersen with an *e-n* in case Jessie had mistaken the spelling. No one by the name James Andersen.

She tucked the paper into a pocket of her purse. On the bed next to her, where she'd left it, lay the morphine. She buried that in the bottom of the purse and in doing so unearthed the hunting knife she'd stolen in Cincinnati. Her fingers touched its untextured solidity. She drew it out and flipped it open and stroked the smooth brow of its curving blade. Everything was falling into place.

Just after ten o'clock she turned out the light, her body heavy with exhaustion, her stomach queasy with it. Sleep came fitfully. At one in the morning she sat up and read a magazine, not taking in a single word of it. She dozed awhile, but by three thirty was wide awake again, staring up at nothing in the dark. Night thoughts: there ought to be some justice in the world, so she intended to hold this man responsible. The morphine was too iffy and way too kind. Forget the morphine. Castration with a green hunting knife—that sounded just about right. That was justice.

On the bedside clock, the red numbers crawled toward dawn.

At five she clicked the TV remote and drowsed while the morning news chewed over the grim aftermath of the bombing in Oklahoma City. Rescue teams were combing through the wrecked building, but no new survivors had been located in the past several hours. The death toll so far stood at eighty, but it could climb to twice that number in the days and weeks ahead. Rain expected, a possible hindrance to the rescue effort. Dogs were being used, a hound specially trained to search out infants. Only a handful of children had been pulled alive from the rubble of America's Kids, the day care center. A still photo flashed on the screen, brightening the room: in the brawny and impossibly tender arms of a fireman, a baby was cradled, improbably small to be dead. Claire squeezed her eyes shut and curled herself into a ball, bedcovers pulled up over her head. For all the world's misery, she thought, there had to be some reckoning. She was here to be its instrument. The warm, familiar smells of her body consoled her, and she slept.

16

From the eighth of Jessie's notebooks

The place: West Tulsa, Oklahoma
The time: December 1944

Once there was a girl named Singing Dove who was captured by the Little People on a warm spring evening when it got dark too quickly and she didn't want to leave the woods to go home for supper. The Little People were only three feet tall, but they looked like whiskery grown-ups and dressed like the Cherokee in round hats and ribbons. They took her to their cave and fed her strawberries, the reddest, juiciest, sweetest strawberries you ever tasted. The Little People danced in a circle singing pretty songs, and she ate strawberries for three years, three months and three days. When she got home and told her grandmother about it, she got sick, and three hours later she died.

    This is the story Hetty tells me at our meeting spot near the big boulder. She is breaking a quartered apple into pieces for the Little People, so they won't play any tricks on her. Ants are taking an interest, running back and forth across the fallen brown maple leaf where she sets the specks of apple. Sometimes if you're lost, she says, the Little People might help you find your way home.

I don't get it: are the Little People kind and loyal, like Americans, or treacherous and evil, like the Germans and Japanese? I don't get how they might trick you or help you, how they might give you strawberries and then make you die. Hetty says, "I think they're like white people."

I'm white, but we'll have to talk about that another time. The Boy Scouts are waiting for me.

Teddy and John Ellis have been collecting newspapers for the war effort. The Boy Scouts send them on, I don't know where to or what for, but Gramp says you need a mountain of paper to conduct a war. Old Mrs. Grayson has a barn full of *Tulsa Daily World*s and *Tribune*s, so I am going to help bring them down out of the hayloft. The old newspapers are stacked every which way higher than our heads, in long rows that curve and lean, and the air has a smell that burns my eyes and the insides of my nose.

We start carrying down piles of papers, but the piles we can manage are so small they barely make a difference. Handing the papers down, with me and John Ellis in the loft and Teddy below, doesn't work any better, so finally we decide to toss down as big a stack as all three of us can manage together, and whatever mess the papers make when they smash apart on the barn floor we'll clean up later. After a while, we go down to get some fresh air, and we have to wade through paper to get outside.

Teddy and John Ellis are going to get scout badges for their work, and of course I won't, but I don't care about a badge. It's still a good deed, and fun, besides. We stack the papers by the barn door, where sunshine has warmed a yellow space in the chilly air. Each of us grabs up a loose page, and we relax there in the light a little while, reading old news.

I find an article called "Girls Study Personality." It is from last spring, and it says each girl is responsible for her own personality, which is news to me. I know I am responsible for feeding the chickens and getting my homework done and going to sleep on time, but nobody ever said personality is one of my responsibilities. The Tulsa Girl Scouts did a whole eight-week course on Personality, What Is It?, showing how you can improve yours. I read how they studied correct foods to insure healthy teeth and hair and lovely skin; washing and setting your hair and getting it styled correctly; simple makeup techniques; posture, speech and dress, with a real fashion show at the end courtesy of Vandever's Department Store. Now scout troops around the state are asking Tulsa for outlines so their girls, too, can learn to minimize their bad points and make the most of their assets.

It makes me stop and think. I assumed people just had personalities, like Teddy has a good one and John Ellis has a peculiar one and Myra and Myrna Daley have bad ones, and that's the way the world is, and the sooner I get used to it the better. But if I am responsible, then I don't have to be who others want to make me. I can make myself who I want to be. Like the report says, I just have to figure out how to make the most of my assets, is all.

When Mr. Draper comes we stop reading and pile the stacks of newspapers in his car so he can take them to the collection point over at the old depot. We fill up the trunk and the backseat, too. Mrs. Grayson brings out some cocoa and cookies, and we don't even wash the black off our hands and faces, just eat as we are. Then we climb back up in the loft and start tossing papers again.

It takes all morning and most of the afternoon to clean everything out. We've got a contest going to see who can find the oldest paper. I fish around until I find a *Tulsa Tribune* I figure nobody can beat, dated June 2, 1921. Mr. Draper makes five trips to the depot—or maybe six, everybody loses count. As we start loading the car for Mr. Draper's final go-round, Teddy is trailing me by a good four years. John Ellis isn't even in the running. He lost interest after finding a front-page story about Nazi troops marching into Austria, dated March 13, 1938. At the last minute Teddy comes up with a *Tulsa Daily World* that's been stuffed into a hole in the barn floor, dated May 21, 1916. So Teddy wins, but Mr. Draper says we all did such a good job, we can each have the paper we found as a prize.

When I get home Grandma tells me she was looking for me, Uncle Jimmy stopped by earlier and waited awhile, then had to leave. I breathe a sigh. Like Mrs. Thompson in Sunday school says, good deeds are their own reward. Grandma tells me I look a sight and dabs at my cheeks with a damp corner of her apron. I ask her might I join the Girl Scouts.

"Whatever for?"

"To improve my personality."

"Why, Jessie, your personality is sweet as the roses in May."

I tell her no one is ever perfect and there is always room for improvement. That's what Grandma told me one day when I thought I finally set the table perfectly, so it's a good point.

"You have enough to do already."

I tell her about the personality classes that will improve my skin and hair and posture.

She says she doesn't know but I might be only a Brownie, and anyway I'm too young for those classes, I'll have to wait for that until I'm older. "No sense joining now, Jessie. It'll be years before you have to think about such things. Now, be a good girl—will you?—and bring Gramp his slippers."

A girl's personality must be like a girl's body, it develops later on. Still, I think it would be handy to join a troop, and learn first aid and earn a badge, and then I could go back to New York and take care of my mother when she is sick from diabetes.

Gramp is sitting on the davenport with his newspaper open to the farm column. I sit down and rustle my paper of June 2, 1921, folding it in half the way he does, and slapping at it. Some barn dust flies into the air. The front page says—it says a riot in Tulsa. It says houses burned to the ground, people shot, people lynched. I wonder if Gramp knows about this. White people killing colored people, and colored people trying to get out of town, trying to climb onto trains at the depot, the same depot where today the Boy Scouts have been collecting newspapers for the war effort.

I look up and start to say something, start to ask Gramp. He is sleeping, his head tilted back, breath softly whistling in and out, his paper still open in his hands. In my mind I am seeing Hetty's people, scared, running away, and lots of other people cooped up tight together behind iron bars and barbed-wire fences and high stone walls wondering what will become of them. Three days of rioting, a whole section of the city burned down, that's what the paper says. And yet I never heard tell of it. Nobody ever mentions it.

I stare at Gramp, peaceful on the black davenport, his head lolling against the wall, mouth open, his stocking feet on the floor next to the slippers I've left there. An army of white citizens, that's what the paper says. An army of white citizens marched up Greenwood Avenue to avenge the outrage against a white woman in a downtown elevator. Was Gramp in that army?

Not Gramp. I don't want to think Gramp would do that. You never can tell, though. I once thought Uncle Jimmy was my friend, and look what he does to me. But I don't want to think about that. Period.

17

Jim

Oklahoma City, Oklahoma
April 19, 1995

By the time Tripp Martinez ran into Jim, they'd both been hauling ass for way too long. Neither one was anywhere near ready to quit, although both had been told to pack it in and head home: Jim by the official rescuers who now controlled all movement at the site; Martinez by his boss, the news director at station KTBO. The networks had resumed regular broadcasting hours ago, and most of the other reporters, even the locals, had given up and left when the wind picked up and the rain began falling heavily. The area had been cordoned off a full three blocks around. Nothing much left to shoot, and not much in the way of news, either. Several hours had passed since any new survivors had been found.

It was just chance that placed Tripp six blocks away on the morning of April 19th in the truck with Teague, probably the best cameraman the station had. A total newbie, barely half a step up from intern, Tripp would never in a million years be there except that even seasoned reporters have to take time off to have babies, and Jennifer Starr was hugely pregnant.

Her beat, her cameraman, and being here, it dropped right in his lap. It was the story of the decade, and he was making the most of it, wringing it dry, interviewing anybody who would stand still long enough, though not many did. Until this encounter, Tripp's best segment had been thirty seconds with the search dog Tonto, who had obligingly sniffed Tripp's shirt cuffs and licked his hand.

He'd found Jim drinking coffee at a Red Cross station not far from the YMCA. Lanky and slow moving, the man had been so covered in dust and gore that Tripp hadn't realized his age. The rescue teams coming in were professionals, equipped with silicone masks, protective gloves, multilayered Nomex suits and fire-retardant undergarments. This guy, he was still in what was left of a flannel shirt and a pair of khakis. Just a guy who'd been happening by when the bomb blew and hung around lending a hand for oh, fourteen hours or so. His hand shook as he lifted the cup to his mouth.

"Fucking war zone," Tripp said to the man.

Jim nodded, met Tripp's eyes, then returned to his coffee. Almost as an afterthought, he said, "'Ceptin' nobody talks Italian."

Italian? A war zone to this man meant *ciao bambino*, for Chrissakes? Where did they talk fucking Italian? Not Bosnia. Not Kuwait. Somalia? Wasn't that French? Anyway, too recent for this old guy. Must be longer ago. Not Panama, not Lebanon, not Vietnam or even Korea. The only American war zone Tripp could think of where the paisanos talked Italian—was Italy. Wasn't that so? Wasn't it? And if so, then here was the human-interest story he'd been waiting for, the story that would distill and frame those breathtaking acts of generosity he'd witnessed all day, the spectacle of sheer nerve he wanted to report.

It took persistence, persuasion, and finally out-and-out pleading to get the old geezer to agree to the interview, but in the end he'd let them clean him up a bit and give him a fresh shirt to wear. They set up in front of the blown-out window of a toy store, everything in shambles, except for one shelf of smiling, button-eyed teddy bears seated all in a row, peppered in glints of glass and fine, silky dust but otherwise unharmed. What a backdrop. News director was going to cream his pants when he saw it.

Teague counted down, signaled him, and Tripp announced, "For the past half century, Americans lived uneasily with the dark dread of nuclear annihilation. When the Berlin Wall came down, and the Soviet Union disintegrated, we celebrated the demise of our fear of mushroom clouds. But yesterday's blast here in Oklahoma City has shown us a more insidious threat arising: the spread of terrorism through the heartland of America. Death arrives not from a sophisticated missile descending on us out of the sky, but from an ordinary van parked seemingly at random on a downtown street."

"Cut!" the cameraman screamed. "Tripp, what do you think you're doing?"

"Roll the camera, Teague. I'm doing my story."

"Nuclear war?"

"Context, Teague. Humanity has always been capable of random acts of violence. This guy—" he threw his arm across Jim's shoulder. "This guy stands for all those people coming in here doing random acts of kindness, random acts of courage. It's a great story, Teague, but it needs context."

Teague sighed. Waste of tape, but it wasn't his call. "We're rolling," he said.

"Two adults and one child are alive tonight because of the man standing next to me. Countless others have been helped by his efforts and the efforts of other volunteers here at the blast site. Jim is a Tulsa boy, a homegrown hero who fifty years ago landed with the U.S. Army on the soft underbelly of Europe. He showed his courage against the Nazi oppressors there. Today, this winner of two Purple Hearts and a Silver Star has shown that time doesn't dim courage, or honor, or self-sacrifice. Fifty years ago, Jim risked his young life to save the lives of five of his platoon brothers. Not one of them was yet out of his teens. Today, he has done something even more extraordinary. Today he has risked himself hour after hour, fourteen hours straight, for people he doesn't even know.

"Jim, what made you decide to do it?"

"I didn't decide. Just did it."

"You could have turned around and walked the other way."

"Nope. Not with them babies under that heap I couldn't."

And so on. Not a terrible interview, all in all, the cameraman thought when it was done. Maybe he'd offer the cub reporter some advice. "If you're ever going to make it in this business," he said, "you'd better learn to identify the person you're talking to."

The gleam on the kid's perpetual grin dimmed. "Didn't I call Jim by name? Sure I did."

"Yeah, but you never said his *last* name."

18

More from the eighth of Jessie's notebooks

The place: West Tulsa, Oklahoma
The time: December 1944

When all is said and done, Grandma doesn't need any whistle to call her. I can help her listen for the water to boil in the teakettle, and I can make her some other present for Christmas in shop class.

I ask Miss Forrest for the patterns for a corner shelf. She says it's a good idea, and anyone else who has finished his or her clothes hook can do one, too. So I get to make something useful for Grandma, and it comes out real nice. I put on six coats of varnish, sanding lightly in between each coat. Miss Forrest gives me an A because I never once break a coping saw blade, and I never split off the edge of the wood. I never ever drip glue the way Margie Hollis does, and I even think to drill the holes for hanging the shelf by putting one sidepiece on top of the other and drilling both at the same time so they'll match.

Gramp sets up the tree in the living room corner. Grandma and I are kept busy in the kitchen baking up boxes and boxes of Christmas cookies. I want to send a box to New York for my mother, but Grandma says it'd all be crumbs by the time it got there, and anyway, Mama can't eat them what with her diabetes

and all, so it'd just be a waste of time and money and good food.
I know I shouldn't let on, but to myself I confide that Grandma
is just covering up a secret: that my mother is coming to Tulsa
for Christmas so she'd never get the cookies anyway. I figure the
thing about the cookies crumbling is a little white lie to keep up
the surprise. I know the cookies wouldn't crumble, because the
German cookies my mother sent me that time all stayed whole.
Besides, at Thanksgiving I made a wish on the wishbone, and it
broke in my favor.

My mother couldn't come for Thanksgiving because she
had practically just been here for my birthday and couldn't
possibly do the trip again. Uncle Cubby and Aunt Cissie were
supposed to come, but Aunt Cissie was barfing and couldn't
even think about food. I wanted Gramp to take her some medicine from the Rexall to make her well, but he said, "She's just
going to keep on doing it until she's good and ready to stop.
It's because of expecting those twins."

"Doesn't she want the babies?" I asked Grandma.

"Why of course she does, Jessie, what an awful thing to
say."

So it was just Grandma and Gramp and Uncle Jimmy
and Aunt Nedra and me sitting down to dinner. Gramp carved
the turkey and gave me the wishbone, and afterwards, while I
patted the wishbone dry between folds of newspaper, we listened to football over the radio. Then I scrubbed my fingers so
as to get a good, unslippery purchase on my end. Gramp won't
allow any choking up, and he pulls hard. Our arms snaked in
the air, and the wishbone shivered, but I just held my breath
and kept concentrating on my wish that everybody would
come for Christmas and my mother would tell me she's taking me to live with her forever in a new home, one with red
Chinese wallpaper and lots of bookcases and a tall Victrola
in the middle of the room. And then it snapped my way, and
now sure enough, just like I wished, everybody is coming on
Christmas Eve—Aunt Cissie and Uncle Cubby and Sammy
and even some cousins of Grandma's from down south—and if
they can all come, my mother must be coming, too. Best of all,

Uncle Jimmy and Aunt Nedra aren't coming. They've dropped off their presents, all wrapped and ribboned, and gone up to Nedra's mother in Kansas.

I go straight home after school every day to help Grandma get the house ready. Grandma huffs and puffs while we wax all the furniture and whip up mounds of mashed potatoes to go with the candied ham. I watch little droplets bead on her upper lip, worrying how many of those drops will fall and ruin all our work, but she catches them in time every time with a swift back of her arm across her mouth.

Two days before Christmas I get home from school, and Grandma is looking cheery. She grabs me up and hugs me tight and says, singsongy like when kids at the playground do ring-around-a-rosie, "I've got some new-ews. Guess what's my new-ews. New-ews, good new-ews."

Ha! I knew it! "Mommy's coming!" I spin out of her arms and start jumping up and down. "Yippee. Hooray! Mommy's coming!" My wish is coming true, all of it, and we're going to have a Victrola in our living room so tall I'll need a step-ladder to get my records stacked and turn them over. I start my own singsong. "Mommy's home for Christmas! Mommy's home for Christmas. Yippee, hooray!" I'm jumping and singing so hard I don't see Grandma's face when it changes, just afterward when it's already sagged and closed in on itself so tight I stop dead still.

"No, Jessie. Oh, I'm sorry, hon. No, it's not your mama. It's your uncle Jimmy." With the corner of her apron she wipes the wet away from my cheeks. "I'm sorry. I should have realized. He and Aunt Nedra are coming after all, and they'll be here tomorrow to have Christmas with us. Now, isn't that something?" She jiggles herself up and down again. I guess she can't help it.

Hetty has a charm string. I find her at the Eugene Field Elementary School playground sitting in the center swing. She can always be counted on to turn up when I need her. The charm string is a long cord, longer than her arm, almost as long as from her waist to the ground. She is quiet like the nuns at Monte Cassino fingering their rosaries. She shows me a glass button that looks clear except if you wiggle it in the sunlight, where it twinkles rainbows. It came off of Hetty's great-grand-mother's wedding dress and is the first thing on the charm string, proving the string is older than her mama or even her gran, though they have added to it. All along the cord are other buttons and charms and trinkets that the women in her family have saved for her. There's a teeny pair of moccasins the size of my thumb, made of red and yellow beads no bigger than John Ellis's nose freckles. It comes from Hetty's gran when she was a little girl on her way to Oklahoma from North Carolina. She got sick and everyone thought she was going to die. She lived, but her brother died. And then an old Potawatomi woman gave her the little moccasins to keep her company on the trail and bring her good luck because she didn't die and had good medicine.

Someday the charm string will be Hetty's, but she's not even supposed to take it out of the house, much less let somebody else touch it. She lets me, though, after I promise to be very very careful. There are three round wooden flower buttons with three rows of petals, and you can run your fingernail around inside between the petals. Someone carved them as a gift when Hetty's mama was born. There used to be a fourth button, but they put it on Hetty's baby sweater, and it fell off and got lost.

Grandma keeps a box of buttons, a tin box that says Talequah Boot Company on it in green and gold, but hers are not story buttons, just some old strays that might come in handy sometime.

The swings are no fun, I've forgotten my mittens and the chains are cold. Instead, we fool around at the seesaws. We ride one for a while and then we try to get the board to float parallel to the ground and not tip one way or the other, the two of us moving forward and back on our seats, but we can't get it right. I practice walking the seesaw. You start at the bottom, where everything feels solid under your feet, but as you heel-to-toe your way up, it starts falling away under you, and you have to edge along sideways and spread your legs out for balance. I'm real careful balancing there right in the middle, with one foot planted on either side of the bar, but not planted too hard. If the thing tips, you have to be light footed and ready to jump.

When the air around us has turned blue, Hetty says it's time to go home. I don't know who is more surprised at what I say next. "Not me. Nobody knows where I am, and I'm not going home."

"Pshaw, Jessie. It's Christmas Eve."

"So what? I don't care." To show her how much I don't care, I plop down on the bare ground and sit there cross-legged, goose bumps all over.

"You gonna stay out all night?"

I shrug.

"Santy Claus won't find you here."

"Neither will my uncle."

"Your uncle? The man at the watermelon shack? What's your problem with him?"

I try to say. I really try, but all I can do is stare at the ground.

She hunkers down beside me and takes my hand. "You'll work it out."

I pull my hand from hers and slap her, hard across her cheek. Tears start in her eyes, but she doesn't move. Me, I'd slap back, or anyway run off and never be friends again, but Hetty says, "What you want to hit me for like that?"

"Because you're a liar, that's what. I'll never work it out. I can't."

Hetty gets up and goes over to the swing where she's hung her charm string. I kind of follow her, but kind of don't. "Tell you what my gran tells me."

I slash long, hard marks in the dirt with my shoe. Why should I care what some old washerwoman says? Crazy old washerwoman and her stupid buttons. I toe five in a row, six. The ground is cold.

"You want to hear or don't you?"

I mutter something that maybe sounds like guess so.

"Gran tells me, 'Hetty, you're a smart girl. God give you a good brain. You got a problem, figure your way out of it. All that energy you spend telling yourself you can't is pure wasted. Child, you can.'"

"Not true."

Someone is coming toward us across the playground. It's nearly full dark now, but I can recognize John Ellis from the funny way he has of running, pumping his arms with his elbows almost straight, his fists down by his sides.

Hetty says, "Jessie, it's pure fact. You can do anything you want to do."

"Not true at all. I can't take out my own appendix, can I?"

"You want to do that?"

I don't have to answer, because John Ellis is here, all heated up and breathless. "Jessie, your grandma says for you to come on home right now." He looks right at Hetty but doesn't seem to notice her, which is okay with me because I am so mad at her I could spit. I don't know why I ever played with her or listened to her stupid stories or so much as gave her the time of day.

"Jessie? She says come right away. No lollygagging."

Hetty turns and walks away from us, to a place on the far side of the seesaws where the boys sometimes squat in the dust and play marbles. She stands there, the charm string looped a couple of times around her neck, and stares at me, like that night last summer at the watermelon shack when I saw her for the first time on the opposite side of the invisible color line. "You can," she mouths, and I turn away.

Maybe she wouldn't be so quick to say *child, you can* if it could be that night last summer all over again. I'd make her come with me, invisible line or no, and take her out back where I got caught alone.

Out back was a bathroom with a sign on the door. The door was lit by a weak overhead bulb, and the sign said Lavatory Whites Only. A narrow path led you there, and after dark the cornfields and pasture beyond were like ink. The moon wasn't up, and the stars looked pale and far away. With a full moon, of course, I could have seen into the cornfield plain enough. But on this night when I came out of the door, I had to stand at the edge of the yellow pool of light and wait for my eyes to adjust to the darkness.

"Fancy meeting you here," a voice said, and I jumped about a mile. "Did I scare you?"

"No, sir. Or maybe just a little. I didn't think anybody was here."

He touched my cheek with his thumb. "You don't ever have to be a-scared of me, sweet pea. You know that, don't you?"

I nodded, shifting my face away from his rubbing.

"You are looking mighty pretty this evening," he said.

A mosquito buzzed in the air between us. Before it could land on me, I reached up and clapped it between my hands. "Ha!" I said. One less mosquito in the world to give me trouble.

Uncle Jimmy squatted down. His hands formed a little chapel above his bent knees. There were dark rings under the arms of his shirt and a small circle of wet in the center of his chest. His top button was open, and I could see the damp curls of hair glistening under the light. He didn't try to touch me again. "Look at you," he said. "Just look at you, how purely gorgeous you are. And you don't even know it, do you? Heck, you're not even trying."

I wondered if I could say something about getting back to the watermelon, or if that would earn me a reprimand.

"Where did you come from?"

I twiddled a loose strand of hair. Was he starting a new game? Was it a riddle? *Where did you come from? From my mother and father.*

"Wherever did you come from?" he repeated.

"New York City?" I said, though I didn't think Uncle Jimmy meant that, either.

He laughed. "Whoo-ee. You are a precious wonder, you know that? In all this screaming, mean world, show me anything as pure and sweet as you are. Not by a long shot. Not by a country mile."

"I think I hear John Ellis calling," I said, which I hadn't, but I yelled out, like answering him, "I'm here, John Ellis."

"And you never have looked at another man, have you?" He put his big hands on my shoulders and drew me toward him. "Want to know why?"

Automatically, I said, "Why?" The heat of his palms and the wetness leaked through the thin cotton of my dress.

"Because nobody else will ever love you better—"

"Jessie?" It was John Ellis, interrupting. He'd come looking for me, after all. "Jessie, where are you?"

Quicker than you can say Jack Robinson, Uncle Jimmy turned me so my back was against him and his loud breath was next to my ear. "Jessie, see that sign on the door? What does it say?"

Did he think I needed glasses? Did he think I couldn't read? I said, "Lavatory. Whites Only."

"Whites only," he repeated, like it was part of a lesson he'd been giving me or a question he'd been in the middle of answering. "You know what that means, John Ellis?"

"It means whites only." John Ellis was looking sour. He doesn't like it when he thinks someone is talking down to him.

I felt the scratch of Uncle Jimmy's nod. "No coloreds, no Chinamen, no red men, no kikes. Just us white folks."

He couldn't mean it. "No Indians?" I said.

"Nope."

He sounded like he meant it, and John Ellis looked like Gramp in church, not expecting anything interesting to happen until the preaching stops. I was like the child in the story watching the emperor strut by in nothing but his birthday suit. "No Jews?"

"Read the sign," said the emperor.

I knew I had him now, because I knew it wasn't so simple, never mind the sign. I am part Cherokee Indian and part Jewish, too, but Grandma says I am white as Wonder Bread, not like that Mr. Shapiro at the Jew store across the river where Gramp buys feed. Mr. Shapiro has sad raccoon eyes and is all Jew. I said, "Says you, smarty-pants. I beg to differ with you, because—"

"Jessie, that's enough now. I swear you'd drive a body to drink." Sounding just like Grandma.

"But I—"

"You and John Ellis go get yourselves another slice of watermelon. Do something useful with that mouth of yours."

"But you—"

"Go on. Off with you. Last one there is a rotten egg."

Now, as I cut across the grass trailing John Ellis, he is talking about Christmas, but I don't listen. I don't want to think about Christmas. I think about being colored. I think about being Hetty. It occurs to me maybe being colored is something like walking a seesaw. Start at the white end like me, add in some Indian, add in some Jew, you're still white. Somewhere along, though, there's a point where a person adds in a smidgen too much Indian or Jew or Chinese or Negro and tips suddenly to black. If a part-Indian colored person like Hetty, starting from the other end, added in some Jew and lots of white, I wonder if the seesaw could tip the other way and the person get to be white. One time I heard Uncle Jimmy tell Gramp those Negro troops in combat fought like the dickens, good as whites, no lie. Well, what if you were real heedful, could you get a perfect balance in the middle of the seesaw and not be white or black? If you could do that, I wonder what you would be. Once upon a time I might have asked Uncle Jimmy, but not anymore. Not ever again.

19

Claire

Far from being out in the country, Monte Cassino was located at a busy city corner. The school had the circular entrance Jessie had described, lawns and farther over to the side, the grotto: a scattering of crocuses and an appealing statue of the Virgin, all backed by an arching stone wall. No children at play, nor was Claire able to conjure a pigtailed girl climbing in new shoes. A new brick school building stood to Claire's left, architecturally matched to the original stone building beyond the curve of the drive. She'd come looking for something stark and severe. What she found was altogether warmer, more gracious, more human in scale. There were gardens in the back, a small greenhouse and, despite the hectic intersection hidden just beyond the line of evergreens, a pleasant calm about the place. She'd only meant to spend an hour or so walking the grounds until the end of office hours for James Anderson, DDS, but she found herself drawn inside, seeking help at the visitor's desk.

Earlier in the day, she'd followed her map northward into Greenwood and parked across the street from a ranch house with forest-green shutters and a split rail fence, clematis vine in purple bud all over it. There was no answer when she rang the bell. Fifteen minutes later she rang again and tried knocking at the door, which was dandelion yellow. For the next three hours from her car, she watched a door stolidly not budge, watched nobody going in or out. Dark-skinned passersby glanced doubtfully at her, a middle-aged white woman loitering in a parked car smack in the middle of Tulsa's African-American neighborhood.

Why on earth would Uncle Jimmy live in the middle of a black neighborhood, especially this one? The smidgen Claire knew of Greenwood's history occurred in 1921, when a rumor ripped through Tulsa that a colored man had attacked a young white woman in an elevator downtown. The alleged sexual assault never in fact happened, but the report of it was sufficient for a mob to burn Greenwood down, murder over a dozen African-Americans and send tens of dozens more scrambling to find safety elsewhere.

Bottom line, Claire knew she was a fool to spend all morning in Greenwood waiting to confront the James A. Anderson who lived behind that yellow door. But only two James Andersons resided in all of Tulsa, this one and the dentist, and she wouldn't rule either of them out without confronting them face-to-face. Forget probabilities. She was the instrument of justice in the world for Jessie. Her objectives: to search out Uncle Jimmy wherever he might be, and to kill him.

About noon, a green Ford pulled into the driveway. The driver was in his midthirties, tall and stocky, a light-skinned African-American. In response to her inquiry, he told her he wasn't James A. Anderson, but Earl. James was his father. Claire had a moment of wild hope. Had the grossly improbable actually happened? Had Uncle Jimmy divorced Nedra, married a black woman and fathered this son?

Earl led her to the garden out back, where his father had been working all morning. James Anderson of Greenwood was putting in a row of kale, and he was very black indeed.

Nice work, Sherlock.

Monte Cassino had yearbooks going all the way back. Claire singled out 1944 and scoured the faces of third and fourth graders seated in their rows, hands folded on varnished desktops, happy girls and boys in neat sailor suits, as winsome a school uniform as Claire had ever seen. In one of the notebooks, isn't Jessie ashamed not to have a uniform to wear? She doesn't mention boys in her class, though. In fact, she says something about being free to climb the monkey bars, no pests around peering up under her skirt.

"Did the children attend class together, coed I mean? Did they play and have meals together? Boys and girls together?" *Me and Mamie O'Rourke. Shut up, Claire, and let the nice nun give you her answer.*

The nice nun was going way out of her way to help Claire find any trace of Jessie. On short notice—on no notice at all, actually—she had pulled out the yearbooks and class lists, names, addresses, contacts back to when the school had been founded in the twenties. Now she smiled in answer to Claire's question. Originally a school for girls, Monte Cassino had been ahead of its time, she said. They'd pioneered coeducation in the 1940s, admitting boys as day students starting in the primary grades. In Jessie's class, Claire reasoned, it was possible that there were no boys. So far, so good, but wouldn't she have seen them on the playground and in the lunchroom? The nun said boys did everything along with the girls; except sleep, of course. The residence hall was girls only.

Claire said, "May I see the dorms? Are they open?" The sister's laughter was bell-like and cheerful, as if she loved laughing for the pleasure of it, as someone else might love dancing or cooking or poking around antique shops. She laughed now because there were no dorms, never had been, if by dorms you meant large rooms housing any number of girls. The bedrooms she showed Claire along a quiet, curving corridor accommodated just two girls each, or three at most—homey, sun-tinted nooks, with a closet and dresser for each child and long windows overlooking the gardens. Claire had never been to boarding school, but she was sure that if she had, she'd never forget these rooms, not even decades later.

Downstairs again, in an old-fashioned sitting room—pale-green broadloom carpet, mahogany table, paisley sofa, loden wing chairs, fireplace—they spent another hour poring through old documents. Not a single hint emerged that Jessie had ever been a student at Monte Cassino. They tried Jessica Langley, Jessica Desmond, Jessica Friedman, even Jessica Anderson. They looked for the name of a contact person, Amos and Lula Langley, or Nancy Ann Anderson, or Nancy Ann Desmond, or Nancy Ann Friedman, or even James Anderson. No luck, not in 1944. Not in 1943 or '45 or '42.

"If she started midyear, say October, and left before the end of the term, say April, you would have a record of her?"

It was so long ago, fifty years, the sister couldn't be sure. Rosters were made before the beginning of the school year, class photos taken usually in the first few weeks. Claire scrutinized the yearbooks again, searching the images for Jessie's steady gaze, her straight-cutting eyebrows, her crooked smile.

"It's very dedicated of you to do this for a friend," said the nun. "Coming all the way out from New York."

Keep it smooth, Claire told herself. Keep it light. "Yes, well. I thought I might publish her recollections as a memoir." Some memoir: graphic acts of perversion as told by the victimized child.

"A woman on our board was a resident here in the war years. Would you like me to give her a call? See if she remembers your friend?"

"I'd appreciate it," Claire said and returned to the photographs. She wanted to believe in Jessie.

The nun reached someone at the other end of the line, had a brief conversation in which Jessie's name figured, caught Claire's eye, shook her head and replaced the receiver in its cradle. "I'm sorry," she said with a regret so deep and sincere that Claire almost apologized in return, almost apologized for Jessie. Was any of it real? Had the whole story been made up one dark and stormy night, a fistful of stereotypes fished randomly out of a sack like Scrabble tiles and lined up all in a row? The more she thought about it, the phonier it all seemed. And yet the grotto was there, just as Jessie described it, albeit smaller and cozier than it must have appeared to a child in a pair of unscuffed Mary Janes.

Nothing was turning out the way Claire expected. So little of what she found matched what Jessie had written. So little of what Jessie had written could be confirmed. She had to consider the possibility that Uncle Jimmy was a delusion on Jessie's part. Or a fiction? But why? Jessie was not one to attempt the Great American Novel. She almost never read fiction. She read books about film, because she loved the movies. And otherwise she read books about bridges: suspension bridges, rope bridges, covered bridges, ancient Chinese bridges—how they were built, how they were used, why they failed. She read about the people who designed them and the people who built them. When *The Bridges of Madison County* came out, she'd picked it up at the library—and tossed it away in disgust the instant she realized it was fiction. Brooklyn was bridge heaven, of course, but any bridge would do where she could cross—including those little garden arches that spanned nothing but an ersatz stream of stone. She'd walk out to the middle just the same, lean over the rail and stare down.

If only Claire could find a bridge to her now.

The notebooks ought to be her bridge. Jessie had left them for her where Claire would find them. It would be better if the things they told were not true. Yet they couldn't be fiction. Jessie didn't do fiction. Jessie was the most straightforward, honest person Claire had ever known, and with a phenomenal memory for detail. Maybe she was good at remembering things because she had to keep straight so many schools she'd attended, so many places she'd lived.

But sometimes she forgot things, and she could be wrong sometimes.

Wrong, yes—but not delusional. Not crazy. Jessie didn't make up stories about herself.

Yet didn't she see, in the kids she saved, what wasn't actually there to be seen? Maybe that was why she was able to save so many of them. Take a kid who was a total fucked-up disaster, who would as soon cut you as look at you—Jessie saw a scared little waif with a talent for macramé or field hockey. Sure, she'd bring about miracles. But how much was it bringing out what was in the kid, and how much because the kid would do anything to be somebody in her eyes?

Questions and more questions, and no good answers. To think you could put a lifetime's experience under your belt and still be so full of doubt. Claire was a numbers person: things added up or they didn't, proofed out or didn't. This inconclusiveness was driving her mad, and the key to it all and the cause of it all—was that bastard Uncle Jimmy.

———

The office of James Anderson, DDS, was near the university in a row of garden apartments, the last unit on the left. She got there at four and stood outside until four twenty-five waiting for his office staff to leave. *But Uncle Jimmy, a dentist?* He could have gone to college on the GI Bill. After the war, lots of veterans did. Claire's stomach turned picturing that creep's big-knuckled hands in people's mouths.

Why wasn't he retired, at his age? He didn't seem the type to keep working for the joy of it. Drinking for the joy of it, yes. Drilling and filling, no.

She had a neighbor in the apartment below who'd never retired. At age ninety-two, Mr. Fritzhand was still practicing law. He left for the office at ten every morning, battered briefcase in hand, and returned at four thirty every afternoon. Imagine wanting to work at his age and not even needing the money. Claire was envious of people who loved their work that much. Mostly, she disbelieved it when someone professed that kind of devotion.

But Mr. Fritzhand was the real thing. Every penny he earned as an attorney was donated to medical research. His wife had died of Parkinson's disease; now his daughter suffered from it, and he was hoping to fund a cure. You could say he went to the office every day out of loneliness, or out of an obsession to defeat this awful malady. You might be right. Nonetheless, he genuinely loved his work. That much Claire knew from the way he talked about the law. When things had been touch and go—the chemotherapy not yet shrinking Jessie's cancer and everyone worried that it never would—Mr. Fritzhand had sat by Jessie's bed, a short, round-bottomed man with a head of shoe polish-black hair, tangled white eyebrows and jutting nose, and regaled her with courtroom stories. She accused him of inventing them on the spot: they were far too juicy to be true, she said.

They were far too juicy to be anything but true, he countered.

Then it must be you, she said, who's too good to be true.

That amused him. "I've been accused of many things, my dear, but never before of being imaginary."

"Don't you laugh. I had an imaginary friend once. Saved my sanity. Damn near saved my life."

Worn and withered, she looked old enough to be Claire's mother. Mr. Fritzhand took her papery hand in his. "Jessie, what do you need to be able to die at ease?"

Claire felt herself blanch, but Jessie didn't hesitate. "I want Claire to find peace." Remembering now, Claire felt a hot rush of anger rising in her chest. Peace? What peace could there be in life for her once Jessie was gone?

As soon as Jessie got well, they'd started envisioning their retirement. Claire was going to master the art of French cooking; Jessie would learn to make Windsor chairs. The rain forest awaited their footsteps, and the Imperial City. Planning for it was such fun that Claire was able to wipe from her mind the time when dying of cancer had looked like the thing ahead, when Claire could only flap her hands if Jessie so much as mentioned death: as if an acrid smoke were stinking up the room and a lot of brisk arm waving would make it go away. She put that terrible time behind her, believing in the adventure ahead—and then came the car crash.

Peace. She would find peace when she got Dr. James Anderson, DDS, alone in his own dentist chair. One of those luxurious chaise longue models, she imagined, vinyl covered in some designer color like raspberry sorbet. Just her and him and the raspberry chair, a complementary garish pink print on the walls casting a blush across his wolfish face. And the drill, of course, not forgetting the gleaming stainless-steel drill.

Little Jessie? she'd say, Uncle Jimmy strapped into his fancy chair, undulant and helpless under the glare of the light. It's the scene from the film *Marathon Man.* She gives his bloodless cheek a playful slap. *Remember her? Your sweet pea?*

He denies it.

Am I touching a nerve, Uncle Jimmy? He denies everything.

Ah, but the body remembers what the mind will not. This molar, perhaps, will remember. The drill throbs in her hand. *Zzzzzzt. Zzzzzzzzzztt.*

An electronic bell rang when she pushed open the door. She entered a small waiting room furnished with three chairs, a magazine table and a tropical-fish tank. No one was there. The reception desk was empty.

When he heard the bell, Dr. James Anderson was closing up for the day. He had let Marta leave early, something about her babysitter taking ill. Whoever had come in would have to wait. A salesman, no doubt, or a patient who had the wrong day marked on the calendar. He wondered why he bothered to print up appointment cards. Patients never looked at them.

The floor creaked. He swung around and, sickle probes in hand, was startled by a middling-aged woman standing just behind him. She looked like she was sizing him up.

"James Anderson?" she said. She had feathery brown hair and a pretty, bow-shaped mouth in a moon-shaped face, and her shadowed eyes were stony.

What she saw was a pair of wire-rimmed glasses that magnified leonine eyes and an old-style dentist's blouse that buttoned at the shoulder, with a high collar and loose sleeves. It was snowy, like his crew cut, and as crisp as if it had been bought yesterday. He might have stepped out of a dentifrice commercial, circa 1960. A name tag in the shape of smiling teeth was affixed to his chest pocket.

"Dr. Jim?" she read aloud.

"The same," he said. "And you are—?"

I am your nemesis. If he could be taken at all, it would have to be off guard. He was close to six feet tall and a good 170 pounds. But she was aware of something awry.

She was staring at him, frowning. He prompted her. "Having a problem with a tooth, eh?"

Something in the way he talked. He had no reason to affect foreignness, having no idea who she was or why she'd come. "Are you—" Her hand flew to her throat.

He touched her elbow, radiating a confidence that was purely for show. The woman looked mad as a cut snake. "You know, I was just finishing up here."

"I—this is a mistake," Claire said, backing away. "I'm sorry." And she fled from James Anderson, DDS, because he wrenched his vowels like an Aussie, and no one talks like an Aussie unless he is one. At her back the closing door mocked her. *Ding-dong-ding* it singsonged: *down un-der.*

For the longest time she huddled in the car, fending off tears that rose in great, choking spasms, fighting them with clenched fists that she rammed against the seat and the dashboard. The sun had begun to set by the time she gained control enough to start up the car and get herself back downtown. She parked in the motel's lot and, still unsteady, stalked grim faced toward the library. She was beyond angry, beyond heartsick. Jessie had to show her something. Jessie had to show her something now, or Claire was through.

The Rexall where Gramp worked had a listing on Quanah Avenue. There it was, there in black and white, printed in the book for the year 1947. And Gramp, too, he was listed: Langley, Amos, 2212 S Phoenix. One narrow line in an old phone book plucked from a stack of old phone books in an out-of-the-way corner of the third floor of the Tulsa Central Library. She ran her finger under it and in a circle around it. A line in a phone book, an intimation of flesh and blood and being.

She looked up the next-door neighbors, the Ellises. There were five listings under that name in the 1947 book. Hiram Ellis lived at 2210 South Phoenix. He must be John Ellis's father, the guy who Jessie said could bull's-eye a spittoon from anywhere in the room. In the *D*s next, searching out Jessie's friend Teddy, she found six Drapers, two of them in West Tulsa. Surely one of them had to be Teddy's father. Heartened by this accumulation of data validating Jessie's story, she turned finally to the crux of the hunt: the *A*s.

James Anderson was not listed. Nor the alternate spelling, James Andersen. Nedra either, not in the 1947 book, and not in the current one. *Show me, Jessie.*

On the library's computer, the Internet turned up ninety-four James Andersons in Oklahoma, more than two hundred thirty in Texas, in Kansas forty-nine. She gaped at the outsized numbers, which didn't even include any J. Andersons, or Jimmy Andersons, or Jimmie Andersons. If Jessie had any hand in this, she was showing Claire a fool's errand. The man (supposing he existed) could be anywhere. Worse, even if she could spend the rest of her life tracking down every James, J., Jimmy and Jimmie Anderson in the whole United States, she might come up empty. Think how many more might be unlisted, or in old age homes. In hospitals. In prison. *Yes, oh yes,* she could hope for that: Uncle Jimmy, somebody's little sex slave in a jail cell somewhere, learning each and every night what rape is all about.

She rubbed her sandy eyes, irritated by the flickering CRT. She was tired and hungry and just about ready to give up. There might be other, better ways of finding this man, but she couldn't come up with a single one, unless you counted those two boys, Jessie's friends. John Ellis or Teddy Draper, they might conceivably know where Uncle Jimmy could be found. Her fingers hovered over the keys, holding back. It was a long shot, in any case, but what if she got their phone numbers, called each of them up, then suffered the pain of explaining herself—only to hear that they didn't remember any uncles? What if Jessie's tale should prove untrue by their recollection? Well, of course recollection can be faulty. Whose, though—theirs or Jessie's? On the one hand, Jessie molested by her uncle; on the other, Jessie bedeviled with false memory. Was it any wonder Claire quailed at having to choose between the two? Both were unspeakable.

But she'd come to a dead end, and those two men were her last, best shot. So she made her reluctant fingers type in the searches, but neither John Ellis nor Theodore Draper had a local listing.

Claire crossed the motel lobby to the restaurant. Another first: dining out alone. No, not dining. The word reminded her of the time they'd stopped after work, she and Jess, for a quick bite before an early evening movie at the mall; and of the college kid in a McDonald's cap and yellow apron who took their order. Assembling their Big Macs, their fries and Cokes, the kid inquired, "Will you be dining here, ladies?"

Merriment shot between them. *Dining?* "Would that one could," Jessie said, befuddling the kid, who couldn't parse out whether that meant a tray or a paper bag.

Claire viewed the word differently now. Eating together, never mind where, never mind what—most certainly constituted dining in luxury. Eating alone added up to something else entirely, and eating *out* alone was not to be calculated without dread. There'd be a roomful of coupled-up people, animated, happy. There'd be her, crushingly lonely in the haze of self-satisfied, oblivious chatter. She'd peck glumly at an unpalatable meal while life effervesced around her, beyond a scrim discernible only to her.

Claire was shown to a table, and when the waiter took her order, the room was nearly empty. Claire ate steadily. Nothing tasted good, but at least sitting by herself was okay, not half as bad as she'd feared. Steak sandwich medium rare, side salad with Italian dressing, peach ice cream: it was all so much cardboard topped with Styrofoam. She ate it to keep up her strength, though for the life of her she didn't know why bother. She told herself she'd need strength if ever she came face-to-face with Uncle Jimmy. A big *if* that was.

After the meal, back in her room, the TV aired more news of the Oklahoma City bombing: the search-and-rescue operation was proceeding, though hopes were dim that anyone else could be found alive. When the Red Cross called for blood donors, volunteers lined up for blocks. She went to the window and gazed down at the parking lot. Wasn't anything happening anywhere else in the world? Was there no other news? To judge from this anchor and his reporters in the field, all news, like all politics, had to be local. On the monitor Tulsans could watch a crawling line of cars three blocks long delivering gear to the site. Piles of raincoats and boots filled the screen, piles of blankets, a row of wheelbarrows, one of them loaded up with flashlights. An interview followed, some guy from the American Legion who explained in boundless detail how that organization of war veterans was helping coordinate all these donations. Claire came back to the bed and sat down. She stared openmouthed at the TV. Then she picked up the phone and asked the motel operator for the American Legion.

20

From the ninth of Jessie's notebooks

The place: West Tulsa, Oklahoma
The time: Christmas 1944

Christmas Day Grandma's distant cousins La Junta and Pedro arrive. They give me a cowgirl lariat because they're from Texas, which must also be why they're called distant cousins, because they came a long distance to get here. Pedro's name is pronounced Pee-dro, so it's hard not to giggle when I say it. La Junta is old like Grandma. Below her real chin she has two other chins that shake when she talks. She likes what I'm wearing, a brand-new kelly-green corduroy ice-skating outfit my father sent me. I don't know how to ice-skate. La Junta says I should learn.

Sammy brings me an autograph book tied up in gold ribbon. The leather is maroon, and the pages inside are creamy, with gold edges all around. Sammy says Doc picked it out for him, so I give Gramp a kiss, too. Then Sammy borrows Gramp's Parker pen to write on the first page in spidery script:

Merry Xmas 1944
Samuel Wellington Birmingham III.

I never had an autograph book before. I hand it to La Junta, and she writes *Yours till the butterflies.*

Pedro tells me he knows Cherokee and is writing an old Cherokee saying for me. I don't know if I can believe him. *Sit on the tack of success, and you will surely rise* doesn't sound anything like Indian to me. Word of honor, he says, trust him. I don't.

Uncle Cubby and Aunt Cissie come in with armfuls of presents. I open mine while everyone is touching Aunt Cissie's belly, which is nowhere near as big as Gramp's belly. It's a cherry-red cardigan sweater Aunt Cissie knitted for me, with five red buttons down the front. It's warm and soft, and I'm wearing it when Uncle Jimmy and Aunt Nedra arrive. I'm hoping their present isn't something else to wear, because I don't want Uncle Jimmy's big hands helping me put it on. I rip the paper off and open the box, and it's a Little Lady doll wearing a yellow organdy ball gown with puffy sleeves. Uncle Jimmy drove all the way to Marshall Field's for it, and our guests pass it around saying how beautiful it is and how big, they never saw the like, and what a fortunate little girl I am. But I never wanted to play dolls, not since I outgrew them in first grade, and you'd think Grandma would know I don't play dolls, instead of making like I've been moping around the house whining for just this ribbony one, which is something I never do anyway, mope and whine.

When I ask for Uncle Cubby's autograph, he chews on the end of the pen for a good two minutes before writing *from a Secret Admirer. Guess Who?* Aunt Cissie takes even longer just picking out her page to autograph. *May your joys be as deep as the ocean, And your sorrows as light as the foam,* she writes, and makes a row of x's and o's and signs her name.

Grandma is too busy with the food to write an autograph now. "You wash up, Jessie."

I help the women serve dinner, and when we're all eating, I ask Pedro if he knows where the Cherokee came from.

"Out of a log or something. It's an old story."

"Straight from the Great Spirit." La Junta makes a half

circle over her head, the skin of her arms flapping like Grandma's sheets on the line.

"Is it true they were forced to come here all the way from Georgia and Tennessee and all?"

"The Trail of Tears," murmurs Aunt Nedra.

"But is it true? They were hungry and sick, and children died? And nobody helped them?"

La Junta sighs. "Everybody's got their troubles."

"Why do people hurt other people?"

"That is not a subject for Christmas dinner, Jessie," Grandma scolds.

"Then it's true?"

But no one answers me.

We're having dessert when the telephone rings, my mother calling all the way from New York to say Merry Christmas. I wait while everyone gets a minute with her, and when it's finally my turn, I tell her about my autograph book and my red sweater, and she tells me she's mailed Grandma money for her gift to me. She sounds tired. She sends me a kiss over the wires.

After I hang up, I find Aunt Cissie and La Junta helping Grandma clean up in the kitchen. The men are in the living room, and Aunt Nedra is at the dining room table with my autograph book. "Come here, Jessie. See what I'm doing." Along the top edge of a clean page Aunt Nedra has drawn a tree branch where a monkey sits, his long tail hanging down. At the bottom of the page she draws a tree stump with small tufts of grass around it, and in the center of the page she writes:

> *When you stand upon a stump*
> *Think of me before you jump.*
> *When you see a monkey up a tree,*
> *Pull his tail and think of me.*

I am barely finished reading it over her shoulder when Uncle Jimmy grabs the book out of her hands and dances away with it into the living room. On the glued-down paper inside the back cover, beyond the very last page in the book, he writes: *If anyone loves you more than I do, let them sign on the next page.*

"That's not fair," I say.

Gramp says, "All's fair in love and war."

"Hear that, sweet pea? You listen to your gramp. He's a smart man."

And Gramp is. He closes the book and writes on the back cover, right there on the leather: *I do! Love, Your Grandpa. Amos Langley.*

I start pestering Grandma since she's the only one who hasn't given me an autograph. Finally she comes out of the kitchen and sits on the davenport with the book in her hand, thinking. Gramp says instead of jumping from foot to foot in front of her why don't I open their Christmas gift. I have been trying for days to guess what's inside the big square box wrapped in crisp red-and-green stripes, a box way too light for its size, one that doesn't rattle at all when it happens to acci-dentally-on-purpose get shaken each time I happen by. Now I'm allowed to tear it open, and it is what I hoped for, a rattan basket for the handlebars of my bike.

"I need a kitten to put into it."

Gramp chuckles and says we'll see—which isn't a no, and might turn out to be yes.

While Grandma is still shilly-shallying over the autograph, I give out my presents—pot holders for Pedro and La Junta, genuine rabbit's feet key chains for my aunts and uncles, and a cross-stitch sampler for Sammy. Gramp gets the clothes hook I made in shop. He runs his hand over it and says it's exactly what he needs at the Rexall to hang up his white coat.

Grandma is conscientious about my wrapping paper. She runs her finger under the tape at each end and unwraps and unfolds and smoothes until I can't abide it one second longer and have to beg her to lift open the box lid. She does and tells me I did a real good job on all my gifts and can be proud. In my autograph book she writes: *Dear Jessie, Thank you very much for the corner shelf. It is very pretty and I know it will come in handy.*

Then Grandma gets her whistling teakettle for Christmas, after all. Uncle Jimmy goes out to the car and brings it in for her all wrapped up in ugly-flowered paper and floppy loops of ribbon with dark finger smudges, the kind you get from sweaty hands.

As soon as she opens the box Grandma lets out a whoop. She grabs hold of Uncle Jimmy and hugs him and rocks him, and then unlocks him except for still holding onto his face. "I declare, James Abner Anderson, you are the sweetest, cleverest, thoughtfulest son these old eyes of mine ever did see." She lifts out the teakettle. "Looky here, we can see ourselves in it, just like the mirror in the fun house. Jimmy, you look too skinny, I'd best fatten you up."

My corner shelf lies pushed off to the side. Six coats of varnish on it, sanded between each coat. And not a single drip mark. I ease a sheet of used wrapping paper over it. Let her look for it.

21

Claire

Tulsa, Oklahoma
April 22, 1995

The American Legion was chartered by Congress in 1919 as
a patriotic, mutual help, wartime veterans organization. Tulsa
Post 1 was founded when a group of World War I veterans
got together and formed a league for the good and welfare
of American boys who had fought to defend their country.
The American Legion has grown to well over 14,000 posts
worldwide, all of them dedicated to fostering one-hundred-
percent Americanism: making right the master of might,
combating the autocracy of both the classes and the masses,
promoting peace and goodwill on earth, and so on and so on.
These fun facts were visited upon Claire by her newfound
voice mail friend, a mellow soul whose unrelenting patter left
Claire anything but soothed. She paced out the length of the
telephone cord, to the foot of the bed and back, and waited for
someone living and unscripted to pick up the line.

The woman who finally did so informed her that they
don't trace soldiers, nor do they give out any data whatsoever
concerning their members. Having faithfully delivered

the party line in clipped tones, she slipped into the throaty confidentiality girls share with other girls. "Some of these guys don't want to be found, you know." Claire asked to be connected to the person in charge and was told no one was available, it was a madhouse there, the post commander off somewhere organizing things for the Murrah Building. Claire tried for an information officer, a membership chairman, anyone who could help her. The woman said, "I'm sorry. I have to take this next ca—" and the line went dead.

"Shit, no. No, you don't!" Impotent, Claire hammered the receiver against the rumpled bedspread, shrieking, "No, no, no, no, no!" She darted to the rain-flecked window, and no sooner there, hurled herself back onto the bed, which shimmied violently beneath her. The narrow room was too small for this sudden, red-hot fury. She erupted out the door and stalked the shadowed hallway to the streaming gray pane at the far end. But she couldn't hold there either, not possible. She about-faced and tore back, remembering only at the last that she'd had no mind to grab the room key. She saw at once for certain she'd be locked out in her thigh-high travel robe, barefoot, uncombed, a half-naked raving harridan, a lunatic.

No: blessedly, the door hadn't latched. *First good thing to happen here.* Inside again, she forced herself to stop and stand still and breathe. In-through-her-nose-out-through-her-mouth, managing a count of two, then four, and six, and eight. Slowing down, slowing down until finally she could sit on the bed, until she could dial the phone. A busy signal set her ablaze all over again. *It's impossible no it's not. Breathe. Now dial.*

Breathe.

Dial again. On the third redial, the ring tone, the chipper voice mail imparting the same tired information, and finally, the woman who was blocking the way to Uncle Jimmy.

Ragged words tumbled over themselves. "Listen, I'm at my wit's end, you have to help me."

"Madam, I've told you. I can't—"

"Not officially. Not in your, your—what is it? your—

capacity at the American Legion. James Anderson. Just by chance. If you've come across him."

There was a silence.

Make up a story, make up a story. Can't fudge one up. Then don't. "Sometime over the years? A man by that name? James Anderson."

A sound came, guttural, smothered, minute.

Catching it, Claire let the moment lengthen, desperately mouthing silent pleas.

"Mmmm, I once knew a guy over in Red Fork," the woman said. "Spelled his name different, though."

"Different how?"

"With an *E*. E-N-D-E-R-S-O-N."

22

More from the ninth of Jessie's notebooks

The place: West Tulsa, Oklahoma
The time: December 1944

Gramp is late at the Rexall doing inventory, and Grandma is working night shift at the war plant. That's fine, I am old enough to go to sleep by myself, and I don't get scared because I'm allowed to leave the lights and the radio on in the house, so it almost feels like someone is home.

I sit at the kitchen table doing my homework for extra credit over vacation. It's map study, which I like because of the different views that different maps can give you of the places people live and how they are connected. I'm up to the section on Mercator projections, where you cut up the globe like an orange if you wanted to flatten out the peel without tearing it. I answer the questions in my geography book, and when my brain gets heavy, I wash my face and brush my teeth and get into bed.

It takes time to settle because of the cold. I have to pull my feet up inside my nightgown and wait some little while for the bed to warm up. I picture a skirt like a Mercator projection, the equator at my waist and the curved blue leaves of the Southern Hemisphere falling just below my knees. The

Northern Hemisphere could make a mother-daughter match, maybe a floppy stole across her shoulders. I say a prayer for my mother and everyone else who cares about me and all people everywhere, and stretching out, I turn over to go to sleep. It's then I hear footsteps on the back porch and the creak of the screen door being pulled open.

Lickety-split I slip out of the covers and crawl into the shadow under the bed.

"Sweet pea," I hear him whisper. His feet in their ugly fancy shoes stop in my doorway. He whispers my name, waits, and then the feet turn away, go clattering across the kitchen. When it gets quiet, I know he has gone to the front room and is treading on the rug.

I slide along the floor—I'm going to catch it from Grandma for dirtying my nightgown—and lift the trapdoor to the root cellar, just enough to lower myself inside. The stairway down is rickety, hardly more than a ladder. It's pitch black, but I know where I'm going. All along the walls are shelves and shelves of fruits and vegetables that Grandma has canned. On the floor below them are barrels of turnips and squash, and the vats of eggs that Gramp and Aunt Nedra filled. In the center is an old low table that must have been used for something sometime, but now is piled with potatoes in crates, the potatoes piled up over the tops of the crates. Making no more noise than a garter snake wiggling under a log, I edge past the table and crouch down behind a barrel, and I listen.

I listen to Uncle Jimmy's feet coming into the room, then going out to the kitchen, then back through and out to the back, and then he is in my room again, not moving for ages and ages. Then I hear a shuffling and a grunt, and the color I see on my shut-tight eyelids turns from black to yellowish brown, the color of his shoes coming after me, and the ladder creaks, and I try so hard not to, but I sob, so he finds me and I scrabble to get free, but he lifts me onto the potatoes. He shoves me onto my back. My knees are against my chest, and my lower legs are over his shoulders, and my nightgown is twisted up. I am screaming and kicking at him, but he clamps one hand over my mouth and holds my both hands with his other, and my kicking doesn't make any difference, and I can feel his prickliness against my cheek, and he is whispering things to me, only I don't know what he is whispering, because he is moaning, too, and then his tongue is in my ear, thick and wet, and he is licking me in my ear and then down my neck and across my shoulder and I try to shove his face away with my leg, but he groans, "Oh, Jessie, you are a wild one," and now he is running his tongue from my knee downward along my thigh, but I am not really there anymore. I am in the woods with Hetty playing in the leaves, gathering them up in a pile and jumping into it and rolling around. But it's too cold. I'm cold, and Uncle Jimmy puts his mouth in my wee-wee part, licking and sucking and nibbling, and I try so hard to make on him, but I cannot. His tongue is pressing hard, and it is awful and then he gives out that gurgling sound, and he leans even further into me, and my back is working right into the potatoes, but where Uncle Jimmy is, his lips have stopped their pressing and his tongue has let up and is soft like a kitten almost not there, but still there, whispering, whispering. And suddenly I feel warm there like when you have to wee and you let it almost go, then stop just before the water comes out, and your stomach is fluttery and your eyes make tears, and when you can hold it in like that, but only just, it feels good, and you alone know that you are doing it, not the girls out on the playground or the teacher at the blackboard or anybody else. But it is awful and I don't want it to feel good because of Uncle Jimmy. Finally I stop fighting and go limp, and I wait and finally he carries me to the ladder and makes me go up ahead of him, and I am afraid he will do something awful again as he comes up behind me—except he doesn't. He makes me stand in the kitchen sink holding up my night-gown and washes me, the water cold and pinkish around my feet when I peek but mostly I keep my eyes shut so I won't have to see him wiping me with his hankie, the linen one with the block letter *J* that I helped my mother pick out the year we did all our Christmas shopping in one day. Uncle Jimmy doesn't dry me, just wraps the nightgown around my dripping legs and takes and tucks me like that into bed and says, "Now, miss, let me hear your prayers."

23

Claire

Red Fork, Oklahoma
April 22, 1995

Enderson, James, had been right there in the phone book all along. His street ran along the base of Red Fork Hill, once a vast emptiness of fields, now a suburban grid rising up the hill's flanks. Uncle Jimmy had taken Jessie to Red Fork Hill, and Jessie's notebook placed it way out in the country. But even in the 1940s, when there had been no highway, even by local roads from West Tulsa, the ride in Jimmy's car could not have taken long. In no time at all, Claire was driving through a neighborhood of working-class homes, the grade sloping gradually upward, spindly trees stepping up the rise. The first tender green of spring fuzzed in their branches, not an evergreen in sight. Jessie had written about pine needles that carpeted the paths from the hilltop. They were gone now, or had never been there, soft underfoot and fragrant. Jessie's testimony belied yet again?

This had to be the right man. She couldn't bear another disappointment. She wanted life to be simple, as when Jessie was sick, and there was nothing else to be done but take care of her. All decisions seemed like bad ones, but you chose the best you could, this bad thing instead of that bad thing, and what you chose sufficed. They'd shared a piercing intimacy then, when Jessie relied on her totally, an intimacy that survived after the cancer released its murderous grip and receded. But the purity of action and intention Claire had known in Jessie's illness did not survive. She yearned for it now, torn between accepting at face value what Jessie wrote and finding the truth for herself; torn between the guilt of not believing Jessie and the self-effacement of denying her own instincts.

The trees were plainly wrong, as was the travel time, a mere quarter of an hour by car from 2212 South Phoenix to the base of Red Fork Hill. But time was relative. Case in point: speeding to the hospital, heart in her mouth, word of Jessie's car accident fresh and terrifying. A twenty-minute trip? No, it had been eons.

Case in point: emergency room procedure, a portable X-ray machine wheeled into the cubicle so that Jessie wouldn't have to be transported. But they had to shift her into position for the pictures, and Claire, loitering just outside the curtain, was drenched by the time they were done, her hands and face slick with sweat, her shirt, pants, socks soaked through. Wet as if she'd run the marathon, and that came from mere minutes of hearing Jessie's agony. Each shriek was a foretaste of eternity.

Final case in point: on a snowy Tuesday noontime in February 1983, Claire and Jessie had made lunch-hour love, taking their time about it, langorous and thorough. Sated, they'd fallen into a doze. A snowplow scraping the street outside roused them, and they'd disengaged in a panic, believing several hours to have passed, meetings and appointments missed. *What time is it?* Precisely nine-and-a-half minutes since they'd fallen onto the bed nuzzling!

Claire smiled at the memory, blinked and swallowed. There would be no more doubting what Jessie wrote. Pine trees could disappear when ham-fisted developers cleared the land. And fifteen minutes in a car on the way to Red Fork Hill could be decades in the heart of a nervous girl with cause to worry.

How many rides had Jessie been forced to take with Uncle Jimmy, to how many nameless places behind a barn, across a railroad siding, under a spreading elm? But Red Fork she knew, Red Fork Hill she could name even all these years later, and why should Claire consider it only a coincidence that James Enderson—sounding just like Anderson—lived here at the end of the block, hugging the hill? She pulled up in front of the house. It was the crummiest little box on the block, asphalt sided in sick-shit brown appropriate to a low-life scum of the earth. The shutters had cutouts of old-fashioned carriages. They were painted baby blue, and the paint was peeling. A battered old Buick was parked in the driveway. The man who lived here, his name glued in reflective letters to the mailbox, must be the very one.

Crossing his straggly front yard, mounting the stoop to his front door, she focused on the pavement, the firm, cold stillness of concrete. Her breathing was too fast and too shallow. Before she'd even found the bell, he had the door open. "Well, what do you know? What do you know?" He unlatched the screen door and pushed it wide. The door squealed on its hinges. "Come right on in, little lady."

Little lady? She hesitated. There had to be something seriously wrong with a person who invited strangers into his house, not even asking their name or their business.

"Figure you're here to sell me something. That's just fine with me." He was gap toothed, smiling like a great fool. She didn't appreciate him guessing her thoughts. "Ain't nothin' I'm lookin' to buy, but I don't get company all that often, so come on in for a cup of coffee, anyhow."

He was five foot seven or so, shorter than she'd pictured, with a barrel chest and a drooping belly and large, loose hands. His hair was gray and thin, his nose a ski slope between close-set eyes.

Now or never, she thought, and stepped into his living room, which was dim and stale, smelling of cigarettes and old soup. The room held a liver-colored tweed sofa and two recliner armchairs in faded avocado plaid. A battered coffee table and a TV stand were of darkened pine, and the walls were paneled in four-by-eight sheets of wood-printed vinyl. The only relief from a sea of brown and brownish came from hundreds of salt and pepper shakers crowding a wall of shelves opposite.

He'd been waiting for her to gape, and when she did, he said, "My pride and joy. Figure they might be worth something, someday. Leaving the whole shebang to the museum in my will."

Pink flamingos, neon-yellow oil wells, flowered hula dancers, spangled jazz singers with wide-open mouths, skiers with tiny poles askew, their crimson scarves streaming, and every tourist attraction in the Union represented in duplicate, Pikes Peak, the Washington Monument, Mount Rushmore. Their cheerful polychrome wackiness drew her. She studied them, searching for some clue to his character, as if Paul Bunyan and his blue ox Babe or Mickey and Minnie would provide the key to how he could have done what he did to Jessie. "Souvenirs of your travels?" she said.

He didn't answer. He was no longer in the room. Through a doorway beyond the couch came the Mantovani sound of golden oldies radio, James Enderson whistling along. "Gingersnaps," he called to her. "Made fresh yesterday."

Her plan had been to accept nothing from the man, on principle. Not so much as a penny's worth, and she ought to have said so first thing, ought to have told him not to bother with coffee. Now, he emerged carrying a tray loaded with cookies, two steaming mugs, sugar and creamer. "Course they're best for dunking when they've had a few days to get stale."

Gingersnaps were a favorite of hers, and how often did she get them? Brooklyn's Park Slope offered an amazing range of exotic foods, but not gingersnaps made from real molasses and ginger, instead of corn syrup and artificial flavoring. She sat down on the scruffy sofa, fighting temptation, gripping her purse in her lap. Inside was the knife. Her license, a credit card and a twenty-dollar bill were locked in the car, and the car key was in her skirt pocket.

He sipped coffee out of a chipped mug, watching her. "So what are you peddling, little lady?"

"Nothing."

He drew in his chin, cocked his head and grinned again. "Collecting for charity?"

She said no, her fingers running across the nubby tweed cushion just like Jessie, like Jessie's fingers would have.

"Good, 'cause I gave at the office." His laugh, a sudden bellow, head thrown back, was exactly what Jessie had described, wasn't it? Claire gripped her purse. He said, "Help yourself to those cookies."

"Who baked them? You?"

"No, ma'am. Not me, not a chance. Gal down the block, she's a little sweetheart, brought these by still warm from the oven." He moved the platter toward her. "Well, go on and have one. I can see you want it."

"I'm here about a girl, Jessie Desmond." Claire on alert for a reaction. None came. "You knew her once? Long ago." Long ago was a good touch. Long ago would put him at his ease, statute of limitations expired, ancient history.

"Sure I must have. Known lots of lovely women in my time." He looked damn pleased with himself. "This was a child, not a woman."

"What was the name?"

"Jessie Desmond. Beautiful little girl."

The grunt he gave was noncommittal. She wanted to cut the stupid gap-toothed grin off his face. Did Jessie write about his teeth? Had she forgotten, after so many years?

"Or Friedman. Jessie Friedman."

"Got married, did she?"

You lying bastard. You prick.

She fixed on his tarnished eyes and knew the very moment they turned crafty. "What's this about?" he said, setting down his cup.

"Jessie passed away recently. I'm looking for her uncle, name of James Anderson. Or Enderson."

He touched his chest. "That's my name."

"Uncle Jimmy."

"Remembered her uncle, did she? Remembered her family ties."

She was having trouble breathing. "How could Jessie forget those unforgettable times out here at Red Fork Hill?" Her voice broke when she named the place. An odd crackling filled her ears.

He said, "Family ties are all anyone's got. Push comes to shove, can't count on nothin' else."

After he said that, it all went so fast. Scenes came sweeping through her head, like life passing in front of one's eyes before dying; only these weren't the scenes of her life, these were movie scenes, from *Reservoir Dogs, The Godfather*—scenes drenched in blood, blood streaming down faces, blood spraying from chests, blood-guts-brains splattering on walls and pavements, blood gushing from the stumps of arms and legs.

He said, "Sure do wish I had me a niece like that. Someone to give me a call every so often and talk about old times. Me, I got no family. 'Cept a cousin up in Montana, and he's a useless piece of—. Sorry, almost forgot my manners."

"No, you can't do that. You can't say you don't remember her. Nancy Ann's daughter."

"Never knew them. Never had no nieces, nephews, brothers, sisters. It's a lonely life without family ties, that's for dang sure. —Here, you need a refill," picking up Claire's half-empty mug. "Let me hot it up for you."

A trick. Surely she hadn't touched the coffee. Rising, she shook her head, as much to clear the awful dinning in her ears as to refuse his offer.

"No trouble. Got plenty made," he said over his shoulder, heading into the kitchen.

She should have lost consciousness then. It would have been so much easier. Decent people who go crazy have blackouts. An hour or so later, coming to, they can ask, "Where am I? What happened?" and be told the hideous news.

She should have lost consciousness right after he told her, "Don't rush off, now," but she never did. She trailed him into the tiny galley kitchen, trapping him in there, howling Jessie's name and flailing at him through the screaming in her skull, clenched fists beating at him because he was wrong to be within arm's reach of her while Jessie was not. She battered him with angry hands, her purse slamming into his hunkered shoulder, into his back, the purse flying open and the knife jouncing out. With preternatural timing like a hawk on a sparrow, she swooped it right out of the air and gave herself over to its keenness, her intentions blackening, but never, oh never, her blood-drenched mind.

How she struck at what kept her from Jessie—it was he keeping her from Jessie, he pretending Jessie didn't exist—and Jessie had to exist for him she had to, he couldn't disown what he'd done. The knife found his flesh and ripped it. Ripped it, so he must have cried out. Claire couldn't hear him over the roaring in her head. But she knew, she was present in each harrowing moment, and each moment had its own terrible awareness: of him turning to meet the attack, of the knife biting into him again, of him grasping her hand, twisting her with an iron fist, of him forcing her to her knees, of her cheek against the soiled vinyl floor. Of him reaching up under her skirt and she kicking him while he pulled her panty hose down around her ankles, hobbling her with a few deft twists of the nylon. "Hush, now," he rasped. "Not going to hurt you."

When the police arrived, she was curled on the dirty kitchen floor sobbing uncontrollably, a poor demented creature dripping snot, drooling spit. She knew she'd go to jail. It would be the final degradation, and a fitting one for an outflanked assassin. But no, it seemed even that meager satisfaction was denied her. He said she'd caught him across his collar bone, missing the artery, and he didn't want to press charges, as long as she promised never to come back. One cop thought he ought to have the cuts looked at. He said not necessary, the little lady hadn't done him nary as much harm as she'd intended, and his first aid kit would do the job just fine. It was only a few scratches, after all. The bleeding had pretty well stopped on its own.

She told herself not to lose sight of who the bad guy was in all this and who the avenger. She'd thought she commanded the situation. He hadn't looked that quick or that strong. Yet somehow she was the one shamed, she the one responsible. It was all coming out wrong. The creep didn't even admit to being Uncle Jimmy. The taller policeman, the freckled one, quietly asked her if she needed bus fare to be able to leave town. They took her for crazy, so she was dismissible. James Enderson, he was home free. She hadn't hurt him, not in his stumpy body, certainly not in his shit-heel soul. And she didn't dare go back to confront him again, or she'd be arrested for stalking. Some avenger. Some scythe-wielding sling blade she turned out to be.

24

From the tenth of Jessie's notebooks

The place: West Tulsa, Oklahoma
The time: January 1945

Teddy Draper and I walk down to the Rexall to buy Valentine's cards for our mothers. We're a couple of weeks early because I have to mail mine to New York, and better safe than sorry. The day is warm, and I am wearing the thick red sweater Aunt Cissie knitted me for Christmas. Soon we will be past the real cold weather, watching for crocuses to start peeping out around Mr. Ketcham's porch, and soon Gramp will be getting the incubator ready for the chicks. Already he is talking about making the barn ready, scalding and scrubbing everything and putting down fresh oat straw and laying in feed.

I get a beautiful card for my mother with lace and flowers and lots of pink. It's perfect, so I don't even mind it costing a quarter. Besides, Gramp throws in a few Guess Who's to send to my friends. Teddy keeps pestering me to tell who I'm going to send them to. Once when I was at boarding school in Westchester—my third school—before the night my mother came and drove me away and never took me back there, we had a Valentine party and I got cards from three boys, and later they each took me on a sleigh ride and gave me candy hearts just as if I was popular. I tell Teddy I haven't made up my mind yet, but really I already know I am sending my cards to Isaac Smith and PeeWee Swenson because Isaac is nice and PeeWee too, except not so popular that everyone will send him cards.

Gramp drives us home and we get to ride alone in the rumble seat even though we're not supposed to without a grown-up. Grandma is on the front porch when we get there, and she no sooner looks at us than she puts her hand up to her mouth and runs into the house. I figure she must be mad as anything, and we're going to get it hard. Gramp drives the car up the driveway and parks it out back in front of the barn. Grandma has made it through the house and now she is standing on the back steps, her face all wrinkled up and her eyes blinking and twitching, her hands twisting her apron.

As soon as Gramp sets me down on the ground I try straightening out whatever the wind has blown apart in my hair and clothes. I can't feel a whole lot of wildness there, but I keep patting myself in place walking over to where Grandma is standing. I try, "Hi, Grandma." She's having none of it. She whirls back into the house and lets the door slam at me. Teddy Boy says, "Thank you, sir," to Gramp and hightails it over across to his house.

"Jessie, you go sit on your bed while I find out what's got your grandma in such fine fettle." Gramp pushes me up the porch steps and into my room. "Sign your cards. That'll make good use of your time."

My room is dark, except if you sit right up against the window, but that's where the footboard is, so there's no real place to be comfortable for writing. Everything is quiet. The icebox in the kitchen is humming, but even so, I expect to hear something through the closed door, above the sounds from the kitchen. I expect Grandma scolding, "Let me tell you a thing or two, Amos Langley. Rules were made for a purpose, and not for the purpose of you ignoring them." I expect Gramp muttering, a groan, a sharp laugh, or every once in a great while, "Woman, desist!" But there is nothing, and then Gramp opens my door. He isn't careful, so the door bumps hard into the bed and my pen slides and makes a blop of ink where the *i* belongs in my name. "You'd best come in now, Jessie."

I screw the cap back on my pen. I get off the bed and smooth out my dress and straighten my socks. I'm taking my time, wondering if Grandma is mad at Gramp, too, or if he told her riding in the rumble seat was all my idea and he couldn't do a thing about it unless he left me up Quanah.

Grandma is standing in the dining room archway, not fixing dinner, not setting the table, not wringing out the clothes, not doing anything. Just standing there, her hands hanging still. I've brought my mother's card to show her, and I hold it out for her to see. Grandma shudders and grabs me tight. "Oh, my poor Jessie," she wails.

"Lulu," Gramp whispers, except loud like a prompter in the school play.

"Oh, Jessie. It's our Nancy Ann. Our Nancy Ann has gone and died."

I pull away. They're both staring at me. I try to think what Nancy Ann they mean. A chicken? The Guernsey Gramp keeps out at the farm? The only Nancy Ann I know, besides my old Nancy Ann doll named for my mother, is my mother. So I ask, "Who's Nancy Ann?"

Grandma squats down beside me and takes my hands in hers. "Sweet Jesus, Jessie. Your mama, Nancy Ann. It's your mama we're talking about. She's passed away."

"Passed away?" No, Mama's nearly always away. So maybe she hasn't really died? She'll still be coming back, and I can see her when she passes this way again?

Nobody says. They just look at each other the way they do when I am being impossible, so I know I'm wearing out my welcome. "If I may be excused please, ma'am. I'd like to go address the envelope for my mother." The edges of the Valentine card have gotten wrinkly and soft from my fingers rubbing them. They threaten to fall apart, and I don't want to add mussing up the carpet to the things I've already done.

Grandma takes the card in her hands, but she never even looks at it. She hugs it to her, bending the corners as she jams it to her bosom. My hand shoots out to rescue the card, too late. She crumples up the lace in a tight fist and says a curse, says a whole string of them, "Damn, damn, damn, damn, damn," then pitches the poor sad thing onto the floor.

Now Gramp is hugging her sidesaddle, the side of his belly to Grandma's hip, his inside arm loosely wrapped around her neck. "Easy, Lulu. It'll be okay. Easy girl," like Uncle Cubby trying to calm the bay mare when she was skittish from the lightning and he was scared she'd drop the foal too soon.

Passed away is bad, bad enough to make Grandma's eyes red and blurry with tears behind her glasses, bad enough for runs from Gramp's nose to bubble on his lips. Bad enough that I squeeze my eyes shut and try to cry along with them, but I can't make the tears start. I'm scared though.

Once when I was real little my father took me to the beach in Brighton and left me there alone while he went swimming way far out. He got so small and stayed under the water so long I thought he'd never come back. Hot stinging tears came like soap in my eyes. People crowded around me and I was still sobbing hard when he finally did come back.

"You made a fuss over nothing," he told me.

"I couldn't help it."

"Not true, Jessie. You wanted people to feel sorry for you. That's always why people cry."

My father may know things nobody else in the world knows—like that you don't have to be scared in the movies because the hero never dies—but Grandma and Gramp are crying hard now, and when they reach over to pull me next to them, I never for a minute believe they are trying to make me feel sorry for them.

The house fills up with people. The Ketchams come over with a casserole and Mrs. Ellis brings a pie. Late in the afternoon Sammy comes into the front room and pats my head, and then Uncle Cubby helps him back to his porch rocker, where he sits for a while wrapped up in lap robes crooning to himself.

The minister comes by with some church members, and somebody from the war plant where Grandma works brings me a Tootsie Roll. There isn't a room that doesn't have people in it, and there isn't a person who isn't nodding or talking or both. I watch everybody without trying to listen in on anybody particular, and I wonder why they all have so much to say. The whole world is filled up with people from one end to the other, and everybody talking, everybody with something to tell somebody else, but I don't feel like there is one whit I want to say to anyone.

The minister sits on the davenport with Grandma. He is always telling jokes that start out, "A minister walked into a bar," or "A minister and a priest arrived together in heaven," or "A minister, a priest and a rabbi were out in a boat." Grandma says everybody likes a person who laughs hardest at himself, and the minister certainly laughs hard at his jokes, right along with Grandma—but not this time. This time she stares at her lap, and he pats her hand as he talks quietly to her.

The Drapers bring a basket of fried chicken. Teddy's hair is water-combed flat, and he stands real close to his mama, fidgeting with his tie. He says, "I'm sorry, Jessie," and I nod, and he says "I'm sorry" again, and then he scratches the back of his neck and fishes around in his pocket for something to keep busy with, but I guess nothing is there, because he returns to playing with his tie again and staring at his shoes. I go out to the back porch and watch the crescent moon rise up over the barn until the kitchen empties out, and then I go in and crouch in the shadowed space between the icebox and the wall.

I don't know if my mother is really dead. If she is dead, where is her body? Gramp says she is being cremated in New York and her ashes will be sent us in a jar, but those could be anybody's ashes, even Picadilly, my mother's black cocker spaniel who died when I was five and got cremated, too.

I used to take Pic into bed with me and whisper in his ear, and he would look at me with his damp eyes that seemed to understand everything, even the things I didn't know how to say. Then he got blind, his eyes milking over, and he couldn't find his way around the apartment too well, some-times trapping himself among the legs of the dining room table and chairs. He started making in the house, soft gobs of diarrhea laced with blood, and one morning when the kitchen smelled badly of Pic my mother said enough, it was time to put him to sleep.

I didn't want to go to school, because I was afraid I would come home and find Pic gone forever, but my mother made me attend, promising I would go with her to the vet and have my chance to say good-bye. Sometimes my mother made prom-ises she couldn't keep, like when she said she would be in the audience for the Christmas pageant to see me playing a wise man, but then she had to work instead. I didn't know whether this was a promise I'd have to understand about my mother not being able to keep, so I was itchy all day in school, and I got in trouble for scribbling all over Martin Leinweber's paper when he called me a monkey.

My mother kept her promise that time. She was there when school let out, waiting with Pic just inside Mrs. Grace's red door because it was raining outside. She had an umbrella, and I took the leash, but Pic didn't want to come down the stoop stairs, padding from paw to paw, maybe not knowing which foot to lead with, maybe not seeing his way down the three steps to the sidewalk. I gave a good hard yank on the leash to help him decide, and Pic came tumbling down, land-ing with a squeal upside down at my feet.

"Jessie," my mother scolded. "How could you?"

"What?"

"Don't be cruel, Jessie. Don't ever be cruel. It doesn't fit you."

I didn't mean to hurt Pic any, and I said I was sorry, but to this day I can't figure out why I was the one who got to be called cruel when she was the one taking Pic to get killed.

Pic always seemed to know where we were headed a whole block away from Dr. Kabnik's office, and sick as he was he set his haunches down on the wet sidewalk and would not budge. My mother had to lift him and carry him in, and poor Pic was trembling all over when they put him on the examining table. The shot seemed to calm him, though, and he went to sleep peacefully enough while I soothed the sleekness between his ears.

I thought maybe Pic was going to get well after all, but my mother sat down on Dr. Kabnik's rolling stool, the leather seat heaving a sigh as she slumped onto it, and dragged her arms over her head. I remembered a long time back when she slumped against the door to the apartment and slid to the floor and dragged her arms over her head in just that way. Then it was because my father shook my rag doll and threw it on the floor and yelled at her and jabbed his finger at her and jammed his hat on his head and slammed out of the apartment. Then it was Pic who crept down the hallway and tongued my mother's bare feet with his soft doggie kisses until my mother reached for him and buried her face in his fur. But with Pic now on the table wetly snoring, I went to my mother's side and took her limp hand and kissed it and waited for her to show me what to do next.

"What are you going to do about Jessie?"

In Grandma's dining room, finally it is just family left around the table, where a yellow linen cloth has been laid. All the neighbors are gone home, and it might be a holiday like Thanksgiving or Christmas, except Grandma keeps dabbing at her eyes with the corner of her apron and not yelling at Gramp for smoking his pipe in the house. Every once in a while Gramp gets up from his chair and goes and stands behind Grandma and pets her shoulder and says, "There, there. Hold on, girl."

I'm half-asleep in the dark in the kitchen corner, my arms wrapped around my legs and my head resting on my bent knees, when I hear Uncle Cubby say, "What are you going to do about Jessie?"

The soft lilt of Aunt Nedra trading recipes with Aunt Cissie stops. Gramp's pipe wheezes. Grandma's teacup clinks in her saucer. "What do you mean?" she demands. Uncle Cubby doesn't say anything, just cocks his head and stares at her. She stares back trying to stare him down, I guess. "I don't see why anything has to change," she says.

"Lulu," Gramp says gently, "we took Jessie in for the summer. Then Nancy Ann asked couldn't we keep her a few more months. We never agreed to a lifetime."

"A lifetime! Why, *there's* a man talking for you," pointing at him like she has an audience of thousands witnessing it. "We'll blink an eye, Doc, and Jessie'll be grown. She'll be grown, and you'll be mooning around the house crying, 'Where's my little one gone to?'"

"Ma, the girl is not your responsibility."

"I raised you, Cubby. Raised Nancy Ann and Jimmy. No reason I can't raise Jessie, too. No reason we can't go right on just as we are."

Aunt Cissie reaches over and strokes Grandma's arm where the sleeve is hiked up to Grandma's elbow. Grandma looks like she'd just as soon pull the arm away. "We're worried about you," Aunt Cissie says. "At your age you shouldn't be working at all, let alone the night shift."

"There's a war on," Grandma says. "We all got to do our part."

"Like Nancy Ann?" says Uncle Jimmy.

Splotches of red are climbing Grandma's cheeks and forehead. "Nancy Ann had her problems. No point dwelling on them."

"Did Nancy Ann do her part for Jessie?"

"Nor any need to talk ill now she's gone."

Uncle Jimmy snorts louder than Mr. Harden's prize hog, and Uncle Cubby raises his coffee cup like he's making some kind of toast to Grandma.

Grandma says, "Anyway, the war will be over one day soon."

I close my eyes and feel the hum of the icebox vibrating through the floor. Icebox is what Grandma always calls it, even though it's really a refrigerator, the old-fashioned kind with a motor in a cage up on top that gets warm while the food inside stays cold. With my eyes closed I don't have to see Grandma's hands trembling, fingers picking away at the balled-up corner of her apron.

Uncle Cubby is getting louder. Above the hum of the motor I hear him say Pa is slowing down, too, and you can't expect him to keep going like gangbusters, either. Gramp coughs, a soft hem, then a deeper hacking like he has a bone caught in his throat. My eyes fly open watching for trouble. He's okay, though. It's Grandma who is rearing and sputtering, and I wouldn't want to be Uncle Cubby for anything.

"Tuck us up with old Sammy in his lap robes, why don't you?" she shrills.

"Now, Ma—"

She presses both palms against the table and stands up and tromps her feet hard against the rag rug. "Looka here," she says, trooping her way all around the table, pausing behind each person's chair to march in place. "Both feet right here at the bottoms of my ankles." Tromp, tromp like one of the Cherokee dancers except without the rattles. "Nary a one of these feet in the grave that I can tell." Tromp, tromp. "So I'll thank you not to be laying my parts in the ground just yet, nor Doc's either." Then she says Uncle Cubby needs more milk for his coffee, and let's see if her addled old brain can remember where she put it. She tromps right past me to the icebox door and never spies me folded up in my narrow corner between the icebox and the wall.

They are quiet until she comes back, and then Aunt Nedra says, "Jessie has people in New York."

"Jessie doesn't need to be taken in by strangers."

"He's her father."

"He's a Jew," Grandma says. "With a Jewish wife and a Jewish stepchild."

"He's her father," Aunt Nedra repeats.

Uncle Cubby shakes his head. "They're strangers to her, with strange ways," he says.

Uncle Jimmy's fingers move around like some fat spider's legs on the tabletop. "Well, are you going to take the girl home with you, then?" he says.

Aunt Cissie kicks Uncle Cubby under the table. "Maybe you haven't heard the rumor, little brother," he says. "My wife's expecting twins. We're 'bout to have our beds full up."

Somebody ought to point out what a big help I could be to Aunt Cissie. Two babies at the same time could be a lot to handle, and think how an extra pair of hands might help. Grandma can make me up a bedroll, and I can sleep on the floor with Clancy, or maybe out in the barn with George. I know if I suggest going there to help, they'll only say Aunt Cissie has enough on her hands without me underfoot. I hope I'll remember when I get to be a grown-up what a big help kids can be and give them a chance, the way Gramp lets me help with his chicks. If only Uncle Cubby and Aunt Cissie were expecting a brood of chicks, maybe they'd want me there with them.

"Has anyone called Jessie's father?" Aunt Nedra says. "Does he even know about Nancy Ann?"

"They're not nice people."

"Now, how would you know that?"

"How would I know? My Nancy Ann was a good girl. Everybody knows that. Everybody." Grandma is truly on a tear now, the words trying to tumble out faster than she can chew them. "A fine-and-proper girl. Till New York. Till she took up with that man. Running around to nightclubs. Living the high life." Tears are streaking down her wrinkled cheeks but she isn't paying them any mind. "Then he up and leaves," she says. Aunt Nedra draws in breath to say something, but Grandma holds up her hand against interruption. "I blame him for everything after. I blame him. He took my Nancy Ann from me. He can't have Jessie."

Nobody speaks until Grandma takes off her glasses and wipes her eyes and blows her nose. Aunt Nedra sighs. She might be singing a lullaby, her voice is that careful, telling Grandma how they are obliged still and all to contact my father, for he has a right to know and be involved.

But Gramp clears his throat and tells her nope, the man gave up his right a long time back, because he never paid one cent to support the child—meaning me, of course. He is more sad than angry, shaking his head like there's something he can't understand and will never figure out. "What a pair, the two of them, one worse than the other," he says. "Big presents, but don't mention doctor bills."

"I won't have you speak of Nancy Ann in the same breath with that man, Doc," Grandma says. "You know she loved us all dearly, and most especially that little one asleep in her bed."

Uh-oh. They're going to realize now that nobody has put me to bed. Nobody has heard my prayers, nobody has tucked me in, nobody has so much as seen me passing by on the way to the bathroom in my nightclothes. The room goes silent. I stay frozen in place, not breathing. Then Uncle Jimmy speaks.

"Nancy Ann was never coming back for her," he says, and Aunt Nedra strikes the table with her hand and cries, "James Abner Anderson! You hush, now!" and I'm forgotten in the quarrel.

Grandma says he oughtn't to say such things, but Uncle Jimmy says, "Well, whyever not? It's the god's honest truth. Nancy Ann was my sister, and I loved her and all, but don't let's forget her selfish ways now she's gone."

Grandma says they've been through all this before, and she'll have nothing bad said because Nancy Ann was sick and couldn't help herself. But Uncle Cubby says the sickness was from not making enough insulin, and he never heard tell that not making enough insulin had anything to do with going through all that Desmond money like it was chicken feed. "Bankruptcy ain't a sickness, Ma. It's a damn sin. And so is drinking yourself to death."

Grandma stands up, but something goes wrong. First she says, "I'll not stay here and listen to this. Jessie stays, that's that." Right then, the ladder-back chair tips over backwards behind her, and her hand reaches out and grabs the tablecloth like she's fixing to try one of those magician's tricks where he pulls the cloth out from under the plates and glasses and silverware. Grandma moans and sighs and slumps, and Aunt Nedra jumps up and catches Grandma in her arms, and the men jump up too, Uncle Jimmy shouting, "Ma! Ma!" and Gramp moving fast to help Aunt Nedra with Grandma.

"Lay her down," Gramp shouts. "Lay her down!" He has Grandma by the arm and could lay her down himself, yet even so he just keeps yelling, "Lay her down," and not doing anything about it.

I feel like when the tiger is chasing me in a bad dream and I open my mouth to scream, but nothing comes out, and I try to run away but my arms and legs are paralyzed. Afraid like that, though it is only moments until Grandma lifts her head and says, "Land sakes, what's all this commotion?"

"You fainted, Ma."

"Nonsense! A little dizzy spell is all."

"Lulu, you need to lie down," Gramp says. He's examining her face, his hand cupped under her chin.

She pulls back from him and smooths her apron over her dress. "Now, Doc," she says, "can't a body trip over her own feet without the world coming to an end?"

Gramp throws his hands up and says he doesn't know what to do with her, she's a stubborn old mare. Grandma bends down and lifts the chair, righting it, setting it close in under the table. "We've had a long day," she says, and then she seems to stifle a yawn. "I guess I'll turn in now."

Aunt Nedra tries to help her, but Grandma brushes her away. "The rest of you ought to go, too," she says. "There'll be no more talk of Jessie, hear?"

But there is more talk. No sooner does Grandma close their bedroom door than Gramp says, "You see how it is, boys." Boys—as if Aunt Nedra and Aunt Cissie aren't there at all. "Lulu's in no shape to be caring for a young'un. Even one as good as Jessie."

Uncle Jimmy says Grandma had a point, though. "When Nancy Ann couldn't pay for that Catholic school, she sent Jessie here. Nancy Ann surely intended for Jessie to stay with her people."

"Well, I've made it a rule never to interfere between Lula Langley and her children. Not my place," Gramp says. "Only now it's her health I'm worried about."

"Her health will not be improved by knowing you've sent

Jessie away," says Uncle Jimmy. "Nor yours either, I might add. I wouldn't want to share her bed after that, no sirree," and everybody laughs, except Aunt Nedra. She stays quiet, her fingers woven together in her lap. She is staring into the kitchen, but not at me, at something above the icebox, or maybe at nothing.

Then Uncle Cubby says they really ought to be getting home, and he and Aunt Cissie get up to go, and so does Aunt Nedra, but Uncle Jimmy asks if there isn't some more of that apple pie. Aunt Nedra says they'd ought to let Gramp get some rest, but Uncle Jimmy insists one little slice for the road won't take long.

Aunt Nedra brings his plate into the dim kitchen and finds the pie on the table and uncovers it and begins cutting into it. In the dining room, Uncle Jimmy says, "Well, if Jessie gets too much for you folks to deal with, Nedra and I will take her." Aunt Nedra stops cutting.

"It may come to that," Gramp says. That's when Aunt Nedra turns and faces me full on and stares me straight in the eye, like she's known I was there all along.

"Over my dead body," she whispers.

I am so surprised and confused it doesn't occur to me to be scared about being caught out of bed at this late hour. I'm surprised that Aunt Nedra doesn't want me. I thought she liked being with me, the way she always joins in our outings whenever she can. Could it be she knows about Uncle Jimmy? If she does and hasn't said anything, then I best not say anything now to her, either. Yet how in the world could she know? It just must be that I've worn out my welcome with Aunt Nedra, and she would rather be dead than take me in—which makes me sad, but also glad, both at the same time.

If you asked me to guess, I would surely have guessed I'd wear out my welcome with Grandma before anybody, but Grandma wants me to stay, while it's Gramp who wants me gone. I imagined Gramp would always have time for me, the way he clucks over me like a giant, round-bellied hen. Sometimes you can be wrong about people. Sometimes it's really hard to know.

Uncle Jimmy is the only one who doesn't surprise me one bit. I know I will never wear out my welcome with him, not Uncle Jimmy. But Uncle Jimmy has worn out his welcome with me.

Gramp says I will make Grandma sick if I stay. I made my mother sick, and I got sent away to school. Then Uncle Jimmy made me do what was bad, and my mother died. I don't want to be sent away, but I don't want to make Grandma die. I've heard Grandma say she never saw bad things come but they come in sets of three. If Grandma dies, or if I'm sent to Uncle Jimmy, that will be the third bad thing to happen since Christmas. I have to hope something else bad will come instead, and very soon, or it will be up to me to make a different bad thing happen. Because I will not go to live with Uncle Jimmy, I swear it. Not ever. Like Aunt Nedra said: over my dead body.

Maybe I will get sent to Brooklyn. I don't know if Brooklyn would count as a bad thing. I was born there, and Aunt Nedra said I have people there, so it should seem like going home, except I don't know anybody in Brooklyn other than my father. My father once told me, when I said divorce is bad, "Nothing is good or bad but thinking makes it so."

I'm thinking I would much rather stay put and go to the Eugene Field Elementary School. Maybe I could do more to help Grandma and Gramp so they would find it easier to take care of me. Then we could all go back to things the way they were.

I dream of things being the way they were. I dream of Easter coming and my mother taking us by surprise, stepping out of a taxi and up onto the porch in a big white hat and a trim gray suit draped with her marten stole, paws and tails and triangular heads of soft brown fur. In her arms, a huge basket with a bright-green bow, which she'll set on the drop leaf table and bend down to hug me, crooning, "Oooh, Jessie, ooh ooh Jessie, how I've missed you."

25

Claire

Tulsa, Oklahoma
April 23, 1995

What had she been thinking? It was one of those questions that didn't beg an answer; it provided one—namely, that in her spectacular folly she hadn't been thinking anything. *What in the world had she done?* served a similar self-flagellatory purpose. Nothing sensible was the answer there. Nor was Claire's court of personal opinion inclined to let her off with a plea of temporary insanity. You can't plead temporary when you haven't been in your right mind for months. You can't mount any convincing defense when you're unsure whether you erred by trying to cut a man's throat—or by trying too feebly.

It occurred to Claire that Jessie had good reason for not telling her about Uncle Jimmy, and better reason for telling her to destroy the notebooks—something Claire couldn't do, and Jessie had probably understood that as well. For all Claire knew, Jessie might purposely have disguised Jimmy's last name, knowing Claire would never rest until she'd found the man and made a fool of herself over him. Now, convinced she'd done both those things, Claire meant at last to rest. But couldn't. She tried everything: breathing exercises, relaxation techniques, even counting sheep. She tried the TV with the sound turned low. She could neither watch, nor lull herself to sleep. Most of the night she spent wrapped in a blanket in a chair by the window, staring out, musing into the darkness.

The man had hurt Jessie, wounded her deeply. Claire's intent had been murderous, even though Jessie had survived his savaging and, with Claire, had thrived—Jessie could never have written those notebooks if she hadn't somehow become whole again. Claire had wanted to put the man to death, been wholly consumed in that moment with his death. And yet, that same moment, the knife rushing toward his hunched neck, she saw that it wasn't him she wanted to destroy. Something malign had plucked out of this world the only one she unshakably loved—leaving an absence behind without the least gash in reality to show for it. She couldn't hit back at whatever evil was responsible for this tormenting and unreachable void, so she hit at him. He had the advantage of flesh that tore and blood that flowed. And what he had done had a name, it had a beginning and an end.

Uncle Jimmy, he had done something monstrous, but so had she. She'd gone on living: how very weak and passive of her to have kept breathing out and in after watching Jessie stop. She'd witnessed Jessie's torn body turn to husk, Jessie's pinpoint eyes go lightless, and Claire survived the moment, the minutes, the hours, days, weeks, months. *As Jessie wanted, as Jessie wanted.* But how contemptible it was to be able to cope so well, to be able to get up in the morning, dress, eat, go to work, plan a trip, board a plane, find her way around a strange city. All this seemed to assert Jessie's inconsequence in her life. An honest inability to cope would at least have demonstrated how upside down Claire's world had turned. And yet it was only the strength she'd gotten from Jessie that made the going on possible.

In the deepest reach of the night she took the pouch of morphine into the bathroom and stood for the longest time at the sink weighing the thing in her hand. It was uncertain. She needed certainty, and it had none. She got the knife from her purse—strange that the cops had let her keep it—and brought it back with her to the bathroom and extended her arms over the toilet. Then she slit the fleshy plastic and let the narcotic run down into the bowl until nothing was left but a desultory drip. A grim little smile twisted her face as she pressed the flusher. *If only you could step in and follow the stuff down.*

When day began hinting it might arrive, Claire crawled out of the chair, her arms, legs and back aching as if they'd been pummeled all night with bricks. She called the airport and booked a seat on the ten-thirty flight out of Tulsa. Then she showered, dressed, packed her bag and went down to breakfast.

Weekend buffet: boat-like aluminum pans were choked with runny scrambled eggs, triangular slices of French toast snowy with powdered sugar, mounds of glistening sausage, mountains of muffins and sweet rolls, acres of soggy toast. Claire trekked past it all to the far end, where she organized a small bowl of fresh fruit and some instant oatmeal.

The dining room's crisply draped tables had been arranged in long rows, conference-style. Most of the chairs faced a large-screen TV just in front of the waiters' station at the end of the room. She'd seen those images during the night: the same pictures of Timothy McVeigh and Terry Nichols, who'd been arrested for the bombings; the same shots of the Murrah Building, nothing new to show now after four days of rescue operations, but you were going to have to watch it all over again—the building falling, the rescue squads, the interviews with police, firemen, distraught relatives, survivors—because it was a day of national mourning. President Clinton was flying in for the memorial, along with Billy Graham. Hours ago, people had begun lining up for the service at the fairgrounds arena. With the whole state in mourning, the stations had canceled regular programming, and the local channel was airing warmed-over background stories and other lead-ins to the afternoon ceremonies. The motel had seen to it that their guests could come down to eat without missing a single excruciating moment.

Claire took a seat way in back and with ducked head concentrated on her spoon. On both sides of her, strangers chatted over their rolls and sausages in the bluff friendliness that comes of sharing a meal and a tragedy.

"You believe the FBI? Two skinny little creeps planned and executed the whole operation? I don't think so. That guy look like a baby killer to you?" This from a florid man a few seats to her right, addressed to the room in general. Claire wondered what a baby killer looks like. If you cannot imagine blowing children to smithereens, how can you picture someone who would? The young guy to her left said wait and see, there would be more of the same: the millennium was coming in smoke and fire. Except for his navy-blue suit, the guy looked a lot like Terry Nichols.

A woman set her tray down on the table and took the vacant seat next to Claire. "Hard to watch it over and over again," she said.

"Very," Claire agreed and went back to her oatmeal.

"But not as bad as being there. I guess if those people could go through it, the least we can do is give them the dignity of watching."

Claire nodded, though she wondered how her watching would change those people's lives one iota.

"I hope I haven't offended you."

"Not at all. Why would that offend me?"

"It's just that you looked so—I don't know." She stirred a packet of sweetener into her coffee. "I wish I could be part of the rescue effort. I called my office, asked my boss if I could stay on here a few days. No way—I have to get back. Otherwise I'd go over there and help."

Claire said, "It never occurred to me to help."

"Where are you from?"

"New York."

She nodded. "That's why."

"I lost my partner."

The woman went rigid. "In Oklahoma City?"

"No, no. Eight months ago." To stop the tears from spilling, she stared up at the screen. Why had she told a stranger her business? She hadn't meant to; it had just spurted out.

"How awful for you. Seeing all of this—" she swept an arm toward the TV. "It must be hard."

This exchange would go no further. Claire tightened her jaw, clamped down on her tongue and feigned interest in the reporter on camera, a handsome thirteen-year-old from the look of him, preppy haircut, smooth swarthy cheeks, fatuous smile. Up in her room, everything was ready to go, her bag packed, Jessie's notebooks in her carry-on. One last run-through of the drawers, instant checkout, and she'd be on her way back to New York, her home, where evidently people were known across the country for never helping anyone do anything. The fatuous reporter was interviewing some old guy. He was being too chummy, and the guy didn't like it. In New York that young man wouldn't make it from busboy to waiter. Here, he got to interview people for the news.

A name flashed across the bottom of the screen. JAMES A. HENDERSON, it read. And Claire's day changed, and her life changed, just like that.

———

"James Henderson?"

"No more reporters." The sound going away from her. He was hanging up. If she called back, he'd likely take the phone off the hook.

"Jessie!" she shouted into the mouthpiece. "Jessie Desmond." A faint shh-shhing along the line. "Hello? Mr. Henderson? Uncle Jimmy?"

"Jessie? Is that you?"

"I'm Jessie's friend. My name is Claire Bramany. I'd like to meet with you, Mr. Henderson."

"What for?"

"I have a message from Jessie."

"Go ahead, then. What is it?"

"When may I meet with you?"

He paused. "Is Jessie coming along?"

"She—can't be here."

"Well. Then there's no point."

"For old time's sake?"

"'Fraid I'm too busy," he said, and hung up.

For the second time in as many days, she found herself scolding a dead telephone receiver. "No," she told it. "No, you are not."

26

From the eleventh of Jessie's notebooks

The place: West Tulsa, Oklahoma
The time: February 1945

Peanut butter and jelly sandwiches are almost always my favorite, and even when I am not in the mood for them, I can usually roll them into balls and stick them in my coverall pocket to feed to the chickens. JoAnne Forehand and I are over at Teddy Draper's in the kitchen eating peanut butter and jelly sandwiches, but the peanut butter is greasy, and the jelly runs in sticky strings down my arms. Mrs. Draper's kitchen is getting hot, and her oven isn't even lit. Soon as I reach over to the wall, it burns my hand like the pipe that comes out of our water heater. In Grandma's kitchen it never gets this hot, not even at Christmas or Thanksgiving or high summer.

Mrs. Draper goes out back, and almost at the same moment, we hear four blasts and then one, the emergency whistle screaming over and over again until we have to clamp our hands to our ears. The sky out the window is black with angry red fire jumping up after it. Mrs. Draper is hosing water on the roof and sides of the house, and spraying the chickens lest they fry up right there without ever plucking their feathers. She lugs the hose into the house and guns water at the ceiling.

The smell of hot, wet paint keeps getting stronger until it is like another person in the room.

"Teddy Boy," she yells. "You and JoAnne and Jessie—out!"

"What's happening?"

"Never mind, Teddy. Just go out front and wait by the curb till I come."

"We haven't finished our milk," I point out, because the rule is to always finish your milk before leaving the table. But then the glass windowpanes all start snapping and crackling and falling into little pieces, and we skedaddle. The doorknob is almost too hot to touch, and outside, blasts of heat feel like they are sunburning our faces. We find an empty piece of curb and sit down. JoAnne has to stretch her legs out lest someone see her underpants. Her mama never lets her wear anything except sack dresses for play. Flour sacks are soft as anything and make easy dresses, but they are not good for curb sitting. She is right to take caution, because Frank Reilly is hunkered down across the street grinning at us. He is the boy who once tried to show me his thing when he said we should play married. I have on coveralls, so I can sit with my chin resting on my knees.

JoAnne's mama comes to her at a full run and hugs her strong enough to squeeze the stuffings out of her, and next she lights into her hard telling her not to budge, a terrible thing has happened, the oil refinery is on fire and to stay put. JoAnne looks like she'll hold here now even if the fire burns clear through the houses and comes running right up to our toes.

The men start trailing home. Down past the general store there's a wall of pink and gray smoke, and they seem to pop out of it one by one like soldiers in war movies. Their faces and clothes are smudged black, and they get their wives and kids all mussed and dirty hugging them, but no one minds, and then they grab hold of a hose or a bucket and start doing their bit to wet down the houses. JoAnne's daddy comes home, and Mr. Harden. Then Old Man Johnson, who I didn't think even worked at the oil refinery anymore.

Aunt Nedra doesn't come by. "She works in the refinery office," JoAnne's daddy says, like he's been reading my thoughts. "She probably just went on home." We try phoning, but there is no answer. I promise not to worry, but when I see the fire start over the edge of the roof of Teddy's house, I can't help it, I start screaming for Aunt Nedra. I have to find her, make sure she is okay, so I run straight for the gray wall of smoke. At once my eyes start trying to close on me, and I can hear my breathing hard and hoarse inside my head. Somebody's hand grabs for me, but I smash past it and keep on running straight into the wall of smoke. I trip and fall down, but nothing hurts, I am too scared for Aunt Nedra. I get back up and run some more until I can't see where I'm going.

I reach out to find my way, and now I don't know if I have turned around or which way I'm headed. It is too hard to stand, so I drop to my knees and I am coughing and my eyes are not streaming wet anymore. They are prickling hot, and it's a worry maybe they will crackle and come apart like the Drapers' windows. I don't know which way to go, and there is no one near me to say. All I know is I have to keep going to find Aunt Nedra, because she said over my dead body, and because we don't need another bad thing happening, the fire makes three. I have to find her because she loves Uncle Jimmy the way I used to.

I am crouched on a patch of lawn where the grass is short and very scratchy. A voice says, "Jessie," but it's not Aunt Nedra's voice. It's a man's voice, but not Uncle Jimmy, either. The big man lifts me in his arms and says my name again, and I recognize the minister. He puts a wet something on my face, which feels cool, but it is creepy, too, having my face covered so. I start sucking at the cloth, and that is the last thing I know until I wake up in my bed and ask Grandma for my peanut butter and jelly.

She tells me I kept trying to get away and run back into the fire, and finally Gramp had to give me something from the Rexall and put me to bed. But I wouldn't stay asleep. Every little while I'd wake up screaming about the fire until finally

Aunt Nedra came. She is all right except for her hands. If I concentrate hard I can just remember her holding them out to me swaddled in gauze, huge and impossibly white against the singed and smoke-smidged stains of her tan dress. Then I must have gone under, lulled asleep by Aunt Nedra's soft chant, "Sorry, little one, I was taking a message to the foreman. Sorry, little one, there was an explosion. Sorry, little one, I couldn't help it." They say I slept almost two days, but I don't remember anything else except waking up and wanting my sandwich.

The minister stops by to see me every day. He has to bend his head when he comes through the door to my room. He sits down on the edge of my bed, and I have to lean back into my pillows so as not to fall toward him, but then I am looking straight up into the hairs that stick out of his nose. They are brownish and bristly like the hog hairs in Hetty's two bracelets that her daddy braided for her, the same deep color as her skin.

The minister doesn't stay long. He tells me a joke, and he says I am a brave girl, and then he goes and talks to Grandma in the kitchen, unless she's at work at the war plant. Every day he has a new joke about a minister. The best one so far is about the minister who saw a boy in front of a house reaching up and trying to ring a doorbell. The minister walked over to the boy and pushed the doorbell for him. "What do we do now, little man?" he said, and the boy answered, "Run like heck!"

Gramp says our minister's jokes are worse than his sermons, and Grandma says how would he know, he always sleeps through church. Gramp doesn't tell her how he knows, he just says anyhow they are better than the Jewish tailor jokes Uncle Jimmy tells all the time. My father is Jewish, but he is not a tailor. Grandma says if Gramp had to go in the army like Jimmy did and live cheek by jowl with those people, he would be making some of those jokes, too, like as not.

One time in the barn I heard Uncle Jimmy up in the hayloft tell some men there's a Jew word that means hello and good-bye. Both! Another man said that's because Jews don't want you to know whether they're coming or going, and everybody laughed, so it must have been a joke. But in Sunday school Mrs. Thompson read from the Bible that a man shall cleave unto his wife, and the word cleave means God wants him to stick to her through thick and thin, and she to him, too, even when he has to go to war or even if he comes home with a terrible wound. Many a time I have seen Grandma use her cleaver to cleave meat and bone, which means cut it apart, so I figure the Christians have a word that can mean its opposite, too. Cleave—cling together and cut apart, both! I don't know if that is a joke, but I think Gramp will laugh if I tell him.

For three days I am only allowed to sit up in bed and not get out except to use the bathroom. After that, I can be outside resting on the porch swing, bundled up in the patchwork quilt that Grandma made when she was just a bride her first time around and still madly in love with the man who was the father of Uncle Jimmy and Uncle Cubby and my mother. His name was Nathan, from Arkansas, and one day he up and left, so Grandma divorced him. She held onto the quilt, though, which is so big and heavy I can't carry it by myself. Grandma wraps me like an Egyptian mummy and tells me to breathe the fresh air and goes back inside. Then I go to stretching and wriggling and kicking until the quilt becomes floppy and tent-like and I can burrow inside its warm darkness breathing in smells of myself and the dusty nest I've made.

That's how the minister finds me, my head where my feet should be and vice versa, deep under the covers with a flashlight that is getting dim, reading a book.

"Is there a Jessica under there?" he says. I poke my nose out and squint in the bright afternoon.

"Well, Jessica, your grandma tells me you're going to be moving soon."

"No, I'm not."

"To your aunt and uncle's?"

"No, sir."

He'd been raising his hat to his head, and I thought he was about to step down off the porch. Instead, he perches on the edge of the swing and looks at me. I pull myself up and try to meet his pale-blue gaze without squirming. My book falls out of the covers onto the porch floor.

"What are you reading?" he says, bending to get it. "*A Little Book of Profitable Tales*—good choice."

It wasn't my choice at all. The school librarian sent it over because it's written by Eugene Field, who gave the school his name.

"How do you like it?" the minister says.

Why do grown-ups ask me what I think of things that don't make any difference at all, but when it comes to things that matter everything to me, nobody wants my opinion? Like going to live with Aunt Nedra. That is what they have in mind for me just as soon as I am up and about, and that must be what Mr. Howard is here to talk to me about. Aunt Nedra's hands are all bandaged up and they hurt a lot, and everybody says I could be a big help, washing dishes and clothes, cleaning out hairbrushes, cooking, sweeping up the floor. A neighbor lady looks in on her, and a visiting nurse comes to help with personal needs, which means going to the toilet. But Aunt Cissie says there are still so many other things I could do to help out, and Grandma says I'd be such good company for Aunt Nedra, too.

Uncle Jimmy says it's a fine idea, just for a short while, and I won't be in the way at all, what with him away on business so often and Aunt Nedra all alone. "And if it works out good, why then, we'll see." Aunt Nedra has always been fond of me, he says, and Lord knows, I'm devoted to her, running hell-bent for leather into all that smoke and flame like an imp from hell just aching to get home after a long cold time on the road. "Just for a short while," Grandma says. And Uncle Jimmy chimes in again, "If it works out good, why then, we'll see."

Nobody seems to think I would be trouble under Aunt Nedra's feet like I'm trouble underfoot everywhere else. Everyone seems to think I will go wherever they decide. They never think I might run away and hide in the woods and live on berries or whatever victuals I can scrounge.

The Sooners, when they first settled Oklahoma, had to carry all their victuals with them, or perish. Victuals are important for getting through the winter. But I think Hetty would bring me victuals if I asked her to. If we didn't have a war on, I could maybe take a boat across the Pacific and get shipwrecked and live on an island like the Swiss Family Robinson, and live off coconut trees and never be heard from again. Then wouldn't everybody be sorry they wanted to send me to Uncle Jimmy!

"You know, Jessica, Mrs. Thompson tells me you're a smart girl, the best student in Sunday school," the minister says.

"She does?" Mrs. Thompson tells me I ask too many questions, and I would learn a lot more if I opened my ears more and my mouth less.

"Sometimes the things God does are hard to understand. Hard for grown-ups as well as children, even smart ones like you. That's where your faith comes in.

"Trials are meant to try us," Mr. Howard continues, "and they wouldn't be trials if they weren't hard. But you must remember that God is merciful and never sends a trial too hard to bear. With Jesus's help, we find the strength we need.

"Jessica, you have suffered greatly in the loss of both your parents. I didn't know Mr. Desmond, but I've known Nancy Ann since we were both children, so I know that God blessed you with a kind and loving mother. You must believe she is in a better place, and you will see her again someday."

I think of my mother in a better place, a beautiful place full of brightly colored flowers like the picture on my wall in New York, or like the land of Oz with people dancing and singing, except no wicked witches or flying monkeys to scare her, and no diabetes either. Just Glinda the Good Witch and my mother in ruby slippers clicking her heels together three times. *You have always had the power to go home* the witch says, and she touches her wand to my feet, and it is me wearing the ruby slippers, and I open my ears to what she says, and sure enough I learn something.

"God has a plan for you, and He has blessed you, too, with a wonderful family. You are not alone, you are not an orphan, so long as you have your family and community around you."

"Minister?"

He holds up his finger to show me he has a little more to say and please to wait my turn. "Your grandparents, your aunts and uncles love you very much," he says. "Your uncle Jimmy and aunt Nedra are ready to step in—"

"Minster, I'm not the person you think I am. Every time I say 'here' when they call the roll in school I'm telling a kind of a lie."

His eyes widen a little, but otherwise there is no sign I've said anything queer.

"I'm not Jessie Desmond. Chester Desmond was never my real father, even when he was alive. My real father is Albert Friedman."

"Friedmann?" pronouncing it funny at the end, drawing out the *a* and the *n*.

"I'm Jessica Ann Louise Friedman."

"Why did—" he starts. "Why didn't—" he stops again, swallows.

"You see, I thought it was a secret. I didn't know it was a lie. I'm very sorry."

"Where is your father now, Jessica? Fighting for Uncle Sam, I hope?"

I say no, but I don't tell the minister how Grandma says it's a scandal the way my father used his daughter to stay out of the service, positively shameless and cowardly. My silence is another kind of a lie, I guess, but I figure I'm following one of Grandma's rules: if you can't say anything nice, don't say it at all.

"He's not...on the other side?"

What other side? Could Mr. Howard think my father is a ghost? "I'm not an orphan."

"Your mother was such a handsome woman. Sophisticated, worldly. She could have had any man she wanted in this town, you know, before she went east—looking for more, I guess. Yes, I see how it could happen." Something is adding up in his head. Gramp says the minister is the kind of mathematician who adds up two and two and gets five. Tell him you went out to the farm to visit Cubby and Cissie for the day, and next thing you know he's thinking Cissie must be in bed with her pregnancy, doctor's orders, and the Sunshine Committee from the church is bringing over a chicken pot pie for you to take up there. Or tell him you've got hold of some piglets to sell, and next thing you know Mrs. Howard is dropping by with her daughter's winter coat and mittens from last year, perfectly serviceable, but too small, and just right for Gramp's little granddaughter.

"I see it. Your mom was young, impressionable. She met someone with European manners, steeped in old-world culture, the music, the literature, the philosophy. Before the war, I'm saying."

That other side? "Minister, you mean is my father fighting for the enemy?"

"And then, Pearl Harbor. The urge to put it under wraps."

"You think my father would kill Americans?"

"No point in flaunting a German connection."

I don't want to tell him my father is a Jew, because maybe being a Jew would be worse than being a Nazi. Instead I say, "My father lives in Brooklyn, and he's no traitor."

"Ah. Brooklyn."

"I bet he hates the Krauts."

"Of course. I see. Brooklyn." He sighs. "And when did you last see him, Jessie?"

"Maybe...I don't know...two years ago, about?"

"And have you spoken with him? Over the phone?"

"It's long distance."

"Letters?"

"I had a valentine for him, but I never got to send it, because my mother died."

The minister looks around the porch like Grandma when she's lost her reading glasses, open-eyed but not seeing, like he's trying to look hard but trying harder to remember where he mislaid those darn things. "You'll excuse me a moment, won't you, dear?" he says, not waiting for me to answer, not even looking my way, pushing himself off the swing so it waggles crazily after he gets up.

He doesn't even knock, just opens the front door and walks right back into the house like it was his own, and just before the door closes I hear him tell Grandma, "I wasn't aware Jessie has a father living in New York."

27

Claire and Jim

Oklahoma City, Oklahoma
April 23, 1995

Her call had unsettled him, and he'd gone out for a walk. The streets were hushed, everyone out at the memorial service or home watching it on TV. Word was that the president was going to give special mention to all the volunteers, and he had planned on being there for it, he being a volunteer, but her call had disrupted him. The streets were empty, and he kept on walking.

The damp air felt heavy and acrid. It left a greasiness in his nostrils and on his tongue. The ashy, metallic tang was not something a person grew accustomed to or ceased to notice. It stayed with you, like the carnage in the Murrah, like those flashbacks from the war that hung on forever.

One little girl, something about her nose and cheeks, the tender flesh, the sprinkling of freckles, reminded him of Jessie, though not with the pure light of Jessie's complexion, never seen its like before or since. At the bomb site he'd spotted the orange Band-Aid on her knee, and they'd gotten her out, dirtied all over and bloody, but not seriously injured. Freckles that reminded him of Jessie, and her Band-Aid. One or the other of Jessie's knees always wore a Band-Aid. A patch of white to point up the creamy perfection of her limbs. And now this phone call. Jessie's friend, she'd said. Why Jessie's friend?

He was exhausted, his body leaden. The exhilaration of the rescue operation, the high of being swallowed up by the moment and the task at hand, was gone now, supplanted by the letdown of having no job to do. He knew this feeling from the war: critical missions he alone could carry out, and afterward—nothing.

He ought to get a dog, that's what. He ought to get a hound, a good hunter, and quit the city—clear out and spend some time in the woods. A dog would be good company on long rambles. He ought to get himself a brown dog and go hunting.

Claire rode the elevator to the eighth floor, found the apartment, rang the bell. The hallway was dim and quiet. No one came to the door. She hunkered down to wait.

As he stepped off the elevator he saw her seated on the carpet, leaning against the wall, trying to read a paperback book in the shadowed hallway, her head bent over the book, her knees up, her skirt pulled over them. He'd seen Jessie like that on the porch one day, with those boys she used to play with, what were their names? Names gone to him now, but she was the same, leaning against the clapboards in the shadow of the porch, knees pulled up under her sack dress, that book he'd given her, *Cherokee Legends* or something like that, open against her legs, and her nose almost touching the pages.

He was straight: her first impression as he stepped off the elevator. Not straight as in heterosexual. Straight as in tall and foursquare, so squared off, in fact, that he looked almost flat, as if he might disappear when turned sideways, but facing you head-on, no way were you going to get past him. He came at her like an arrow.

She extended her hand, preparatory to introducing herself. He took it and held it quietly between both of his. "I've been expecting you," he said.

She pulled the hand back and, easing it into a fold of her skirt, tried surreptitiously to rub off the feel of his flesh. He watched her do it, visibly amused.

"You know who I am?"

"You phoned. I told you not to come. Women never do what I say."

"How do you know I'm not a reporter?"

"They're all over at the memorial service. I guess I'd've been there too, hadn't been for your call."

He unlocked the door and ushered her into an apartment that was darker than the windowless hallway until he flicked on the recessed lights dotting the ceiling. A small foyer opened out into a spacious living room. Shattered glass doors at the far end were boarded over, the merest glimmer of fuzzy daylight leaking in around the edges of the plywood.

The place was comfortable, simply furnished in shades of ivory and khaki with touches of deep red. She sat down on the three-piece beige sectional couch, he on a striped-linen chair. A square glass-topped coffee table separated them, nothing on it but a skim of dust. Face-to-face with him now.

"I wondered what you'd look like," he said.

On the wall were framed pictures of jungle creatures— monkeys, a leopard, a jaguar, exotic birds. Bookplates, they looked like, colored plates torn from old tomes, mounted and framed, some in gold, some in marquetry. "How is your wife?"

The man's laugh was high, sharp and humorless, like the sudden yap of a dog. "My wife left me years ago."

Claire said she was sorry.

He offered her coffee, tea. She declined.

"Quickie war wedding," he said. "Sometimes they work out. Sometimes—" He shrugged.

"Did Nedra go back to Kansas?" She tried not to put any emphasis on Nedra's name, just let it fall out of her mouth, the most natural thing in the world, the expected thing, so he wouldn't know she was fishing, trying to make sure this time. He didn't answer. She'd bet anything he wore the same greasy leer that day at his mother-in-law's farm in Kansas, the day he'd put moves on Jessie while making a show of drying her tears. But she had to be sure she didn't have the wrong man again.

He said, "Tell me about yourself. Where do you live?"

"Park Slope." No mistake this time. She had to prove he was Uncle Jimmy. "That's in Brooklyn."

He nodded like it fit with his expectation. His hair, the jaundiced color of old sneakers, might or might not once have been blond. "What do you do?" he said. His eyes, unremarkably brown, might or might not have faded from a coppery glint.

"I'm an accountant."

"An accountant! Now, that's somethin', ain't it?" Putting on the yokel accent. He hadn't talked that way on TV. "Good money in accounting, is there?"

"Good enough."

He rubbed at his thighs, the fingers crawling over the verge of his knees, then straightening as he pulled his arms back. Knuckles like gumballs. Fingers bending away from his palms like the legs of spiders. Gigantic, the hands. As Jessie described.

"I had a hard time finding you," Claire said.

"Been right here, twenty years and more."

"I was looking in Tulsa." Up Red Fork Hill: that poor man, she owed him an apology, but didn't dare contact him.

"You sure I can't get you something to drink?" His gaze swiveled away from her as if seeking a waiter to hail. "A Coke? Orange juice?"

She shook her head. "I thought I'd try Cubby, but I didn't know how he'd be listed. Cubby's obviously not his given name."

"Name's Nathan, after our real dad. I used to call him Natty to get a rise out of him. Drove him right up the wall."

Got you now, Uncle Jimmy. Not so cagey, after all, are you? It's you. It's really you.

He was eyeing her oddly. She said, "How did they get Cubby out of Nathan?"

"Bear cub, I think. Mama Bear, Papa Bear, Cubby. He's dead and gone now. Cancer got him."

She started to say she was sorry; he started to say Cissie still lived out at the old place; they stopped at the same time, and she waved him on. He said the twins had moved away. The boy was in Seattle doing something with computers, the girl a nurse in St. Louis with half-grown children of her own, and Claire wanted to tell him she didn't give a rat's ass what any of them did or where they were, only that he was who she knew he was; and suddenly he was choking, then gasping, then lost to a spate of heavy, wheezy coughs that went on and on, until his face was gray and his eyes streamed. She waited stone-faced while the spasm subsided and he got his breath back. "It's just from the smoke," he said, gesturing toward what lay beyond the boarded-up patio doors. He got to his feet, went into the kitchen and returned with a glass of water for himself, and one for her. "So what brings you to Oklahoma?"

"You."

"Me? I'm flattered." He didn't look flattered. Gratified, maybe, as if her purpose in coming was not unexpected, although her admitting to it so readily might be. She was irked that he didn't look flattered.

"Don't be," she said.

"Why not? You here to sue me?"

"What for?" Claire said. She could play cagey, too.

"National pastime," he said. "Nobody needs a reason anymore."

"Bullshit."

"Ah, sweet pea. You oughtn't to talk that way."

He'd called her sweet pea. Too much was happening. She had her proof of what he'd done, he'd just admitted it. He had, hadn't he? No other reason to mention a lawsuit. "You won't deny there are grounds."

"Now, sweet pea, why would I deny you anything?"

Sweet pea. It made her die a little more inside.

"I'm not Jessie," she said. "I'm Claire Bramany."

"Mind you, I'm not copping to anything."

He said he knew all about those people who came back years later complaining and carrying on. He watched the news. Did you see him complaining that Nedra led him on year after year, then left him flat? Did you see him going back and suing her for what she did to him during their marriage?

"What did she do?"

"A lot. Bored me to extinction, for one."

"What did she do that's actionable?"

"Well, now, that's between me and her, because I'm not going to sue her." It was a long time ago, he said. A very long time. What if we all had to go through life looking back over our shoulders for every mean thing we did to one another? For every mistake we made? For times we tried to be kind, only to find out we were mistaken, and our kindness wasn't kindness at all but the reverse? "You ever do something nice, you thought was nice, and it turned out somebody was mad as a bee's nest at you?"

Claire didn't answer him.

"You shouldn't have waited so long to come," he continued. "Pushing your luck here, you know. I might have been dead."

"Ought to be dead."

He'd been lifting his water glass. He froze with it halfway to his lips. "Ah, Jessie," he said.

"I'm Claire. Like I said. Jessie's friend."

He studied her, head to toe, taking his time about it, assessing. Medium height, medium build. Telltale highlights of red in her chestnut hair, hazel eyes flecked with gold. "Sure you are. Just a 'friend.' A friend who traveled—what? two thousand miles?—just to look up an old relative. A friend who never met me before but hates my guts. Happens all the time: friend says guess I'll fly clear across the country then drive halfway across the state, all just to pop in on a guy I've never met, because I wish he would drop dead, and I want to tell him so to his face."

"That about sums it up. Only I was planning to kill you after I said hello."

He laughed, little heh heh heh noises, like wasn't she

adorable. "Well, that is a relief, sweet pea. Here I thought you were planning on suing me."

"Unfortunately, I have no standing in a court of law." She fumbled in her bag.

"What you got in there? Got a gun? Going to shoot me now?"

She pulled out her driver's license, slapped it down on the table and nudged it toward him. He ignored it.

"You couldn't shoot a grasshopper if it jumped in your soup. People don't change, sweet pea."

Her eyes flared. "Don't call me that name. Don't say it again." She flipped the license across the table. "Nobody is your sweet pea."

He picked it up, read it, turned it over and read the back, as if there was something to discover there, as if it wasn't just bureaucratic form. He didn't want to look at her. He'd believed she was Jessie. Now, of course, it was plain she didn't look anything like the vivid girl in his mind. He could tell her to leave.

No, he couldn't do that. "Jessie sent you to me, did she? Remembers her old uncle?"

"Not especially."

"We had great times together. She tell you about those? I took her to the state fair, the rodeo. Taught her card tricks. Bet she can still do those tricks, too. Near drove us crazy with them, Doc trying to get his work done out in the barn, and Jessie trailing him around with the deck." Actually, now he thought of it, maybe it wasn't Jessie he'd taught the tricks to; maybe it was his son. They'd had some fun together playing cards. But the boy never amounted to much. A salesman, like his daddy, though nowhere near as successful. He hadn't the gift of gab. Diabetic, like Nancy Ann, and quiet like Nedra. He should have been a museum guard or something, the way he looked like he always was ready to shush somebody. "The boarder, he was the only one who'd sit still for those card tricks. The old guy."

"Sammy."

He smiled, like he'd caught her, because how would she know the old guy's name? "Never knew Jessie to be shy. Is she feeling shy? Sent you on ahead to break the ice, I guess. You can tell her for me I don't hold a grudge. What's in the past is over and done. I'd be right pleased to see Jessie."

"Jessie—died." That was the hard word to say. It took all the air away.

Jim Henderson closed his eyes. He saw her when he closed his eyes. She had a jump rope in her hand and ribbons plaited in her hair. Luminescent, bone-china skin. Watercolor eyelids: you didn't find violet like that, ever, on grown women, for all the eye shadow they gopped on.

When his eyes opened again, they surprised Claire with their moist red pain.

He cleared his throat. He said, "When?"

"Last August." At three-oh-one in the afternoon on the eleventh, a day that should be banished forever from the calendar.

"From?"

"Excuse me?"

"Why'd she die?"

"Because this is an unjust universe."

"You got that right, Ms. Bramany," he said. Ms. Bramany: the formality of it touched her. The smirk was gone from his lips. He was solemn, all trace of good ol' boy erased. It was hard not to believe this was the real Jimmy showing through, a genuine deep-down, soulful Jimmy. It was hard to remember that this might be the false Jimmy, and the other the true one.

"She was running an errand. A drunk driver hit her."

"She suffered?"

As if I'd tell you.

A silence lengthened between them.

"You got a photo in there?"

Claire had three photos, not that she wanted to show him.

"Only reason I let you in here is I thought you were Jessie. Last I saw Jessie, she wasn't ten years old. Now you tell me she's gone. Why should I believe you?"

"Why else would I be here?"

"Hell, I don't know. My name's been in the paper. All kinds of crazies come crawling out of the woodwork when they see you in the news. Scammers, blackmailers."

"People seem to think you're some kind of hero."

"Last I saw Jessie, guess I wasn't more than twenty myself. Long time ago."

"No, it wasn't."

He shook his head, and his grin flashed. "Takes two old coots to agree to that."

For an instant, there was a kind of sweetness about him.

"So. You going to show me that picture or not?"

Claire had snapped one of the photos while Jessie was watching the Sarajevo Olympic games on TV, and the camera had captured the intensity of Jessie's attention, the beautiful active stillness in her gaze. Behind that photo was one of the two of them at Long Beach taken ages ago. They'd been "helping" Lisi build a fort in the wet sand, forming parapets and moats and outlying fortifications. Long after Lisi had lost interest and gone off to search the shore for shells, someone had snapped them kneeling in the midst of their domain, dirty, wind wrecked, happy in the late-afternoon shadows. The third was only a passport photo from a series of four taken at the beefed-up pharmacy near their office, but it happened to be a good shot. It captured something of Jessie's enthusiasm for everything, even the awkward business of getting passport photos taken in a drab little booth in an overcrowded store by a pimply-faced clerk with big feet. It was this picture, still crisp, not yet worn and curling at the edges like the others, that she pulled from her wallet and held out to him.

He took it from her, nodded at it, nodded again, then turned the photo over facedown and pushed it back across the table toward Claire. "She was a wonder."

"Yes, she was."

Behind his eyelids she was there. Not that woman in the photo. The girl, hair on her body all downy, not a pore showing in her skin, nothing coarse. "She was a wonder, beauty like that...."

"She was a child."

"Nothing self-conscious, either, the way she flung herself into play, into chores, into every second of living. Beauty like that never dies, not long as I'm here to remember."

"She was an innocent child. You destroyed that."

"No, ma'am. Love never destroys."

"Look, you may play hero to the rest of the world, but I know who you are. You are evil. You are an evil man to the depths of your miserable, shriveled, desiccated, puny little soul." What was she doing? She'd promised herself restraint. Now she was tumbling into some hideous third-rate soap opera. His mouth was fixed in a sneer, lips rolled under, yellow horse teeth clenched. She felt powerless to halt the script or change it: how could you, how could you do it, you filthy piece of crawling slime?

She already knew what his answer would be. He'd blame it on Jessie. *She led me on.*

Unbearable, what was coming, yet she delivered her line like a pro, venomously enunciated and resonant. How could you, you slime? Then she focused on his shoe tops and waited for the words that would put her once and for all over the edge into madness: *girls know what they're doing. They drive little boys crazy, and why not me, too? She fluttered her eyelids, she plunked herself in my lap, she giggled and swished. Girls pretend to say no, but they know what they're doing every minute.*

For the longest time she waited, tensed to detonate, scrutinizing his gray running sneakers with their touches of navy suede, orange Nike logo just under his ankle. White cotton crew socks, khaki Dockers, a striped rugby shirt, navy and white. She hung by a thread, waiting, while he only sat there unmoving and mute, studying her, his face gathered in concentration, worry lines etched deep. When finally she met his eyes, he looked as unnerved as she, but he looked, too, as if some conundrum had been untangled, some problem teased out and solved.

"She left word for me."

Claire winced.

"She did, didn't she? I'm not looking for an inheritance, mind you. I'm set, far as that's concerned. Been in sales all my life; life's been good to me. But maybe after all these years she left me word."

"Mr. Henderson, she left notebooks full of words."

"And that's why you're here?"

Her hands, she noticed, were trembling, but the frenzy Claire had been dreading—half dreading and half banking on, too—was gone. She nodded in response to his question, in no way calm or cool, but someway collected. Where was the storm that had nearly overwhelmed her? Evaporated, vanished.

"I knew it," he crowed. "Knew she couldn't run out on me like that and nary a word." His hand reached toward her, eyes searching the cushions each side of her, the purse in her lap, the floor near her feet. "You got 'em with you, don't you? Those notebooks?"

"In the car."

"Good. We'll get them. She wrote them for me."

For him? The idea had never crossed Claire's mind. "They're not for you," she said. "They're about you. About you, and Grandma, Gramp, Cubby and Cissie, Nedra and John Ellis and Teddy Draper. Cousin La Junta. Pedro." She listed everyone, every name she could think of, some he didn't know, Mr. Shapiro, Miss Forrest, Miss Glade.

"But I was her favorite."

The hell he was. To steady herself, Claire picked up the glass in front of her and took a long pull at the water. It was tepid, unpleasantly alkaline. Jessie used to say people don't change; they only get more so. This self-centered bastard was living proof of it. Kids could change, though, which was why Jessie loved working with them, because she could change the more so they were going to become.

It was time, now, to take Uncle Jimmy down a peg or two. "Jessie was my lover. I was hers."

He nodded, but not like he understood. Like his neck was on a spring, and he had hit a bump, and his head couldn't stop bobbing, bobbing, bobbing. Like a damn dashboard ornament.

"This is a mistake," Claire said, gathering herself to leave. Whatever she'd thought to do here or find here, it wasn't happening. A fool's errand, from start to finish.

He watched her as from a distance, saw her collect herself—first her face, then her things—and stand up and move away. She was going, and he was glad of it. He was fed up with her. He nodded when she said, "I never should have come." On that, if on nothing else, they saw eye to eye.

"I'll walk you to your car."

With a flick of her hand, she dismissed the offer. "Not necessary."

But it *was* necessary, because he wanted what she had, and he wouldn't be left empty-handed. For her part, she believed, mistakenly, that all was done, and to drag out the torment would be useless.

They went down, she cold-shouldering him, he loping half a pace behind. Work was in full swing at the bomb site. Through the newly erected chain-link fence they could see the cleanup continuing, although the rescue operation had been called off. No hope remained of anyone being found alive. Above the sound of motors churning, Claire heard the mournful tones of a trumpet. Someone beyond the vast field of rubble was playing "Taps."

In that very field, not two days past, the man walking with her had pulled children to safety. He had pulled young soldiers in Italy to safety at Monte Cassino, in the middle of one of the worst battles of World War II. He was brave, and he had saved lives, which was more than she had ever done. Yet he had blighted the life of the one person she held dear. And it wasn't even how could you look at a child that way. Children *were* gorgeous: he was right about that. How fleeting their beauty was—how soon the body changed, hair darkening and thickening, bones growing prominent. Not that adults were unsightly—just different. They didn't have the faces of children, the bodies of children, the minds of children. They didn't have the energy or the curiosity or the liveliness of children. You could desire a child; that was understandable, if only barely. What wasn't permissible was to act upon it, because you spoiled her childhood forever. Did that even need to be said?

The clouds had lifted, and watery sunlight glinted off the rental car, a white Chevy parked along the fence at the far side of the site. When she stopped, he bent to peer in the window. Nothing at all cluttered the seats. "I don't see those notebooks."

She had her key out, ready to open the driver's door.

He said, "You want money, is that it?"

Furious, she turned on him. "No, I do not want any money."

"You got other pictures?"

"What? No. They're personal."

"I'm not judging, mind you, but you come here saying she was a dyke, a butch, whatever you ladies call yourselves, and I have to know."

"They're pictures of Jessie and me. And Jessie's daughter. I'd rather not show them to you."

"Jessie has a daughter?"

"All grown up. Too old for you."

She was pleased to see him flinch.

"I'm not a pedophile, pederast, whatever. I loved Jessie, and she loved me." He leaned against the car and stared out over the devastation. "I don't know what I did to turn her against me."

"Oh, for God's sake. You ruined her life. Don't you know that?"

"No, Ms. Bramany, obviously I didn't ruin her life."

Damn him, that he could take Jessie's pluck and her good fortune and turn them to his favor. He was right: Jessie's life was anything but a ruin. She'd healed. She'd been that strong, and that lucky. Which didn't let him off the hook. "And the others? How many children have you raped? Count them up on your fingers and toes if you've got enough. How many little girls did you crush in your long-and-despicable life?"

"There were none," he said.

A lie, she believed, though one she was obscenely grateful for.

"None," he repeated.

She looked away from him, across to the fence, where people had been arriving out of nowhere, it seemed, their arms full of flowers. They set the bouquets on the ground or twined blooms through the wire. They tied ribbons to the fence and poked shreds of paper through the slots, pigeonholing their letters, poems and prayers. Claire watched them come and go, people who wanted to talk about people who were dead, strangers nodding to each other, clasping each other's hands, some even embracing.

This man next to her resting his back against the car, this man she'd traveled halfway across the country to confront—he was more of a stranger to her than the wandering pilgrims at the fence, whose pain she knew only too well. The world was peopled with lonely souls who felt diminished, empty and broken in some deep, unfixable way. But Jimmy wasn't one of them. He ought to look more like a Bubba. He ought to have a mouth like a carnival booth, a circus fun house entrance.

"I thought you'd be like Howdy Doody," she said.

"Sorry to disappoint."

She was sorely aware of him contemplating her. An ache swelled in her throat. "What was she like?"

It was the last question Claire thought she wanted to ask this man. Or else it was the reason she'd come all along—just to ask this one thing, just to talk to someone else who'd loved Jessie and, for however brief a time, been loved by Jessie. Oh, God, to be so needy, go so low as to beg this monster for his memories. Yet how hungry she was for every detail. How she ached to take that one little girl in her arms, defy time, space and dimension, and undo her betrayal.

"Like a bird," he responded. "Like a bird I saw in Italy when we sailed up from Sicily and landed near Rome. You spotted her for just one instant in among the foliage, before she was gone. Then two trees over, a sudden—" he faltered, hunting for the word, "—a sudden glory flickering through the branches." All he'd ever known, he said, were genteel ladies and sluts, but Jessie, she was something else again. Outside of battle, she was the only vivid thing that had ever happened to him.

"You can't mean that," Claire said.

But he did mean it, and he was glad to say it out loud after a lifetime of silence. *Outside of battle, she was the only vivid thing ever to happen to me.* If Claire could only see her, a creature who would rather run than walk, rather sing than talk, bursting with life, aflame with questions about everything and answers that just about blew his socks off when he saw how her mind figured.

There was nothing he said that Claire didn't already know, and know better than he. The child he evoked was maybe not so unprecedented a little prodigy as each of them opined, maybe simply your ordinarily precious little girl trying to find her way through a very confusing world. A girl to be treasured, as both of them had treasured her, one rapaciously and to her harm, the other generously and to her healing, but both in ways that society called ugly.

She was gone to them both, though more alive than life to them both; and so they talked on through the April afternoon, because there was no one else on earth who would talk this way about Jessie, not all afternoon, not for no reason except the pleasure of finding her in someone else's mind—thus not so absent after all. They talked until the sun was low in the sky; and still people streamed to the fence. People who carried the weight of loss with them on slumped shoulders. Who delivered their offerings, their benedictions and turned away with suffering faces.

All this time Claire had envied Jessie. Dead meant being past pain and out of all trouble, while Claire slogged on alone. This world, those mourners there, were tormented by common worries—the rent money, or that swelling lump on the breast. In the spirit world she imagined, one saw and understood all. There might be the possibility of wonders and mysteries inconceivable this side of the grave—and never the need to give a single thought to getting dinner cooked or the plants watered. Whatever that world beyond was, she knew she wanted it. And so it had never occurred to her until now, watching a teenager in baggy pants lay his wreath against the fence, that the spirit world might envy us—envy us the fall of snowflakes on our tongues, the savor of honeysuckle in the air, the tang of new wine, the taut stretch of muscles, the trickle of sweat. Even our discomforts enviable, the small aches and twinges that tell us *Yes, I'm alive. I'm alive.*

And still she didn't know what to make of this man beside her. Maybe he'd really loved Jessie in some twisted, puerile way. Maybe he'd gone to war an ordinary Joe, and the war had turned him crazy. Maybe he'd never touched another child, or maybe he'd molested dozens. She couldn't know the truth. If it had ever been knowable, it was long buried. She could only know what was important now: that she had helped make Jessie whole again—a truth to hold dear. But this despicable man? What truth could she know of him? He had acted courageously in the midst of terror and chaos. Because of his daring in those crucial minutes and hours after the bomb blew, some people were safe at home with their families, and some families were spared from loss. He had redeemed those people's lives, and it seemed to her now that, in doing so, he might have redeemed his own. That's why she went to the trunk of the car and withdrew Jessie's notebooks: because he didn't understand what he'd done to her. That's why she left them with him to read: because he was human and might—just might—come to know.

"I don't forgive you. Jessie might have; Jessie could have. I can't."

"No question, Jessie will."

Claire started up the car and turned the wheel, but spoke one last time before pulling away. "Try as you will to deny it, Jessie's never coming back." Her words were her dagger, striking home. "Never."

28

From the last of Jessie's notebooks

The place: Brooklyn, New York
The time: Spring 1945

Belle is my new mother. She says we are going to be a real family, so I must never mention Nancy Ann or talk about her in any way to anyone. But I can still talk to God if I want to. So if my mother is really dead, maybe she will hear me, too.

On my last night in Tulsa I made a wish on a chicken bone how my new home would look. It mostly didn't come true, especially the dining room—they don't have one here—but anyway in a do-over, I wouldn't waste my wish on wallpaper or a Victrola, I'd wish for a second bathroom, because Jane (Belle's daughter and now my sister) spends hours in there on her complexion. She soaks her face with a steaming washcloth and squeezes her blackheads at the mirror and comes out with her nose and cheeks and chin covered in red splotches. I don't tell her about looking worse than when she went in, because Jane is nice to me.

Our bedroom is painted yellow and blue, and my father has promised to decorate it along the borders of the walls and doorways with stenciled men in bright-red coats on horseback. The furniture is not at all like in my father's design books. I have a plain wooden dresser with plain wooden feet and plain wooden knobs and a plain wooden top where I set up my mother's photograph to smile at me in my sleep. The dresser is painted yellow, and there is plenty of room in the drawers, since Belle threw out most of my clothes when I unpacked. I must never wear flour sack dresses again, I will have plenty of hand-me-downs from Jane. I find out later that my mother's photograph was an affront to Belle who has offered me a home out of the goodness of her heart and is treating me just like her very own flesh and blood. The picture is gone. It isn't in any of my drawers, and Belle won't like me asking where it has disappeared to, but I can keep my bicycle and I still have the Indian beaded collar and purse my mother gave me from Times Square, so if my mother is really not dead, she will have a way to recognize me.

The bike got here just like Gramp promised it would. I wanted to bring it with me on the plane, but I couldn't, and probably just as well. I clean forgot my copy of *Cherokee Myths and Legends* right there on the seat when I had to change planes in Washington, D.C., and say good-bye to Hetty and get her name in my autograph book, which is filled up now on every page. My last day at school Miss Forrest sent it around the room for the whole class to sign. She wrote: *I shall miss you, Jessie. Sincerely, Agnes Forrest.*

Grandma, too—she said she'll miss me, and don't forget I can always come back to them. Gramp muttered and rubbed his backside in front of the fireplace just as though it had a fire lit and kept going out to the front porch to watch the sky for weather until Grandma chided him to quit banging that screen door. When it was time to go, he carried my suitcase and set it down real slow in the driveway. He kissed me on the top of my head and straightened up. Then, like he'd just thought of it, he bent and kissed me again where my hair is parted down the center. I held onto his hand, wrapping it across my throat. Pretty soon, he grunted that the hens needed looking in on and loped off to the henhouse, and I got into the car.

Uncle Jimmy and Aunt Nedra drove me to the airport in silence, no singing, no jokes, no rhymes. Aunt Nedra's bandaged hands were still hurting her, and anyway she's always quiet. Uncle Jimmy was mad at me, that's why he was acting nothing like himself. Not that I cared, as long as he wasn't planning on fussing over his good-byes, or making me hug him or anything. Still and all, the miles go slow when not a word is spoken and the only sound is the phut phut phut of his fingers thrumming hard against the steering wheel. I hummed a little until he said it was getting on his nerves, and then I kind of wondered half out loud to myself about my father's family and how they might be saving buttons for me.

"Saving what?"

"Story buttons, Aunt Nedra. Telling where my ancestors lived and what they did."

"Who knows, child. They must have lived in Europe somewhere. Or worse."

Uncle Jimmy grunted and stretched his neck like Gramp waking up after a snooze behind his newspaper. "Probably sold the buttons right off their clothes."

"Jimmy!"

"Those people wouldn't save nothin' unless it was worthless now, would they? They'd sell it."

"That's enough, James. You're being ugly."

He caught my eye in the rearview mirror. I looked away. "No buttons, Jessie. All sold, sealed and delivered. Just like you."

Aunt Nedra sighed, and nobody made another sound all the way to the airport. At the curb, he got out of the car and handed the porter my suitcase, my ticket and a fifty-cent piece. "See that the little missy gets to her plane all right." Then Uncle Jimmy ran his thumb along my cheek from the outside corner of my eye to the bottom of my chin, a slow line that wouldn't stop prickling my skin till I wiped it away. His lips twitched into a stiff grin. "So long, sweet pea," he said. I looked at the curb, and he got back in the car and screeched away like there was something important he had to do that couldn't wait another instant.

Belle says I will have to learn the rules here. Don't I know, for instance, that here we call Saturday the Sabbath, even though the stores are mostly open and on Sunday mostly closed? And I must take a bath every night whether or not I have been playing in the dirt, which there isn't so much of, only some vacant lots. But I can read in bed for half an hour before lights-out, and I am allowed to take out an armful of books at the library every week, not just one.

It is not polite to say Nigra here, or Jew you down.

The super walks with a limp, and Jane says keep away from him. The landlord always tips his hat to Belle. Belle doesn't seem to mind that it's a pork pie. She nods, her corkscrew curls squiggling up and down. Jane says the landlord is afraid of Belle. Belle doesn't look like someone to be afraid of. She has a pointy nose and a pointy chin, and the tops of her ears come almost to a point, like a pixie. Her hair is the color of dried apricots.

My school doesn't have a name like Monte Cassino or Eugene Field Elementary School. Here the public schools have numbers and are called P.S. In Tulsa, a P.S. is an afterthought in a letter, but you are impolite to write one because P.S. shows you haven't taken the care to think through beforehand what you planned to say to the person. I figure in Brooklyn you can say P.S. and not be impolite because here P.S. means your thought after you are in school, and you cannot always plan what you will think beforehand. That way you can learn more.

The lady behind the counter says I am way behind, being from Tulsa, so I must go back in fourth grade again, even though I already know all my explorers, and here they don't even do explorers until sixth grade. Not even Verrazano, whose Narrows we might visit in nothing flat if we had a mind to! The lady rests her arm on the counter and her bosoms on her arm, and she isn't mean, just bored. I start to explain how good I am at division, both kinds. Her fingernail taps the records in front of her. She says if truth be told, I am on the young side even for fourth grade.

Belle's orange-colored lips dip down at the corners. Her eyes fix on the lady like she's something Belle wants for breakfast, but the lady tells Belle those are the rules, nothing she can do. Belle's nostrils widen, and she tosses her head, and I have already learned what that means, and I get out of the way. Next minute Belle is grabbing up my records. Waste of time, she growls, and drags me around the counter, right past the lady, into the principal's office. He is sitting at his desk drumming a yellow pencil against a green blotter. Hello, she trills, nice to see him again. He stands, bending his tall, sloping shoulders into something like a bow.

Jane is doing fine, she says, almost fourteen already how time flies, and this little girl (meaning me) is going to be registered today into the fifth grade, Belle will brook no arguments. Those are her words, which I repeat in my head while she talks a lot more, fast and loud. Brook no arguments. The principal fingers his Adolf Menjou mustache. He has one of those Jewish noses. Belle is like Mr. Draper's truck pulling out of his gravel driveway at forty miles an hour. Brook. No. Arguments.

The school has bricks on the inside just like the outside, and you can tickle your fingers running them along the wall. I tickle mine clear down to the end of the hallway, going with Belle to find the very last classroom on the right, where on this very day I start my new school in the fifth grade. Jane says the principal is afraid of Belle, too.

Belle doesn't go to work. She's a homemaker, and that's different from a housewife. Any wife can keep a house, but making a home is a much tougher job, which I will learn if I pay attention. I don't have chickens to feed anymore, but I have chores to do all the same. Like once a week on Thursday afternoons, Jane and I pull out each and every book from the shelves in the living room and dust them all off and replace them so the backs line up perfectly straight, and if they're not perfectly straight we have to do it all over again until we get it right. And every night before dinner when I hear the drawer rattling in the kitchen, that's my cue to start setting the table. Grandma didn't want me underfoot in her kitchen, so I had to wait to be called, but Belle says she shouldn't have to call, I should know I'm wanted without having to be asked, so as soon as I hear the tiniest squeal of the drawer starting to slide open, I report for duty.

I could make the table prettier, but Belle doesn't want it that way, you can tell about things like that. In my head I can see the spoons turned over, cloth napkins folded in a fan across the plate, the dessert utensils set above the plate, a vase of fresh-cut garden flowers in the center. With other tables in my head, it's okay to have paper napkins and the dessert spoon in size-place order outside of the soup spoon and no butter at all with our dinner. Imagine my mother dabbing at her lips with a paper napkin, or Gramp taking bread without fresh, sweet butter on the table, but in Brooklyn that's the way we do it.

The store on the corner is Greenbaum's Dairy, except nobody calls it Greenbaum's, or even The Dairy. It's The Appetizing. Inside, it is dark and cool, and it smells funny, like fresh sweat, only oilier. One afternoon Belle sends me there on an errand to buy a quarter pound of pickled herring in cream sauce. I give the order, and Mr. Greenbaum starts spooning something ugly from a large glass jar.

"Is that pickled herring in cream sauce?" Nothing in it is red like the time Chester let me taste his Cherry Heering, red and sweet. Nothing in it is green, either, like pickles ought to be. If you took gray rubber erasers and threw them in milk with broken shoestrings, you would have what is in Mr. Greenbaum's jar.

He lifts his toad eyes and stares over his glasses at me like he'd forgotten I'm there. "You want maybe a bite? It's good."

"No thank you, sir." No matter what people want to call the store, this doesn't look at all appetizing to me.

"Quarter of a pound, you said?" He frowns, wiping his gnarled hands on his long white apron. "Quarter of a pound. No can do. Sorry."

I can't go home empty-handed. Have I insulted him, like the time Mrs. Ellis served her chipped beef in pink gravy, and I got up from her table and said I wouldn't be staying to dinner, after all? Mr. Greenbaum holds up a wax container, pointing to an invisible line halfway between the top and the bottom. "I could do half of a half. Will that do?"

Half of a half? Isn't that the same as a quarter? Maybe in Brooklyn they measure differently, like in England, where things are weighed in stones, not pounds. When an Englishman says pounds he means money, not weight.

I repeat his words, a wobble in my voice. Half of a half. I shift from one foot to the other trying to make up my mind. On my first day in Brooklyn, when Belle took my sack dresses away, I asked to keep one just for play. Her nostrils widened, and her orange mouth puffed out, and she ripped the dress to shreds in front of me and made me pick up all the tiny scraps and threads until you'd never know there had ever been a dress. At dinner that night she wouldn't talk to me or pass me any food. And that was for asking a question. What will she do if I come back today with the wrong thing?

I reach for the red button hanging on a string around my neck and think of Hetty. Then Mr. Greenbaum winks at me. It's a slow wink. His upper and lower lids meet lazily over one eye while the other stays fixed on me never blinking, moist and bloodshot. Bloodshot, but kind and—yes—brimful of a joke he wants me to get. I heave a sigh that is a return joke of my own. "Oh, dear," like he's broken my heart, but what can you do. "A half of a half then, if that's really all you have."

He never cracks a smile, but along with my package for Belle, he hands me something to eat, says it's a special treat just for me, don't tell anyone where it came from. I get home and tell Belle I've just tasted my first bagel and my first lock, and she sits down in the kitchen chair and laughs till she cries.

Maybe everything is going to turn out all right, after all, the way Hetty said it would. I didn't notice her on the flight from Tulsa until everybody was settled with seat belts fastened and ready to go and the pink-cheeked stewardess had shown us how to put on the oxygen masks and exit the plane, and the army officer in the seat next to mine said he would help me if it came to that, which I could be sure it wouldn't. Then the plane started to rumble and shake, and I was pressed backward into my seat as we sped down the runway fast and then even faster, and up into the air, rising and swooping, my stomach dropping, everything in the plane creaking, until at last we climbed steadily and were good and truly on our way. Just as we broke through the clouds, coming out over miles and miles of cottony white below, blue sky and sunshine above, there in front of me was Hetty saying, "Shift over so's I can sit with you."

I let her borrow *Little House on the Prairie*. I had *Lad: A Dog*, and we sat together reading. After a while we slept, curled up around each other like two kittens all the way to Washington, D.C. When the plane landed I told her, "Just wait here with me. The stewardess will be along any minute to help us change planes."

"I won't be going to New York."

"Where, then?"

She shrugged. Her lips were crooked from biting inside.

"Stay with me. My father will let you. You can stay."

She bent an arm around my waist and kissed me. Then she took my hand, and that's when she told me, "You'll be all right now, you hear? I promise everything will turn out right."

"But they'll make room for you in Brooklyn." I swore up and down they would.

She kept shaking her head, pulling away. "You have to leave me behind now, Jessie."

Something was pressed into my palm. A red button from her clothing. Hetty was never anything but imaginary, yet the button was real enough, an ordinary button like you can buy on a card of eight in any dime store. It shouldn't make me cry, this simple gift from a make-believe friend. A true friend. "Thank you, Hetty," I called, but she was already past hearing, gone away that fast and silent, and the pink-cheeked stewardess was bending over me, offering to buy me a hot chocolate on the way to gate three and the plane bound for New York.

My father has a whole family I never knew about. First there is my grandmother, Bubbie. She lives downstairs from us with my uncle, who never got married, so he never left home. Bubbie cooks chicken soup and potted meats and poppy seed cookies. On her kitchen wall are two photographs—Douglas Fairbanks Sr. in *The Thief of Bagdad* and Douglas Fairbanks Jr. in *The Prisoner of Zenda*. Bubbie says we might be related to them, because Fairbanks starts with an *F* just like Friedman, and you never know whose relative changed his name coming through Castle Garden. She says it proves we are just as good as any movie star.

My father says my uncle is a business genius, so don't make fun of him. He made his mark in advertising, printing ads on cardboard shirt bands that he sold at wholesale to Chinese laundries all over the city. That's how he made his fortune, before he got so fat and took to his chair in Bubbie's living room, where he listens to the radio and drinks tea with sugar and lemon all day long. When I am taken to visit, he struggles to unrecline himself, and he asks me, "What are you taking up in school?" His voice is the smallest thing about him. The only taking up I know is hems, and we're not doing any sewing, so I don't answer.

Jane says he never listens for your answer, all you have to do is say English or civics or any of your other subjects, and next he'll ask, "Are you making good grades?" and you say yes, and he'll hand you a butterscotch and go back to his radio.

Every night when my father gets home from work he stops in at Bubbie's, then comes upstairs and takes off his suit jacket and the tie he wears now because he sells furniture instead of making it. He puts on his smoking jacket and settles down in his easy chair with the newspaper, but he doesn't smoke in his smoking jacket. Belle won't let him. Jane says my father is afraid of Belle, everyone is. I tell her not Daddy, he's her husband, so how could he be afraid? But she says he is more afraid of Belle than anyone, and he will do anything to dodge out of a fight with her.

I like to stand next to him and stroke the soft green velvet of the smoking jacket while he works the crossword puzzle. He never makes a mistake, you can tell because he does it in ink. I want him to teach me crosswords, but Jane says we mustn't disturb him when he's relaxing in his chair. Just bring him his Manhattan and help Belle get dinner on the table, and don't ask for anything.

Conversation is for dinnertime. My father always starts it by saying how glad he is to have his little girl with him again. Then he asks Jane what she learned today. Jane has an answer. Jane has an unused answer every night of the week. She plays the piano, so there is always a new bar or two she can learn, or a new phrasing.

He looks over at me, head cocked. "And you, Jessie? What have you learned?" Today, *ablution*. Tomorrow will be *abnegation*. I never fail to be *abloom* with a new dictionary word, ever since the *abashing* time he quizzed me and I answered "Nothing, sir." He was taken *aback* like an *aardvark* without a termite. His bushy eyebrows swung up like the gates on a pinball machine.

"Nothing? In all this livelong day?"

I tried to dredge up some scrap of something learned. Finally, I shook my head.

"What have you been doing all day?"

In school we were reviewing, and after school, some of the kids were making fun of the landlord's son. He is my age and chubby and has a runny nose, and kids say they don't like him because he is a crybaby and a tattletale, but I think the kids have it the wrong way around. I think that boy is a crybaby and a tattletale because they don't like him. Sometimes they purposely trip him, but that afternoon it was only a harmless game they were playing, calling out *Make a shimalecha on the old man's back*, and still he ran home, hollering "I'm telling, I'm telling." I wasn't in on the teasing. I was trying to figure out how to sneak in and out of the cellar without the super seeing me. But none of this was anything I could tell my father.

He was inspecting me like I might have a fever. "You were awake all day? You had your eyes and ears screwed in?"

I allowed that I did.

"You had your head buckled to your shoulders?"

I gave a small grin, which he returned.

"You remembered to crank the ignition and put your brains in gear?"

I thought I'd try saying no to that, and was caught speechless when he shot back, "Well, then, how did you manage to pull your socks up?" There and then, I made up my mind to start the dictionary and go all the way through, so I'll have a new word every day for a long, long time.

This particular night, though, I don't need a word. This night, the twelfth of April, President Roosevelt is dead. My father has been listening to the radio. He hasn't looked at the crossword. The smile is gone everywhere from his face. I help Belle serve, and when we are all seated no one speaks. My father gazes at each of us in turn. Belle tells him eat while the soup is still hot. Jane picks up her spoon. I don't wait for him to ask me, I tell my father I learned today that grown-ups can be out of doors, walking up and down the sidewalk crying, not even wiping the tears away, just letting them drip.

He nods. "A great man is gone, Jessie, a great leader. Let's hope his successor can do the job."

"Fat chance," says Belle.

Jane says that "President Truman" will seem funny, when her whole life it's been "President Roosevelt."

I think about Mrs. Roosevelt alone in the White House and feel sorry for her, having to leave her home. I know how she will miss things and wonder about things after she is someplace else. I miss the sound of chickens, miss their stiff-legged walk and the way they'll come right over and peck between my toes if I stand still long enough in the yard. I wonder how Sammy is keeping warm without me to pick up his lap robe when it falls to the porch floor while he's taking a catnap. I wonder how many war bonds John Ellis has now and how Teddy is doing on his scout badges. I eat my dinner fingering the red button hanging on a string around my neck.

I keep watching, but I can't figure out if the super has a schedule, so I can get my bicycle out of the basement and back in when he's not around. Finally I tell Belle I need someplace else to keep the bike, might it be in the foyer across from the coat closet? People could be careful opening the front door to the apartment so as not to hit the bike. Belle says the answer is no unless I will tell her why I won't go to the basement. I haven't ridden the bike in well over a week. It's because Jane says all the girls have to watch out for the super, he's a groper. He'll feel you up if he catches you alone down there. *Psshhht*, Belle says, with a flick of her fingers. There's nothing to feel up, not even buds yet. She sticks out her large pointed bosoms, one hand at her waist, the other behind her head. Wait a few years until I have a figure like hers, and then come talk to her. I go into the bedroom and sit down on my bed.

After a while Belle sends me out to play. I watch the other kids until a new girl from the next building lets me take turns playing A My Name is Alice with her Spaldeen. Propping a hand against the wall isn't allowed here, so I lose a few turns until I get my balance right, but I've caught up to her on Q, and I've used Quito, and she hasn't thought of Queensland but doesn't want any hints—when her mother calls her home.

I go upstairs. There's a glass of milk waiting for me on the kitchen table, and Belle sits down beside me while I drink it. "Jessie," she says, "you don't have to be afraid of going down the basement or anywhere else, because everyone knows who you belong to."

"They do?"

"See this finger?" She holds up one manicured hand and waggles her coral-tipped pinkie at me. "If anyone tried to sprain this finger, they'd have to deal with me, wouldn't they? But they don't want to have to deal with me, so they leave my fingers alone.

"You're no different than my little finger," she says. "No one is going to touch you, but if anyone ever tries, you're to come immediately and tell me. Immediately, you understand?"

She says everyone, but everyone, is afraid of Belle Friedman. Finally, I believe it.

Except one overcast afternoon in May, I begin to think maybe Mr. Greenbaum at The Appetizing is the exception that proves the rule. It is V-E Day: the war in Europe is over, we have beat the Nazis, and now the children there will have food to eat. In school we have a victory assembly. A color guard marches down the auditorium aisles and onto the stage while the school band plays "The Star Spangled Banner." We pledge allegiance to the flag and sit down. The music teacher sings "God Bless America," drawing out the final swe-e-et ho-o-ome while we clap and shout, because everyone in school knows she's better than Kate Smith, even though she is only our music teacher. After the sixth graders read poems, we sing some songs.

There's supposed to be a citywide address from the superintendent of schools, except the PA system breaks down. The principal comes out on the stage and clears his throat and says you have to travel across this vast country of ours to understand how great America is. "Most of you children have never seen amber waves of grain, but talk to your teachers, or to Jessie Friedman, who came to us from our nation's heartland—" I wake up from a sort of doze, not really a doze but just not full attention. I've been playing finger games in my lap. Here is the church, here is the steeple, and I hear the principal say my name, and the girl in the next seat pokes me, and I'm suddenly hot from blushing. Amber waves of grain. Yes, I have seen them, but I can't think how I would describe them better than those very words, which were written, somebody behind me whispers, by a Jew, and somebody else whispers yeah, yeah, yeah, like everybody knows that, except I didn't, and then somebody else whispers, "No, stupid, that was 'God Bless America,'" and a teacher comes up the aisle and stands near us, arms folded, eyes hard on us, and everybody stops whispering and fidgeting and then we sing "America the Beautiful" and go back to our classrooms. Everyone is much too excited to work, so we are permitted to play quietly until school lets out.

It's on my way home I hear Mr. Greenbaum through the open door of The Appetizing. I have never known him to shout before. "One year. Is that so much to ask?" He's shouting at Belle. The pole he normally uses to reach high shelves is in his hand, and he is shaking it like a club in Belle's face! I step inside. "Just one year, please God, in the whole damn history of the whole damn world."

Belle is making soft noises in her throat. As my eyes adjust to the dimness, I see his face is raining tears, like the people in the street the day the president died. "Only one year, it's all I'm asking, missus. I'd like to live to see it. And not even a leap year. Three hundred sixty-five days stretched end to end, that's all. Let the world restrain itself that long." He puts down the stick, fishes a handkerchief from his pocket and wipes his face. Then he picks up containers of sour cream and pot cheese and sets them into a paper sack. "One year in which not one Jew gets killed for the plain and simple reason he's a Jew. Give me that," he says, handing the sack to Belle, "and I'll die a happy man."

In the papers there are photographs, in the movie houses newsreels, of walking skeletons in striped pajamas who once were people like me. I want to tell Mr. Greenbaum about the Cherokee on the Trail of Tears. I want to tell him about the race riots in Tulsa, but he isn't talking to me, he's talking to Belle, and anyway, maybe he'd only say that's not his war, the way cousin La Junta said everybody's got their troubles.

He looks so sad I want to give him something to make him feel better, but what would he want with the things in my pockets, a good potsy rock, a stub of chalk? I have nothing worth anything, except Hetty's red button hanging on the string around my neck.

Belle opens her purse. I lift the string over my head and put the button in his hand.

He blinks at me and squints at it through his glasses. "What's this?"

"For remembering the good ones."

"The good ones?"

Ones like him, though I feel too shy to say so.

They exchange glances, Mr. Greenbaum and Belle. She is holding money out to pay him, but he ignores it. He takes my chin in his hands. "A Yiddisher kop you've got, you know that?"

I nod.

"You what it means, a Yiddisher kop?"

I don't.

"It means a Jewish head. You think like a Jew."

"Of course she does," says Belle. "Why wouldn't she? She's family."

It's Saturday. Jane has gone to her piano lesson, Belle is out shopping, and I'm in my room reading. My father comes in holding a battered manila folder under his arm and sits down next to me on the bed.

"I thought I'd paint that frieze around your room today."

"What freeze?"

He smiles. "A decoration." I guess he's realized I'm picturing icicles. He opens the folder, which is full of stencils, and first shows me the toy soldiers he originally had in mind. "But I think you'd prefer something else." We look through the designs—flowers, ribbons, animals—and we talk about colors, and finally I settle on a trail of dark-green ivy to climb the door and window frames and circle the room just below the ceiling. He holds the stencil up, showing me how it will look on the wall.

"Well, then. I guess I'll get started."

"But only if Jane goes along," I remind him.

"All taken care of."

"Really?"

"Jane told me anything you want is okay by her. Don't forget to thank her."

For Jane's sake, I take one last look around, trying to picture how the room will be. I think she'll like it. Nothing will be ordinary anymore, it will all be nicely decorated. Except for the furniture.

"Wait, can you do a matching design on our dressers?"

"Mmm. Interesting thought."

He runs his fingers over the plain yellow wooden surface of mine. "I could paint a border an inch or two in from the edge—or better yet," thumbing through the stencils and plunking down another design, "—an oval. Fight the rectangularity, you see? What do you think, my keen-eyed daughter?"

"Oval. Definitely."

He nods at the dresser, light catching the shine on his forehead where his hair has receded. Then, "Jessie, where's your mother's photo? Didn't you have it here? I'm sure I saw it."

"Belle took it away."

A silence.

"Did she say why?"

"Because *we're* the family now, the four of us."

"So we are," he agrees, slowly nodding. Sometimes, a tough clue in the crosswords makes him frown just this way, his thick eyebrows drawn together. "And happy to be so," he adds, clumsily patting my shoulder.

Then he walks out of the room. I wait, wondering when he'll be back to start the work. The apartment is so quiet I can't read. Ten minutes tick by.

Fifteen.

He strides in, the goofiest grin spread all across his face, and in his hand, instead of paints and a brush, is my mother's photo. "Here, Jessie," holding it out to me, but I don't take it from him. He urges, "This belongs to you."

"Belle is going to be so mad."

"You leave Belle to me." He sets the frame on the dresser, peers at it, nods. Again he says, "You leave Belle to me."

"I will, Daddy," slipping my hand into his. "Only, if you wouldn't mind," I whisper to him, "I think I'll just keep the picture tucked away somewhere in my closet."

His tongue licks at his lower lip as he nods. Good idea, he tells me. No, he wouldn't mind at all.

Acknowledgments

I am grateful to the following for their help: Jerry Gross, Nancy Nicholas, Maggie Cadman, Louise Estrema, Leslie Browne, Sandy Albert, Jackie De Young, Michael Kasky, Fran Medoff, Carol Ascher and Nomi Rinke; Sister Barbara of the Monte Cassino School, the Bereavement Counseling Center of the Parker Jewish Institute, and the Army Medical Museum; and the librarians of the Tulsa Central Library, the University of Tulsa Library and the Port Washington Library.

During the ten years it has taken me to complete *Even You,* I've been fortunate to have the support of so many wonderful people. To those of you not mentioned above, I hope I've been lavish in my thanks in person; you deserve it, and I'd like to think it means more than any acknowledgment I could give here.

I've had lots of assistance in making this narrative better; it goes without saying that the faults are my own.

Also by Marilyn Oser

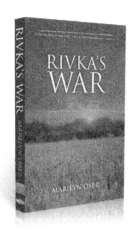

RIVKA'S WAR
A novel of World War I

Russia, 1914. Rivka, daughter of a prosperous boot maker, seems destined by tradition for marriage and the humdrum rounds of shtetl life.

Then war breaks out, and things go badly for the tsar's army. When demoralized troops begin deserting their posts in the trenches, one unlikely officer recruits a battalion of women to set an example for the men.

Rivka seizes upon this chance for adventure as her once-in-a-lifetime opportunity to do something great in the world. She signs on, never suspecting the terrors that await her, or the trials that will test her, or the mishaps that will take her from the frozen steppes of Siberia to the hot, dusty hills of Palestine.

"Rivka...is a compelling heroine, representing both the Jewish diaspora and the precarious politics of the time."
—*Publishers Weekly*

"*Rivka's War* is a must-read." —*Baltimore Jewish Times*

"A figure steps forward from history and shows herself to be a strong and courageous character. In *Rivka's War*, Marilyn Oser gives us a hero to cheer. A thoughtful and inspiring novel."
—Susan Isaacs

"Steeped in historical fact, with a healthy dose of adventure."
—Joanne Harvey, *Kiwi Book Advisor*

"Outstanding...Five stars." —Fran Lewis, *Just Reviews*

CPSIA information can be obtained at www.ICGtesting.com
Printed in the USA
BVOW08s0156240915

419286BV00002B/64/P